K. L. HAWKER

THE DREAM KEEPER

A DREAM KEEPER NOVEL

THE DREAM KEEPER

The Dream Keeper / K.L. Hawker

ISBN: 978-0-9917257-7-9

Written by K.L. Hawker

www.klhawker.com

Cover Design by Design for Writers

www.designforwriters.com

Published by Pages & Stages Publishing

www.pagesandstages.com

For Austin, Kate and Marley . . .

I love you with all my heart.
Follow your dreams,
they will take you to great places.

"The future belongs to those who believe in the beauty
of their dreams." ~ Eleanor Roosevelt

K. L. HAWKER

THE DREAM KEEPER

A DREAM KEEPER NOVEL

PROLOGUE

Five Years Earlier

~ DREW ~

"IT'S JUST UP ahead here," Dad said as he stepped carefully through the wooded, barely visible path. "Watch your steps there, son. Don't make the path wider than it needs to be."

I paid close attention to where his foot left the ground, and made sure that my next step was exactly there. I wanted to do this right. There was so much to learn, and this was just the start of it all.

"Duck," Dad said as he crouched down, narrowly avoiding a branch that reached across the path. I mimicked his movements so as not to disturb the limb or leave behind any evidence that we were there.

"How many feathers do we need?" I asked as I studied the craft in my hands. The silk was woven with detail in, around and through the perfect circle, which was made from melted metal, but not just any metal, Dad had pointed out many times—it had to be the silver-white metal that was called platinum. And the beads—or topazes, emeralds, sapphires and rubies—were carefully hanging from the tightly woven leather strands that hung from the sphere. It was beautiful, yes, but it still needed feathers.

"Three will do it," Dad said, then stopped and sniffed the air.

"Can they be any feathers?"

He chuckled as if this was naïve. "No, no, son. From a blue jay bird. Only from a blue jay."

"Why from a blue jay? Won't feathers from a robin or a sparrow work the same?"

"They don't, actually," Dad said as he stopped suddenly and stretched his arm back to prevent me from running into him. "Now there's a nest just up there," he said, pointing to a branch that was higher than I would have liked. "Think you can do it?"

I scoffed. "Of course I can." Because at twelve, I was a man now, and a little tree climbing never scared a man.

Each branch was just the right height from the last, creating an easy climb to the upper part of the tree. When I reached the nest and peered in, I was pleased to see plenty of feather options. Long ones, short ones, skinny ones, plump ones. It hadn't occurred to me until that moment that this could have been a futile attempt. What if there hadn't been any feathers at all? I supposed Dad must have known before he dragged me all this way so I could finish our little father-son homemade project.

I chose one of each—long, short and plump—and hurried back down the tree. Dad helped me secure them to the leather strands and I held up our masterpiece with pride.

"What do you think, son?"

"It looks cool."

Dad laughed. "Yes, I suppose you did alright."

"Will it really work?"

"Of course it will." He patted me on the back and then said, "Well, let's keep going. We're almost to the clearing now."

After a minute more of careful footsteps, Dad stopped in his tracks. "Well, that's disappointing."

"What is it?" I asked, craning my neck so that I could see around him.

"Looks like someone crossed this path recently. See here? They broke that branch off in there." He pointed to a small tree to our left. "And trampled the new growth here."

"Could it have been a deer?" I asked hopefully, because I knew how important it was that no one ever be able to stumble across this place.

"Not likely. A bear, maybe, but even a bear wouldn't purposely destroy nature."

We continued to tread carefully along the path until we reached the clearing. The tall grass was about knee-high now that it was mid-summer. The large apple tree was sitting confidently still in the centre, draining the surrounding ground of all resources so as to ensure it would be the only tree in the clearing.

"Isn't she beautiful?" Dad admired.

"It is," I agreed.

He nudged me. "Trees are living and breathing too, Drew. She's not an 'it.'"

I nodded.

"Now, Drew, this is a special place. You always remember to keep this place quiet, okay?"

"I know, Dad."

"No friends."

"I know."

"Or girlfriends."

I scoffed. "As if that would happen."

He laughed. "I'm sure one day you'll find a girl that'll steal your heart."

"Can I?" I asked. "I mean, am I allowed to have a girlfriend?" There were so many normal adolescent things that I couldn't do, I had just assumed I wouldn't be allowed this one, either.

His eyes narrowed, suggesting he was putting some thought into it. "As long as you stay focused." He smiled and brought his eyes to mine. "You just have to be careful. When you get too involved—fall too hard in love—you'll lose focus of what's really important. *This* is what's really important, Drew. Your job is important. The world depends on *you* now."

I nodded, regretting the direction the conversation had taken. I should have known better than to ask since this was how Mom had died—Dad had screwed up. He didn't have his priorities straight. He had let his guard down. But I wouldn't let that happen to me. No. *I* was the keeper now. I had a purpose. I had a duty to my people. Earth's people. Even though they would never know it, and I would never get recognition for it—that wasn't the point. The point was, I had a chance to make a real difference, and I wouldn't let my father down. I wouldn't let my mother's death be for nothing.

Suddenly, the silence was broken by a shuffling sound coming from the large apple tree. Dad held his hand out for me to stay and he carefully, slowly walked forward. I could tell by his approach, by his caution, he expected a predator. He expected an invasion.

But in the tree, about ten feet up, a tangled mess of red hair, pale face and bright eyes peeked around the trunk of the tree.

"The girl," I breathed.

Her eyes were curious, full of eager interest as she watched us. Wasn't she at all scared of us? Out here all alone in the deep, untouched part of the woods. Didn't she wonder if we were going to take her away? Maybe that's what she wanted. Maybe she had run away from home. The very thought of it made me sick to my stomach. Was she lonely? Scared? Lost? I struggled for breath as all of these thoughts flooded my head.

Why was she so high in that tree? Didn't she realize she could fall out at any minute and break a leg? And who would hear her screaming from this deep in the forest? My heart was racing now. Yes, she was about my age, but so much more vulnerable than I felt.

This girl was special. I knew that. I knew the first day I laid eyes on her. She was someone I wanted to protect. Needed to protect. By all accounts, I was too young to know such things, so I couldn't explain it, even to my own father, but I knew. And by the look she was giving back to me, I knew she felt it, too. These things I knew. But that was the extent of my knowledge. As Earth's new keeper, I had too much to learn already. But one thing I did know, I was never going to be able to fall in love. Not that I really wanted that anyway, at twelve years old, but seeing this girl sitting high on that branch, the thought was crossing my mind, and it was agonizing.

"There she is, son," my father said. Had he seen it too? Had he seen the look she and I were exchanging at that very moment? Did he know what I was feeling? "Go on. Go introduce yourself."

The girl was climbing down from the tree now, eager to reach the book that had fallen to the ground. Was it a journal maybe? Had she been writing her own life secrets in there?

"Careful!" I said quickly watching her foot fumble for the lower branch.

She smiled shyly and said, "Thanks. I do this a lot. I'm okay."

She was independent. I liked that, but I could tell her independence didn't come with a comfortable upbringing. Her independence was from years of doing things on her own. In her own way. How I knew this, I wasn't sure. But I liked this about her. I admired it. I would have to quash it, of course. If we were to be friends, and I knew we would be, she couldn't be doing these dangerous things all the time. My deep-rooted instincts to protect her wouldn't allow it. I would have to teach her how to shoot arrows and throw knives—she may need these skills one day, as much as it sickened me to think about.

I turned quickly to my father so she couldn't read my lips. "What is this?" I meant the feelings I was experiencing. He would know. He was my dad. He knew all things.

He smiled and laid a hand on my shoulder. "Ah," he said as if he had waited for this moment and just realized what I had meant, "this, my boy, is what you've been trained for."

Trained for? I was trained to feel undeniably attracted to someone who caused me to lose sight of my responsibilities? I was trained to exercise complete self-control?

The girl was beside us now. "Hi," she said, startling me. I spun around and our eyes met. Hers were almost yellow, if that was possible. Blue, or green, but washed out with a bright ring of yellow near the centre. Or was it white?—

She blinked.

I was staring. I quickly looked down and cleared my throat. "Hi," I answered, brushing my hand through the top of my hair.

She watched me for a minute, her eyes darting and thoughts seemingly swimming. Had I not told her my name yet? "Sorry," I said, realizing I had been too captivated by her stunning red hair and bright eyes that I had forgotten my manners. "I'm Drew. Drew Spencer."

Dad gave a deep throaty chuckle. "Uncanny," he said, which was odd, but deliberate, and I wasn't sure what he meant by it.

She smiled broadly and her eyes twinkled. "I'm Sarah."

Sarah. Yes, this girl was special.

"What do you have there?" Sarah asked as she fingered the feathers dangling from the platinum, silk-webbed sphere.

"Here," I said as I handed it to her. "You can have it." She would need it. I may not have known everything yet, but being raised as Earth's keeper meant that I did know the dangers of this world, and she, being as unique as she was, would need protection. No objection from Dad confirmed that my instincts to give it to her were right.

"It's beautiful," she admired. "What is it?"

"It's a dreamcatcher."

CHAPTER 1

Present Day

~ SARAH ~

MY FINGERS TWISTED and turned the dial on my locker as I was acutely aware of the other students behind me hurrying to leave the school. 19-37-15. Click. I pulled open the locker door and slid my textbooks in, but not before letting my eyes fall on the photograph of me and Drew sitting high in a tree last summer. And not just any tree—our tree. The same tree we first met almost five years ago. I let my fingers brush the photo as I reached in the locker for my coat.

"Sarah," a sharp, unfriendly voice said. Unfortunately, I knew the voice well enough to not have to look at her—Holly Haverstock—but gave her the courtesy of a sideways glance anyway.

"Holly," I replied.

Before I had a chance to close my locker, she flicked one of my drawings hanging from the inside of my locker door. "Nice kitty cats."

She and her best friends, Bria and Karley, giggled as they kept walking. I slowly shut my locker, trying to think of a quick, mature comeback, but too much time had lapsed, I figured. I touched the picture of the tiger — not kitty cat — that I had drawn yesterday in Math class. There were only four drawings in my locker, and I was suddenly thankful that she didn't know how many pictures were plastered over my bedroom walls. *Maybe this is immature. I'm in high school. Why am I drawing and colouring pictures of rainbow tigers?* I let my fingers wrap around the corners of the paper, and pulled it from my locker door.

"I think they're nice." Drew's voice was always such a treat, bringing me comfort in a cold world where I felt so isolated. I turned to meet his eyes and he gestured toward the picture.

He took the paper from my hand. "Can I have this one?"

I snorted. "Why? It's lame."

Drew shook his head and nodded toward the group of girls who were now moving down the hall. "*They're* lame." He cocked a smile. "But *these*" — he held up the picture — "are awesome. You're very talented, Sarah."

I thanked him with a sideways smile and closed my locker.

"Does this one have a name?" he asked as we walked down the hallway.

I shrugged. "Lucia," I answered with a laugh.

"Oh, okay," Drew chuckled, "so she has the same name as your dog then."

"Yeah, I'm not very original."

Drew laughed. "Makes sense. It's a nice name. From St. Lucia, right?"

"Yeah. Where I like to think I was born." Of course being abandoned when I was three, I had no idea where I was born, or who my parents were, but I did like to imagine that I was born on a beautiful, sunny island with green mountains and turquoise seas.

We continued together through the halls when I heard the voice of my best girlfriend, Maddy, calling my name. "Sarah! Sarah, wait up!"

Maddy's thin blonde hair bounced as she hopped and pushed her tiny self through the crowd, making her way to us. I couldn't help but giggle. She was small, but she made up for it in personality. My very best friend since the day I moved in with the Robinsons, Maddy was like a sister to me.

"Hey," I said as she leaped and landed with two feet right in front of us.

"What's up, Maddy?" Drew said throwing his hand

into her already straggly hair.

"Guess what I got?" Maddy sang as she hid her right hand with her left, and held it to her chest excitedly.

My heart sank. I knew what it was before she even showed me. And I could tell by the way Drew looked down and cleared his throat that he knew what it was, too.

"He gave it to you?" I asked, hoping I was wrong.

"He did!" Maddy shrieked and thrust her hand in front of my face.

The ring was too big for her tiny fingers so she wore it on her thumb. The large X adorning the face of the ring, and standing for Xavier High, had become, over the years, more of a symbol of relationship status and ownership than the school pride it was meant to represent.

"Congrats," I said, smiling as I lowered her hand. "Did you give him your necklace?" I asked, hoping she hadn't. It was one thing for a guy to give away his school ring to a girl, but it seemed completely foolish for a girl to give away her Tiffany-inspired school necklace to a guy who would likely just lose it or break it anyway. Last year, Emily Goodman gave her necklace to her boyfriend of six months and within a week she found out he was cheating on her with a girl from another school. She broke up with him by giving his ring back to him, but she never got her necklace back. In fact, rumour was that his new girlfriend from Stevenson High was now wearing the necklace with pride. A three hundred dollar necklace. Gone. I wouldn't have been so careless.

Maddy had pulled her necklace from her sweater. "Not yet," she said, twirling the circular pendant with X in the centre between her fingers. "But if he wants it, I think I will." She twisted back and forth with a sickening look of longing on her face.

I fought hard at not rolling my eyes.

"Ring looks good on you," Drew said, saving me from saying something I'd regret and have to apologize for later. "Say hi to Caleb for me." He took my elbow in his hand. "We should get going."

"Will do! Bye!" Maddy turned on her heel and skipped back down the hall.

When she was out of earshot, I said, "Can you believe her? Just last week she was saying how stupid the whole ring giving thing was."

Drew chuckled. "Every girl says that until a guy gives her his ring."

I scoffed. "Pathetic."

Drew stopped and was now facing me, eyes pressing into mine. "Is it, Sarah? Is it really?"

"What? Pathetic? Yes." I held my ground, but as his eyes burned into mine I wasn't sure I wouldn't be thrilled too if he offered his ring to me. But he wouldn't. And I knew that about Drew. We were just friends. Always had been. Always would be.

A grin crept across his face. "Yeah, I agree too, actually. I wouldn't want some girl giving me a stupid necklace to prove she cares about me."

For some reason, his words stung. My necklace burned into my skin where it laid against my chest.

"Besides, I already have a necklace. Don't need two."

I looked down at the black braided cord draped around his neck and trailing down inside his shirt, and imagined the gold key resting cozily on his sculpted chest.

I shook my head and rolled my eyes. "Well, if you consider that a necklace. I'd say it's more of a 'man piece.'"

"Well whatever you call it, I don't need two things wrapped around my neck."

"Well, that's good 'cause you're likely never going to get another one anyway." I turned briskly and continued toward the outside. I heard Drew chuckling behind me as he hurried to catch up.

When we approached the front doors, and more particularly, the ticket table for the end-of-year prom, Drew got quiet. What was he thinking? Would he finally ask me to prom? He had turned down at least a dozen offers so far this year, and I . . . well, I turned down my lab partner in Biology. It was our senior year and we'd only get one prom, and although dances and elaborate social gatherings weren't my thing, I did want to go.

He put his hand on the small of my back, which sent shivers up my spine . . . and then led me past the table and out the doors. My heart sank.

He doesn't love me, I reminded myself. *He just wants to be friends.* He had alluded to it enough times by this point and I wasn't sure why it wasn't sinking in yet. Maybe it was the mixed signals he would give. Maybe it was that he always turned down other girls and made me feel like I was the only one for him. But why wouldn't he just ask me out? Was he afraid it would ruin our friendship? Rightfully so, I guess. What if it didn't work out? What if we couldn't be friends afterward? Where would I be without Drew? I couldn't imagine a single day without him. We were inseparable. Apart from Maddy, he was my only tried and true friend. That was if you didn't count Lucia, who had been with me from the beginning—she was my only true family, and I couldn't imagine life without her, either.

"I'm taking Lucia for a walk down the trail after school," I decided. "Did you want to come?"

"Sure, yeah." He seemed distant, almost as if his agreement was based more on necessity than actual desire. Or maybe that's how I read it since I was still marred with disappointment over the non-invitation to prom.

THE TRAIL WAS still hard underfoot, not having thawed quite enough to make a mess of my hikers as we made our way through the winding path. The air was still cold, but the warmth from the sun that peeked through the treetops every few yards was a comforting indication that summer would soon be here. I wasn't a fan of the bitter, bleak winters in Nova Scotia. It wasn't just the teeth-hurting cold, but the lack of colour was almost unbearable. Everything was either white or grey. For someone who didn't ski or snowboard (not for lack of trying, but more for lack of coordination), winters were unbearably long. But now the ground was beginning to thaw and the birds were coming back from their southern holidays. Soon shrubs and flowers would start to brighten our path with colours that were sure to bring a smile to my face and a renewed energy for a few more months. And then it would be fall—my absolute favourite time of year with all of the brilliant colourful leaves.

"What are you daydreaming about now?" Drew asked, pulling me back to reality.

I blushed. "Colours."

He smirked and nodded. "Should've known." Then he looked at me, almost sad-like. "Maybe this wasn't the best place for you."

"What do you mean?" It wasn't often Drew didn't make sense, but sometimes he'd throw out something like that last comment that had me wondering where *his* mind was.

He brought his gaze back to the path ahead and

chuckled lightly. "I don't know. Maybe you were meant to live in a warmer climate, that's all."

"I could go for that. As long as it still had an autumn."

"Yes, definitely."

Our hands brushed just then and my fingers instinctively twitched toward his. As his pinkie hooked around my two fingers, I nearly lost my balance . . . and breath. Was he really holding my hand? Well, my *fingers*? It wasn't the first time our fingers brushed, but it was the first time his lingered in a deliberate show of affection. The ground swayed as if it would give out underneath me.

A squirrel ran across the path in front of us, and Lucia pulled at her leash to chase after it. Thankfully she wasn't a big dog so I could restrain her with only one hand while still holding Drew's pinkie with the other.

"Want me to take her?" Drew asked as he let go of my hand and reached for the leash. *Damnit, Lucia!*

"Oh, yeah sure." I handed him the leash and our hands brushed again, this time stopping us both where we were. Our eyes met, filling me with an odd rush of bravery. "Drew?"

"Yeah?" his mouth stayed slightly open as his eyes pinned mine.

I took a deep breath. "Did you want to go to the prom? . . . With me?" My heart was beating so wildly that Lucia stopped, cocked her head sideways and watched me intently.

Drew licked his bottom lip and sucked it in, biting on it gently, then let it slip out of his perfect teeth. The illustriousness of it pulled me in, but I quickly snapped out of it, realizing his response time had been too long. Was he thinking of his escape plan? Did I cross the line? We had never been on a date. Never kissed. Heck, I didn't even know for sure if he liked me the way I liked him.

"I . . . I don't think that's a good idea, Sarah." He dropped his eyes to the leash and took it from my hand.

It took me a few seconds to recover. "Yeah, no that's cool," I said as I kept walking, ensuring I was a pace or two ahead so he wasn't able to see my face, which was betraying me deeply with its crimson stained cheeks and glossy eyes. "I was actually just wondering if you wanted to go at all. I don't really care to go. It's cool."

He was quiet. Didn't say another word, making it even worse. I just wanted to dig a hole in the frozen ground and climb in. Cover myself with whatever drab foliage I could find, and stay there until fall.

THE END OF the path couldn't have come soon enough. Drew handed the leash back to me and smiled sideways as I quickly took it and wrapped it around my hand twice.

"Hey, pretty girl, did you have a good walk? You ready for a nap now?" I said, feigning sudden interest in

Lucia. She wagged her tail happily at the sound of my voice—true love.

"So I'll see you later?" Drew said as he took a few steps backward, in the direction of his house.

"Yeah, sure. I'll probably go lie down for a bit. I'm tired. Long day." I kept my eyes on Lucia, still too embarrassed to face the guy who I'd been crushing on for far too long, and who just turned me down to my face. Ugh. My stomach flipped. "I have to go. Bye." I turned and headed toward my house, acutely aware that he hadn't said good-bye and I couldn't yet hear the crunch of his soles on the gravel-sprayed sidewalk. I focused on keeping one foot in front of the other and hoped that my back looked confident and sure, and not at all how I felt on the inside.

I OPENED THE front door, unleashed Lucia, and stripped off my winter attire. Lucia panted heavily and stood patiently by her water dish.

"I know, girl. I got it," I said softly, leaning over to pick up her bowl. "You're a good girl, aren't you? I love you so much." The "l" word nearly got caught in my throat. I looked down at her happy face, tail wagging ferociously, eyes bright with wonder and love. Maybe *this* was what love was. Unconditional. Forgiving. Patient. Kind. Maybe what I felt for Drew was just "like" . . . or "lust." I sighed heavily and headed for the sink while Lucia waited by the spot where she knew I'd return with her water.

Startled by the sound of a mug being placed hastily on the counter next to me, I spun around to find my foster mother waiting peevishly for me to finish with the water.

"Oh, hi," I said. I shut off the tap and brought the full bowl to Lucia who was now drooling with anticipation.

"Mmm," she grunted.

I rolled my eyes. "My day was good, thanks."

She "pfft" and set the mug in the sink. I knew her job was stressful, and I knew she worked nights more often than she wished for, but when was the last time we had a decent conversation? A mother-daughter conversation. One where she looked at me with loving eyes and where it was clear she wanted to hear what I had to say. And now, at seventeen, I needed it more than ever. I needed a mother who cared, and would listen, and would give me advice that I so badly wanted. Was it because she wasn't my *real* mother? Was a girl of eleven too old to bond with? I was too young to remember my first foster family, and I tried desperately not to remember the chaos of the second family, so the Robinsons were the only family I knew. George and Darlene were the closest thing I had to parents, and I loved them. But to them—I was still a foster child. A way to make some extra money. And a painful reminder that they weren't ever able to have children of

21

their own. But still, why couldn't she at least *try* to understand me?

"I like Drew," I blurted, keeping my eyes on Lucia lapping at her water.

"Duh," she replied as she opened the fridge and rattled around with some bottles on the door.

Duh? Really? "But I can't figure out if he likes me back." I wasn't sure why I kept talking. Why I needed so badly for her to *want* to help me. Did I think she could somehow magically fix it all for me?

She let out an exasperated sigh. "Sarah, how long have you known him? Six years? If he was into you, you'd know it by now." She closed the fridge and left the room.

"Five," I mumbled when she was gone. I had lived with them for six years, but I didn't meet Drew until the following summer, five years ago.

I scooped up Lucia and brought her up to my room. She jumped up on my bed, curled up beside my pillow and whined for me to join her. Instead, my walls, plastered with animated pictures of colourful tigers, caught my attention. Picture after picture, each drawn with such care and detail. Probably over a hundred of them as I had been drawing them for as long as I could remember. Each had brought me so much joy at one point, a welcomed distraction from the real world, but now they just represented my childish youth. They stood for another reason why I was different from everyone else.

I ripped the first one off the wall. It was one I had drawn last summer when Drew and his father were away on a trip. The tiger was lying in a grassy meadow, with his head on his paws, a look of loneliness on his face. I tore down the next one—a colourful tiger wearing a tortured expression as dark clouds encircled her head like a wreath. I had drawn that one before I moved in with the Robinsons. I was about nine years old then, and struggling to find myself. The third and fourth came down without any reminiscing, and soon my walls were bare and my floor was covered. My room looked older now, more refined. I was heading into womanhood and I would need to start acting like it.

I slumped down next to Lucia and patted her softly as I rested my head against my headboard, immediately annoyed by the sharpness of an object that stuck into my head. I reached back and tugged the dreamcatcher from the hook that held it in its place, a twinge of guilt striking me as I did. Drew had given the dreamcatcher to me the first time we met, the summer I was twelve. I had gone home and put it up right away, excited over finally meeting the cute boy from down the street. And since that day, the dreamcatcher hung peacefully, feathers and jewels resting gently against the old wood of my headboard. I thumbed the silk web in the centre of the circle. Such a pretty design. It hardly made sense that Drew made it himself, or that he gave it to me that day, or that he periodically made sure that I still had it. I felt an urge to tuck it under my bed along with the rest of my childhood memories, symbolically freeing myself from Drew and the hold he'd had on me since the day we first met. But I couldn't. It was the only meaningful thing anyone had ever given me. It was handmade. And maybe he hadn't made it *for* me, but he had given it *to* me, and he didn't have to. He could've kept it. I resolved to return it to its hook and instead gave my attention to Lucia. As my hand moved along her fluffy coat, my eyes rested on the ring on my pinkie finger. It was simple, but elegant and I always loved that it had my yellow birthstone in the middle, hugged by the birthstones of my foster parents on either side. They had given it to me on my twelfth birthday, just after I moved in with them, and although it seemed an odd gift under the circumstances, I wore it with childish pride. I supposed that was why it was called a Daughter's Pride ring; not a Parents' Pride ring.

"Hmph. Daughter's Pride. Whatever." I pulled the ring from my pinkie and set it on my bedside table, then snuggled up next to Lucia and drifted off to sleep, filling my mind with imaginary thoughts of a pleasant childhood, one that was full of love and fun memories made with a family who treasured my existence.

CHAPTER 2

First Dream

~ SARAH ~

THE WARM, WHITE sand massaged the soles of my feet as I wandered toward the turquoise sea. Bright green-leafed palm trees swayed gently around me, filling the moist air with the sweet smell of coconut. A colourful surfboard rested against the palm tree closest to me, almost begging me to take him for a dip in the soothing water just yards away. My fingers were now on the surfboard. I ran my hand down the colours, allowing them to fill my soul with the most relaxed sense of peace.

"Do you surf?" a deep voice asked from behind, startling me.

I spun around and came face to face with the brightest, yet darkest, blue eyes I had ever seen. Windswept brown hair framed his perfectly tanned face and gorgeous surfer smile.

He laughed and then his gaze lowered, only pausing long enough to make me suddenly aware of the small, yellow bikini I was wearing. I straightened my posture, embarrassed that I had been caught in such a revealing bathing suit. Why couldn't I be wearing a more modest swimsuit?

"Uh, no, I don't surf," I said, finally recalling his question. I pulled my gaze back to the surfboard. "I was just admiring it. It's beautiful."

"I would've thought your standard for beauty would've been set higher." He grinned. "You know, given the flawless beauty that you see in the mirror every day." Was this guy blind, maybe?

I blushed and pushed a strand of hair from my face. Hair that somehow, in this light, didn't just have orange highlights. It shone a vibrant orange.

"Why are you here?" he asked.

I scanned my surroundings. Sand dunes, palm trees, white sand, turquoise sea, rock cliffs. How was I supposed to know *why* I was someplace when I didn't even know where that someplace was?

"I don't know," I answered honestly.

He took a step closer to me, and the smell of coconuts shrouded me like a blanket. A delicious, scrumptious, melt-in-your-mouth coconut. A look of mischief, combined with lust, covered his eyes. He bit his lower lip and I found myself fighting hard to refrain from biting it, too.

I took a step back and felt the surfboard against my back. My breathing was heavy. I couldn't explain why I wanted to kiss this stranger. Pheromones? Chemistry? Whatever the reason, it was a welcomed distraction from Drew.

As if sensing my need, but my reluctance to act on it (mostly due to social protocol), he leaned into me and whispered, "It's your dream. You call the shots."

"A dream," I heard myself say. As strange as it sounded to everyone else, I never dreamed. While I was sleeping, anyway. Daydreaming was not foreign to me, but this—dreaming in a subconscious state and having little to no control over what was happening around me, was definitely different.

"Yes, a dream." He laughed. "You do dream, don't you?" He paused and his eyes darted back and forth between mine, determined for my response.

"This is a first," I divulged, somehow feeling silly for saying it.

He crinkled his brow and narrowed his eyes onto mine.

"What?" I said, suddenly feeling examined and vulnerable.

"You've never had a dream before," he repeated as if

struggling to believe it.

"That's what I said."

"Not even a nightmare?" His eyes were locked on mine, studying me hard.

I shook my head. "No. Why is this so hard to believe?"

"It just makes you unique." He smiled as if this was a good thing.

"You don't need to tell me," I said, feeling the burden of it. "I realize I'm quite different."

"It's not a bad thing," he said.

I raised my eyebrows in protest, but let them fall at his deep blue eyes burrowing into mine.

He took my hands in his and studied my fingers. "No ring," he said, more to himself.

My face reddened. *That's right. I'm single. For the taking.* "I don't have a boyfriend," I said, answering his quiet question.

He smiled and returned his gaze to mine. "Hard to believe."

"Unique, remember?"

"Yes. Yes, you are. The girl who never dreams." He cocked a half smile and my face flushed at the way his eyes twinkled when they looked at me.

"The girl who never dreams," I repeated just so I could convince myself that I wasn't frozen from his stare. "Why does that amuse you?"

"Just think it's odd, is all," he said before sucking in a deep breath and continuing. "But since it is your first time, the pressure's on to make it a memorable one." The side of his mouth curled up and my heart leaped. "Don't worry—it's just a dream."

Just a dream, I thought. *It doesn't matter what I do, when I wake up, it was all just a dream.*

I took a deep breath of courage, then leaned in to kiss him, my eyes closed and heart pounding. But nothing happened. I propped open one eye. Then the other. Dream Guy was staring at me with a most peculiar expression on his face. *Okay, so apparently even in my dreams no one wants to kiss me.*

"I'd love to kiss you," he said after reading my embarrassment, "but I'm more interested in getting to know you first."

Of course you are. Most people are more interested in being my friend.

And as if he read that expression too, he added, "I'm drawn to you, and that fascinates me so I'd really like to get to know you first. But I promise—I will kiss you before you wake."

My knees trembled and a sensual feeling erupted somewhere deep in my belly.

"Shall we take a walk?" He held his hand out for me to take, and I took it happily, feeling his strong, warm hand in mine. It felt so real. I ran my free hand up his forearm. It all felt so real. His skin was smooth, warm and soft. His fingers wrapped nicely around mine, sure of their commitment. When I took in Dream Guy's profile, I realized he had been watching me. I looked away quickly, feeling embarrassed that I had been caught inspecting him so closely.

"Do I meet with your approval?" he teased.

"It's just you look and feel so real."

"Am I not real?"

"Well, it's a dream. I kind of thought you'd be wispy or ghost-like."

"Wispy or ghost-like," he said, nodding and smiling at the same time.

"Well, you know."

"Oh yes, I forgot that you've never dreamed before."

"I may have dreamed once, although I can't be sure. But I have friends who have, and I've been told about dreams. They never seem that believable." I remembered Maddy telling me about her so-called amazing dreams. They never sounded as amazing or interesting as she made them out to be. Maybe this was the same thing. Maybe when I woke up, it would somehow not make as much sense, or feel as real.

There was a moment of silence as we continued treading the warm sand together. When we reached the end of the beach where a rock cliff and high tide prevented us from venturing further, we turned and started back.

"You have beautiful hair," Dream Guy said as he gently swiped a piece of my messy orange hair from my face.

I smiled politely, but didn't say thank you. How could I when I knew he couldn't possibly have meant it?

"And your eyes. They're almost—"

"Yellow," I finished for him. "Yeah, I've been told. Part of what makes me *unique*." I rolled my eyes.

"You don't know you're beautiful, do you?" he said, a hint of sadness in his voice.

I shot him a strange look and then turned my face toward the ocean.

"You're the most beautiful girl I've ever seen here. I promise you that."

He wasn't walking anymore, and I had to stop too, or let go of his hand, which I wasn't ready to do. I kept my face turned to the water, letting the ocean breeze carry my hair from my face.

Then, in one charismatic motion, he reached up and took my face in his hands. His warm body melted against mine and our eyes mated before he brought his lips to mine. Even his kiss tasted like the ocean.

After a moment, he pulled back, perplexed, and said, "Who *are* you?"

"Sarah," I answered in an exhale as I traced his sculpted chest with my fingertips, making mental note of the hard contours and smooth muscles.

"Where are you from?" he asked as he gently pulled

my head back and then kissed my neck.

My breathing became heavy again as his lips made their way up to my ear, and his fingers massaged the back of my head. "Bedford."

He stopped and looked me straight in the eyes. "Where is Bedford? What country?"

I laughed. "Nova Scotia, Canada." Okay, so apparently yes, dreams were very weird. I would have to remember this when I woke up. Remember that it was weird while it happened too, and not just weird when it was retold to someone else.

"And you've never been here before," he said, strangely, as if to himself.

"Right." I pulled away, sensing all the magic of the moment was lost. "And it's just a dream, remember?"

He chuckled and ran his fingers through his hair. "I know. Yeah, I know. I just . . . I'm just trying to figure out what it is that makes you so irresistible."

"Okay." I raised my eyebrows in a display of sarcastic confusion. *Should I be offended by that?*

"What brought you here?" he asked cautiously. He sat down in the sand and pulled me down next to him.

"I really have no idea what you're talking about."

"Okay, that's fair. I'm sorry." He reached for my hand. "You're incredible, Sarah, and I just don't want this dream to end."

"How about this." I leaned over and kissed his cheek

softly. "Let's make the most of the time we have together then." I stood up and went for the surfboard. "Teach me to surf?"

"Ha!" he laughed disapprovingly. "Not until you tell me what your biggest fears are."

I tilted my head sideways, a strange look on my face. "What does that matter?"

"It just does," he said, taking the surfboard from me.

"I don't have any." I almost convinced myself.

He looked down at the ground, mulling something over, then peered out into the ocean. "Sharks? Everyone's afraid of sharks."

"Not me," I said.

"Drowning?"

"Not really."

"Sea creatures?"

"No," I laughed. "Why are you asking these questions?"

He raised his eyebrows and sucked in a breath. "Because I need to know."

"Okay, let me think." I put a finger to my lip and pondered his question. "I'm afraid of dying alone."

"Afraid of dying alone," he repeated, as if deciding how he could fix that. "Okay, I'll tell you what. How about we just take a walk on the beach today? And the next time you come back, maybe we'll try surfing." He dropped the surfboard into the sand.

"Deal." I slid my hand into his and led him down the beach. Because really, as long as I was next to him, it didn't matter where we were. This was the first time I felt special in a long time.

"So do you live here?" I asked, knowing it sounded silly with it being a dream and all.

"I do," he said. "This is my home."

"It's beautiful."

He looked around, as if admiring it for the first time. "Beauty is in the eye of the beholder."

It was an odd thing to say and as we walked down the beach, I wondered what he meant by it.

We came across a checkered blanket spread out on the sand with a wicker picnic basket that sat on one corner. I looked around to see who it belonged to, but then Dream Guy turned me to me and said, "Hungry?"

"Wait. You did this?" I asked, puzzled, but then remembered that it was a dream. Anything was possible, right?

He smirked his gorgeous sideways smile and motioned for me to sit. "I'll get us a snack. You enjoy the sun."

"I think I will," I said, finding a comfortable place to lie out and let the sun bathe my body. "We don't get much sun this time of year in Nova Scotia."

"Is it cold there?"

"Right now it is."

I turned my face toward the blazing, hot sun. "Mmmm . . . this is so nice."

A minute later he was next to me, propped up on his left elbow and running his right hand over my middle. I pried one eye open and looked up at him, a strawberry dangling from his luscious lips. A smile crept over my face as I tilted my head up and met his mouth with mine, gladly taking the cold, sweet fruit on my tongue. He produced another strawberry and slowly traced my lips with it. I licked it once, but he pulled it away as I opened my mouth for it. He repeated this tantalizing game until my mouth watered for the fat, juicy strawberry. Eventually, I closed my eyes and waited, with my mouth partly open, for him to give in. His tongue touched my lips next, a different texture and temperature from the strawberry, but just as tasty. Our lips met and my body instantly arched, calling for his to meet mine. He slid on top of me and I entangled my fingers through his thick, untamed hair.

"How do you do this to me?" he moaned, almost complaining.

My heart smiled. I had never had that effect on anyone before. No one ever seemed to need me the way that my dream guy did. As much as I always wanted Drew to need me like this, he never did.

Suddenly a loud knocking sound interrupted our moment. He slowly sat up, bit his lower lip and looked down, annoyed.

"What was that?" I asked.

He shook his head. "Ignore it." And he kissed my neck.

The knock came again, and louder this time. I looked around and everything started to feel fuzzy and unreal. "What's going on?"

He kissed me one last time. "Come back again," he said.

"Am I waking?"

He nodded. "See you around, beautiful."

CHAPTER 3

Prom Date

~ SARAH ~

MY EYES POPPED open and darted around the room. Lucia was lying next to me, her eyes open too, but head resting on my arm as if she enjoyed where we were and had no intention of getting up. The room was cold and I took notice of my blue fingers and freezing toes. I pulled the blanket over me and curled up with Lucia, trying to bring back the warm feelings of my dream. His face was still etched in my memory as if he was still standing in front of me. I opened my eyes, but he wasn't there. Is that what dreaming was like? No wonder Drew was always so interested in Maddy's dreams. But most of hers lacked detail and realism. This dream was so vivid. So real. I wanted more. There was a slight grogginess to my head, and the images began fading from my memory. *No. Come back.*

A loud knock on my bedroom door startled me, causing me to sit straight up.

"Come in," I said, heart beating wildly.

"Hey, it's me." Drew poked his head around the door. "Were you sleeping?"

"Yeah." I rubbed my head and stretched.

"You okay?" he asked as he carefully sat on the edge of my bed.

"What? Huh?" I fell back on my pillow and yawned.

"You're tired."

"My head is just foggy. I'm fine." Maybe I was tired. I normally woke up feeling refreshed and well. But this time I couldn't free myself from the feelings of my dream. But what even *was* my dream about? A guy. It was about a guy. But . . .

"What's wrong?" Drew had his hands on my shoulders and was sitting me up to face him. "Sarah, snap out of it. What's going on?" He flipped my blanket off my bed and looked around my room, searching for something. "Are you drunk?" he asked, wildly.

"No!" I laughed, pinching my eyes closed and stretching. "I'm fine, Drew! You just woke me up in the middle of a deep sleep. I'm trying to remember my dream."

"Dream?" Drew took my hand in his. He rubbed his thumb across my fingers, and my breath hitched in my throat. I wondered if it was more out of habit.

"Hey, you lost your Daughter's Pride ring," he noticed.

"It's too small. I took it off." I jerked my head toward my bedside table where my ring now lay.

Drew nodded slowly and then said, "What was your dream about?" He dropped my hand and looked down at the floor.

"There was this guy." A smile spread across my lips as I fought through the fog and confusion to recall my dream. "This amazingly good-looking guy." *And a beach. And . . . a picnic, maybe?*

"Was it a nightmare?" Drew pressed. I noticed his eyes went straight to my dreamcatcher. He held up the leather strands and counted the beads quietly, then turned it, inspecting the web.

"What are you doing?" I asked, pulling the dreamcatcher from him. "No, it wasn't a nightmare." *Didn't you hear me? An amazingly good-looking guy. That's a good dream. Maybe it wouldn't be for you, but it was for me.*

"Can't you be more specific? What did the place look like? What was the guy's name?"

"I don't remember, Drew." I pulled Lucia onto my lap and stroked her fur. "Why do you care what the guy's name was? It wasn't Drew." I hoped he would blush. He didn't.

"Did he say anything specific to you?"

"Not really." I thought back to our conversation, which, for some reason, I felt oddly protective over. "Look, Drew, I know you have this weird obsession with deciphering dreams and such, but this was literally just a normal dream. Probably had it because of Maddy's news about Caleb giving her his ring." *And I'm not about to tell you all the details and listen to you tell me it's because I have an irrational love interest in someone who isn't the slightest bit interested in me.*

He nodded slowly. "Anyway, I think your parents would be hurt if they found out you took your ring off." He held the ring out for me to take.

I considered it for a moment, but Darlene's cold words and unloving demeanor flooded my memory. "If they want me to wear one, they'll have to buy one that fits. They gave this to me when I was twelve. They can't expect me to wear it forever."

Drew sighed heavily. "Okay."

"Why are you here?" I asked.

He sucked in a breath, as if summoning enough strength. "I changed my mind about the prom. I think we should go," he said in an exhale.

I studied his face. Duty? Guilt? Did he lose a bet? "Why the change of heart?"

He shrugged. "It's important to you. And it'll be fun."

I smiled. "I think it will be," I agreed. "Let's do it." I hopped up onto my knees and squared myself with him.

"You really want to go?" My excitement was obvious.

He laughed, at my charm, I imagined. "I think so."

"Yay!" I clapped my hands and then propelled myself at Drew. He caught me and stumbled backward, both of us laughing as we fell to the floor. Me and Drew. How it always used to be before things got awkward between us in the last six months or so.

"Stay for dinner?" I asked, knowing it wasn't one of his favourite things to do, but hoping he'd make an exception for tonight. I wasn't looking forward to facing Darlene again.

His eyes bounced back and forth between mine. "Sure."

"GOOD TO HAVE you here, Drew," George said as we joined him at the dining room table. "We haven't seen you around much lately."

"Been busy, Sir," Drew answered, "but it's nice to be back."

George looked from Drew to me and back to Drew again. "Well, good then. Glad you could stay for supper."

"Thanks for having me."

"Self-serve," Darlene called from the kitchen.

George took his plate and stood up. With a laugh, he said, "Can never get good service around here."

We filed through the kitchen and piled our plates with pot roast, mashed potatoes and a vegetable medley.

When we sat back down at the table, Drew folded his hands in his lap. He was expecting us to say grace. He always said grace when I was at his house for dinner, and although I found it awkward at times, I also found it comforting. I put my hands in my lap and waited, too.

George had a forkful of dinner on its way to his mouth when he stopped and looked at the both of us. "Oh," he said, putting his fork down. "I, uh, suppose we should say grace?"

Darlene snorted. "You want to thank the Lord for the food? How about you thank me? I worked five night shifts this week to put food on this table. Is anyone thanking me?"

"Darlene," I said in a tone that she read as disrespectful by the look she shot at me.

"What? You think you know how to say grace?"

"No, I didn't say that," I answered.

"You want to give it a try? You think you're so wise? Let's say grace then. Sarah has volunteered."

I glared at her.

"I'd like to, Mrs. Robinson, if that's okay." Drew reached for my hand under the table and gave it a squeeze. He bowed his head and started, "Here we sit and softly pray, thank you for this food today. Please bless the food we're about to eat, the hands that prepared it and the people that will share it. Amen."

Drew squeezed my hand again before letting it go,

and then we began eating, in an awkward silence that made me wish I had gone to Drew's for dinner instead.

"So what's new with you young kids these days?" George asked before taking a bite of his dinner.

Drew picked up his knife and began carving his meat. "Well, uh, I'll be taking Sarah to the prom." His cheeks flushed a pale pink as he stuffed a forkful of meat into his mouth.

Darlene looked quickly at me, surprise scrawled over her face. "Really?"

I shot her a meaningful look, a silent cry for her not to embarrass me. "Yes," I said before looking back at Drew and smiling.

"Well I'll be damned," she said, eyes wide. "After all these years of begging, he finally said yes?"

"Please, stop," I pleaded.

"Actually," Drew began, "I was the one who asked her. I'm the lucky one here." He gave a quick smile and George relaxed enough to continue his meal.

My jaw was clenched tight and I suddenly didn't feel much like eating. After a few awkward, Drew piped up, "So Sarah tells me that her Daughter's Pride ring is too small now. She can't wear it anymore."

"Is that so, Sarah?" George stretched his neck to gain a better view of my hand from across the table.

I raised my bare hand. "I've been wearing it on my pinkie for two years now."

George chuckled. "Must be time for a new one then, wouldn't you say?"

"She's not getting a new one," Darlene said before taking a sip of her wine.

"Yes, not necessary," I added, trying not to let the hurt reach my face.

"Well, why not?" George challenged, which he rarely ever did.

"She'll be eighteen this year, George. There's no need for us to spend money on a ring that she won't end up wearing anyway. I'm sure it fit just fine. Just not very convenient is all. Besides, she's not even our real daughter anyway." She muttered the last part under her breath, but I was meant to hear it.

I raised my eyebrows in Drew's direction. *See what I have to deal with?*

Drew's eyes softened with an apology, and without any further objections from George, we all continued our meals in silence.

"**I KNOW YOU** were only trying to help, but next time you think my parents have an ounce of compassion and you want to draw it out of them, just don't." I flopped down on my bed as Drew pulled the desk chair next to me.

"I'm sorry," he said, watching me closely.

"S'okay. I'm used to it."

"For what it's worth, George seemed cool with it."

"He's just along for the ride."

"I'm really sorry, Sarah."

"Don't be." I smiled. "I'm totally fine. She's right. I wouldn't wear it anyway. It'd be a waste of money."

Drew eyeballed the Daughter's Pride ring on my bedside table. "Is it really too small? Or are you just being stubborn?"

I grabbed the ring and jammed it onto my pinkie. It didn't glide on easily, but I managed to get it on nonetheless. "I've outgrown it."

"Just wear it for tonight. Maybe you'll feel better in the morning."

I glared at him. "Drop it, Drew. I'm not wearing it." I yanked the ring off, and as I did, I felt the metal separate between my fingers. A momentary swell of guilt punched at my heart as I hoped my parents wouldn't think that I broke it intentionally, but then I remembered Darlene's treatment of me during dinner and realized that I didn't care anyway. "And now it's broken," I confirmed. I opened my bedside table drawer and tossed the ring into it. "I just have to accept the fact that nobody's *proud* to call me their daughter. Even my real mother abandoned me."

Drew sat down on my bed next to me. He traced his finger along my face and behind my ear, tucking a strand of hair with it. My heart beat wildly. "I'm sure your real mother loved you, Sarah."

He meant to comfort me, but it was only confirmation that even he knew my parents were cruel and unloving.

He rested his hand on my knee and squeezed gently. "You're special, Sarah." The action, combined with his words, caused my heart to squeeze.

I smiled self-consciously and occupied my thoughts with a loose string on my bedspread.

"I have to go," he whispered after a minute. "I hate to leave you like this."

Then don't go, I silently pleaded.

"I have a ton of homework to do," he said, as if in answer to my broken desires.

"S'okay," I said.

As he stood, he leaned forward and kissed my forehead. "Sweet dreams."

I immediately thought of my dream guy and hoped I could have that same, desire-filled dream as earlier.

"Dream of me." His words hung in the air, cradled by the silence that followed.

Kiss me.

His stare fell to my lips as he moistened his.

Kiss me.

My heart beat wildly and my breathing was getting heavier and heavier.

Kiss me!

The door popped open and in bounded Lucia, making a run for my bed.

"Lucia!" I scolded, annoyed that her entrance had ruined our moment, but then tried to play it off as though she had just startled me. "What are you doing, girl?"

"I really have to go." Drew stood up and made for the door.

"Drew?" I said, propping myself up on my elbows.

"Yeah?" He turned, hopeful and waiting.

"I'll dream of you."

He smiled wide as a look of relief washed over his face, but as I settled in that night, my eyes heavy and promising a deep sleep, there was only one guy on my mind, and Drew wasn't him.

CHAPTER 4

Letting Go

~ DREW ~

EVEN WITH A sweater and thick coat, the air was bitterly cold as I walked home. I hated leaving her. As much as she pretended that Darlene's indifference toward the Daughter's Pride ring didn't bother her, I knew it did. She just wanted to be loved. She wanted a mother who she could count on, a mother who she could relate to. It was her dream after being abandoned by her own mother at the age of three, then thrown into a foster care system and bounced around for one reason or another, to end up being raised by people who hardly had any time for themselves, much less her. Any other girl would've given up by that point, but she still held onto the hope that one day her real mother would come back for her. The aching feeling in my chest was because of this. I had wanted to give Mrs. Robinson a piece of my mind at the dinner table. How could she be so blind? Sarah was unique. She was special.

I wasn't walking anymore. I stood in the middle of the sidewalk, halfway between Sarah's house and my own. The streetlight was directly above me and I wondered what had made me stop and how long it had been. My stomach churned with the thought of her dreaming. Yes, the dreamcatcher would protect her from the worst dreams, but still, what if she met the wrong person? What if . . . history repeated itself?

This last thought had me jogging back to her house. When I came face to face with Mrs. Robinson in the kitchen, it occurred to me that I had just let myself in, without knocking or announcing my arrival.

"Drew," she said. "Did you forget something?"

"Uh, yeah," I lied. "Upstairs. I'll just be a second." I started up the stairs, two at a time, when a memory from dinner stabbed at me. I halted on the steps, and slowly turned around. "Mrs. Robinson," I began.

"Uh-huh?"

"You're too hard on Sarah. She hasn't done anything wrong to you."

There was a pause before she answered. "I beg your pardon, Drew?"

So she was going to pretend that I was out of line and this wasn't any of my concern. But it *was* my concern. Protecting Sarah and her happiness was my main plight. "I mean this with respect," I said, coming down the stairs and back into the kitchen. "Your words hurt her more than you think they do."

"Then she needs to toughen up," she snorted.

"Has she *done* something to you?" I challenged.

"What? Other than embarrass me by walking around with her head in the clouds and wasting her time chasing after a boy that clearly only has sympathy for her?"

I clenched my teeth to avoid saying anything I would regret. "She's special," I said.

"She's a lost cause. Her only ambition is to draw pictures of cats all day. She'll never amount to anything." Mrs. Robinson sighed. "Doesn't matter. When she turns eighteen, she's not my problem anymore."

"Wow," I said. "You have no idea how lucky you are to have a daughter like Sarah but yet you can't get out of your own way to notice it."

"I'm not saying she's the worst mistake I've ever made." And I knew that was the closest to an agreement or apology that she would ever give. My heart hurt for Sarah, and suddenly I didn't want to wake her from her dream. I wanted her to experience freedom and adventure, and for a few hours not have to worry about the life she was given here.

Once in Sarah's bedroom, I traced the circle of her dreamcatcher as it lay valiantly on her headboard. I always knew this day would come, but it still never quite prepared me for the anxious feeling that crippled my heart.

I knelt next to her bed and took her hand. She looked so peaceful. The worry lines in her forehead were gone, the tense purse to her lips was now relaxed. Maybe this was where she belonged.

"Be careful," I whispered, low enough that even if she were awake, she probably still wouldn't have heard. "I . . . I care what happens to you." They weren't the words ready to slip from my tongue, but I couldn't let her know I loved her. Protecting her was my mission. Loving her would only get her killed.

Chapter 5

Dream Guy

~ Sarah ~

THE WIND WAS thick and whipped mercilessly at my face as I stood on the edge of a cliff peering down the canyon at the wild, rushing river below. I was dreaming. This place was different; I felt free. I *was* free. Free from my parents, free from Drew's elusiveness, free from all the troubles and worries of the world. But I could feel them pressing against me like the walls of a room closing in around me, forcing me to the edge of the cliff.

It wasn't going to take me. Fear wasn't going to win. I sprung from the very depths of my feet and decided that since it was my dream, and it wasn't reality, then I could fly. I flapped my arms and my body twirled in the wind, taking me higher and higher. My body was light and airy as it defied gravity. I flipped onto my back and looked up into the dark blue sky, focusing on a black shadow in the distance, and then heaviness returned to my body and I felt myself fall. Suddenly I wasn't in control anymore. The wind ripped my clothes as I spiralled through its savage breath. I pinched my eyes closed as the sharp, dark red rocks of the canyon drew nearer and nearer. Then, as quickly as it began, it stopped.

I had been holding my breath, I realized now. One eye slowly pried open, confirming a sharp, ragged rock only inches from my face. Then suddenly a voice.

"You always take life-threatening risks?"

I scrambled to my feet, the hard ground only a foot from where I hung suspended in the air, and turned to see my visitor. Dream Guy. His dark hair was windswept, too. Had he been falling alongside me? His deep, mysterious eyes were searching my face for an answer. An answer? *Oh yes, I should probably stop staring and start talking.*

"I . . . I don't normally take risks," I admitted. "I just wanted to feel . . . free, I guess."

He took my hand in his and started navigating us through the rocks. "Well, next time you want to *feel free,* maybe start small. Don't go plunging yourself off the side of a cliff."

"Noted," I said, brushing my free hand through my tangled hair and wiping the wind-given tears from my face. I thought I could do it. I was *sure* I could. Why hadn't it worked? It was just a dream. I was in control, right?

"So you came back," he said after a minute, an element of curiosity in his voice, coupled with relief.

"Why wouldn't I?" I laughed. "It's the one place I feel . . . safe."

He laughed, too, although almost in protest. "Safe isn't how I would describe this place." His fingers tightened on my hand and I felt the warmth and intensity of his touch. "What were you trying to do when you jumped off that cliff back there?" He stopped and turned to face me, a sense of urgency and determination plaguing his face.

"Fly," I said simply.

His eyebrows arched.

"Haven't you ever wanted to fly?" I added, registering his perplexed expression.

"Sure," he said. "I just never expected *you* to say that."

"Why?"

"You're from Earth. Humans don't fly," he said flatly.

"True," I agreed. "But this isn't real and I'm dreaming. There are no limitations in your dreams, right?" . . . *Right?* I wasn't really sure. My limited knowledge of dreams came from the bits and pieces Maddy would share of her odd dreams.

"No limitations," Dream Guy repeated as if considering how to dissect that comment. "I wouldn't say there are *no* limitations. But I think it's safe to say that you are definitely not in control of everything that happens while you're dreaming."

"So you're saying I *could* fly."

"I'm saying it's possible, but only if someone doesn't try to stop you."

I shook my head. "Okay, whatever. It's not like I could die if I had landed on those rocks. I would've just woken up." At his silence, I met his eyes. "Right?"

His face had gone a very pale shade. "Sure."

I kicked at a stone and continued walking, hoping that the motion would bring colour back to his cheeks. "I don't remember much of my mother—my real mother—but what I do remember of her, she was always singing to me. Her songs didn't often make much sense, but I loved to just hear her sing them anyway." I smiled to myself. "Her songs were often about dreaming, probably because she was trying to get me to fall asleep, and I remember she would sing about flying." I shook the daydream from my head. "Maybe that's why I thought I could fly."

He nodded as if understanding and sympathy were united. "Is your mother . . . did she die?"

I shrugged. "Could have. She left me on the steps of the Children's Aid Society when I was three with no information about herself. All she left was my name and birth information. The name didn't match any records anywhere." I felt his hand on my shoulder now. "I don't remember much of her. Just that she used to sing to me." I smiled at one of the only fleeting memories I had of her—kneeling beside my bed, holding one of my hands to her face while she stroked my cheek with her other hand. "She always looked so determined when she sang, as if she were afraid I would one day forget how she sang to me." I shook my head. "I thought she loved me . . . but then she abandoned me." My eyes began to sting.

"Maybe she did love you. People leave their kids for all kinds of different reasons. Doesn't mean they don't love them. Maybe she knew she wasn't the best person to raise you."

I smiled and nodded. This was one of my theories. The one where I painted her as a selfless heroine who had abandoned me because she loved me.

My arm was extended back and I realized that Dream Guy was no longer walking. When I slowly turned to him, his face showed sadness, intensity and a longing that I had never seen before.

"You are special," was all he said, his expression unchanging.

I scoffed. "Well, I would beg to differ, but—"

"Why do you do that?"

"Do what?"

"You're so hard on yourself. Why?"

I pulled my head back a bit. "I don't know," I said dismissively. "I guess it's hard to take a compliment when you don't believe it to be true."

"You don't have to believe it in order for it to be true," he said.

"Ok, well then, thank you for the compliment."

"From what I can see, everything about you is perfect."

"Well, I guess being the guy of my dreams, you would say that, wouldn't you?"

He smirked and then pulled my face to his, connecting his lips with mine. He brought his hands to my waist and held it firmly as I ran my fingers through his hair. *I've never been kissed like this*, I thought. Passion, heat and lust coursed through my body like a train bounding down a steep hill.

He hoisted me up and I wrapped my legs around him, my arms now locked around his neck as we kissed. Blindly, he took us toward the cliff face, and into a cave in the side of the cliff. After propping me up on the ledge, he pulled himself up beside me. We sat in the cave together, breathing heavily, holding each other and staring into each other's wanting eyes.

I didn't mind the time that passed. I was enjoying just being in his arms and him being in mine. It felt right. Safe. Sure.

"I'm falling for you," he whispered, a trace of disbelief in his own voice. "I don't know why or how, but I am."

My heart was light and filled with joy at the sound of his words, spoken to me, all for me, but I couldn't help let my sarcasm show. "Thanks. You're not sure *why* or *how*, huh? Am I too plain to imagine falling for?"

I expected him to laugh, but he didn't. Then I expected him to make a rebuttal, but none came.

"I wish it made more sense," he finally said. "Oh, and you're hardly plain."

He was still holding me firmly, my only view was the back of the cave. My eyes darted around the dark room, wondering what I should say next. He said he was falling for me. This was a dream, I knew that, but he hardly knew anything about me. But I was falling for him, too, and I didn't even know his name yet. Although somehow, it wasn't the most pressing matter. I may have known nothing about him, but at the same time, I felt I knew everything about him.

"It just feels right, doesn't it?" I said, somehow knowing he needed to hear those words. Maybe it was the firm way he held me, or the sharp breaths he was taking, or the shake in his voice. I pulled back and forced him to look me in the eyes.

"It does," he agreed. "It does feel right." His concern was obvious, but why?

"Are you okay?"

His eyes found mine. Like, *really* found mine. They had only been skimming the surface for the last minute. Now, he was visibly calmer as his eyes penetrated with mine. His body relaxed. He was in me now and I was in him. We shared the same thoughts, emotions, feelings. And this made everything clearer.

"I'm falling for you, too," I whispered, the excitement in my chest lifting me higher and higher, deeper and deeper.

Our lips were touching now, but unmoving. Our eyes were still connected, and our souls were too, I knew. I felt.

"This must be why Drew doesn't want me to dream," I said as I softly kissed the top of his head, pushing my fingers through his thick hair.

He stopped kissing my neck long enough to ask, "Sorry?" He pulled back. "What did you say?"

"I'm beginning to wonder if this is what my friend Drew was afraid of—that I'd find someone else to fall in love with. He got a little weird earlier when I told him I had a dream this afternoon."

"How so?" he pulled back and studied my face as I answered.

"I don't know. I guess he was just asking all these weird questions and then made me promise I would dream of him tonight."

"You've really never dreamed before," he said as

more of a statement than a question.

"Not that I can remember. But now that I know what I've been missing out on, I'm definitely going to start going to bed earlier." I laughed, finding myself amusing, even if he didn't. He just wrapped his arms around my back and pulled me in too close to kiss.

"Tell me all about yourself," he said, causing me to wonder what he was thinking. Or do dream guys even think?

I turned on his lap and wrapped his arms around me so that I could lean against his chest and look out across the horizon. "Okay," I began, happy to give him an insight into who I was. "Well, you already know my name."

"What's your last name?" he quickly interjected.

"Marley. Sarah Marley." When he didn't reply, I continued, "It's the only thing I have that's mine, you know?"

I felt his lips rest on my head. He was listening. "Go on," he whispered. "Tell me more about you."

"I'm in grade twelve at Xavier High."

"Where's Xavier High?" he asked.

"Bedford," I said. "Nova Scotia."

"Right." He nodded slowly. "Sorry to interrupt. Go on."

"That's pretty much it."

"Siblings? Parents? Friends?" he coached.

"I don't have any siblings, but I do have Lucia." I

smiled as I pictured her big brown eyes. "She's my dog. We were found together the morning I was abandoned."

"Wow," was all he said to this. It was all most people said. I knew what they really meant—that is sad and depressing, but somewhat hopeful.

"And as for parents, well, I have foster parents. I've had three foster families, but this one is my last. I'll be eighteen in November so I can live on my own then."

He watched me, but didn't ask, although I knew what he wanted to ask me—why three foster homes?

"The first family—the Millers—discovered they were allergic to dogs, and there was no way I was staying without Lucia, so I was only there for less than a year. Then I was with the second family—the Comeaus—for about six years. They had a dozen kids and she kept popping more out, so eventually we were all taken from them and put in other homes, which is when I moved in with the Robinsons. George and Darlene were in their fifties and not able to have kids, so I was kind of like the daughter they never had. . . . Except they treat me more like the stepdaughter they never wanted."

The conversation was starting to depress me. I never talked about my past with anyone, but for some reason it felt okay to open up to the tall, dark and handsome figment of my imagination. Maybe I needed a therapist.

"Where did you live before you went into foster care?" he asked quietly.

"I don't remember and no one knows. It was like my mother never existed. When I was abandoned, there was a big search for living family members, but nothing ever came up. It was like no one knew me or my mother. I only know I had a mother because I vaguely remember a few details of her." A memory of me laughing and running with other children through a thick field of flowers flashed through my mind. I was surrounded by people. By love. But where was my mother? "I know it's stupid, but I still hope that one day she'll come back for me. She'll have a tragic story of her own about why she had to leave me. About how she thought I would find a good home and have a better life than what she could give to me."

He squeezed me. I knew he thought it was farfetched too, but at least he didn't crush my dream like Drew sometimes did. Drew liked to call himself a "realist" in times like these. He didn't like when I dreamed up stories of rescue from my mother.

"Tell me about your friends."

"I have two best friends—Maddy and Drew. Maddy is super spunky and fun. We've been best friends since I moved in with the Robinsons when I was eleven. We can talk about anything. She's always good for a laugh. And then there's Drew. We met the following summer. We were going into grade eight. He's . . . I like him a lot."

"You're lucky to have such good friends."

"Yeah," I agreed, then pushed Drew from my mind.

"Your turn," I said. "Tell me about you now."

"There's not much to tell, really," he began. "I have an older brother. Some friends. But this world can get pretty lonely sometimes."

"Parents?"

His forehead creased and he shook his head. "No."

Feeling as though that was a topic not to be discussed, I moved on quickly. "Girlfriend?" I asked, hoping for a certain answer.

He grinned. "No." And there it was.

"Oh?" I feigned surprise.

"Don't get me wrong, there have been lots of girls, just never met the right girl." He squeezed me tighter and pressed his lips to my ear. "Until now it would seem."

"What makes you think I'm the right girl?" I asked. My heart was beating so loudly I wondered if he could hear it. I was sure he could feel it.

"I don't know what it is," he answered. "When you first came earlier today, I was pulled right to you. It was like a magnetic force that pulled me to the beach and there you were. I couldn't very well ignore it. And your eyes . . . your eyes are just so beautiful. *You* are so beautiful."

I hadn't noticed it coming, but a tear was now trailing down my cheek. Never in my life's memory had anyone ever spoken such sweet words to me.

"And then when you were gone, I know it wasn't for

that long, but it felt like an eternity. And when you came back, I knew it was you right away. I was pulled to you again. But this time I wanted to just watch you. Just see where you went and what you did."

"That's a little creepy," I teased.

"Still, I could've watched you all day long had you not thrown yourself off the cliff like that." He gave a tight, threatening squeeze. A warning not to do it again.

"But I was flying," I argued.

"You were. For about three seconds."

"It was still three seconds."

"And the other eight seconds you were plummeting to your death," he pointed out.

"But the flying part was pretty awesome."

"Yeah, it was impressive," he admitted. "But, if you ever do dream again, just try to remember that not all dreams are good ones. You need to be careful."

I shook my head. He was beginning to sound like Drew. "I'll be back," I assured him.

"I wish that was up to you."

"What do you mean?"

"You won't remember much of this dream when you wake. And whatever you do remember, it'll be distorted and probably won't make much sense."

I turned so that I could read his face. "I'll remember it," I assured him. "I remembered everything from my earlier dream."

His eyebrows came down, puzzled. "What do you mean?"

I laughed. "Did you honestly think I'd forget meeting you? Seriously, you're not a forgettable guy."

"No, I mean, there's a fog that clouds a dreamer's memories when they wake. It's not often that that doesn't work on a dreamer."

I shrugged. "Well, it didn't work on me."

His face reddened.

"What?"

"I probably wouldn't have made all of those admissions earlier if I thought you'd remember them when you woke up."

I suppressed a laugh. "Really? Well, I'm glad you told me. It's not often I feel special, or wanted."

He took my chin and held my stare. "Sarah, you *are* special. Don't *ever* forget that."

"Okay," I said, but as I smiled, a yawn came to the surface. "I'm sorry," I said, covering the yawn.

"You're tired."

"A little."

"Will you stay with me tonight?" he asked, his voice low and pleading.

"I want to," I said, not having really considered how this would happen. "But how do I stay with you if I fall asleep?"

"I can make sure you don't leave," he assured me.

He snapped his fingers and a four-poster bed appeared in the middle of the cave, complete with a blanket and two pillows. Another snap of his fingers and two torches appeared on either side of the bed, casting erratic shadows throughout the cave.

"Go lie down. Get some rest," he offered.

I crawled to the bed and climbed on, groaning as the exhaustion swept over me. "This is nice," I moaned.

He was still sitting against the cave wall. "You look beautiful in candlelight," he said, making my heart warm and sure.

"Will you come lie with me?"

He hesitated.

"I just want to feel your arms around me. Just hold me. That's all." After all, it was *my* dream. If I wasn't so keenly aware that it was a dream, I would never have been so bold. I was enjoying my pretend confidence.

He stood up, crossed the cave and climbed onto the bed next to me. He pulled me into him and enfolded me in his arms. We entwined our fingers and I held his hand close to my heart, where he seemingly belonged.

With his warm breath against my cheek, his strong arms holding me close, and his perfect body cradled with mine, I let myself fall into a place that was so peaceful, so unspoiled, that I was content to never wake up.

CHAPTER 6

The Fog

~ SARAH ~

SUDDENLY A LOUD, piercing siren split the air. Beep, beep, beep, beep.

"My alarm," I said, recognizing the annoying, sleep-shattering sound.

He groaned and lifted his head off the pillow. "I don't want you to go," he complained.

The fog in my head was spreading and everything around me, including Dream Guy, was becoming more and more fuzzy.

Groggy, and with my eyes refusing to open, I rolled over and shut off my alarm, pulled the blankets over my head and let myself tumble back into sleep and back into the arms of Dream Guy.

The world around me became crisp again as the fog cleared my head.

"I think I just experienced the fog," I said as I pulled my arms between us, warming them against his chest.

I ran my hand down his chest and felt something hard beneath his shirt. My fingers traced the line from his upper chest to his centre—a necklace. Our eyes met and he studied me with a heavy look of interest.

"What is it?" I asked, my fingers not moving from the shape under his shirt.

Without a word, he pulled the necklace from the neck of his shirt and let it rest again on his chest. A golden key hung from a thick, black cord. I had only once seen a necklace so distinct. So original. So ornately carved. This was Drew's. But how? Why? What did this mean?

"Drew?" I said, my heart pounding. Could this possibly *be* Drew? Did my subconscious rearrange his physical features and personality so that I could finally be with him, if only in my dreams? My attraction to Dream Guy was certainly similar to my real-life attraction to Drew.

When I met Dream Guy's gaze, he was staring at me intently, eyebrows creased and eyes batting back and forth between mine. "What did you say?"

"What's your name?" I asked, hesitantly.

"Not Drew," he answered slowly. "Have you . . . have you seen one of these before?" he asked, laying his fingers on top of mine, which were tracing the edges of the key.

"Drew has one. Where did you get this?"

"Drew has one like this?" He pressed his thumb into the round emblem at the top of the key, and when he removed it, the design in the middle shone brightly, illuminating the figure of a tornado.

"His is different," I breathed, relieved. This wasn't Drew's key. Drew's key had a tree in the centre. Not a tornado.

Dream Guy sat up slowly, watching me as he did. His eyebrows were puckered in thought as his eyes searched mine. I could tell there was more to me that he wanted, no *needed*, to know. But I didn't know everything about him yet. He knew my name, but I didn't even know his.

"My name's Luke," he finally answered.

My heart leaped, causing my breath to hitch somewhere in my chest. How was it possible that hearing his name could cause such a physical reaction?

"Nice name," I whispered, more than relieved that he didn't say "Drew."

"It means light," he said with a smirk, as if finding irony in the meaning.

"My name means princess," I said, pursing my lips and producing my best royal wave.

"I could see that," he chuckled, nodding approvingly.

I laughed. "Well, you don't know me that well, then. I am probably the furthest thing from prim and proper."

"You're amazing," Luke blurted, his chest rising and falling as fast as mine.

It's just a dream. "This is crazy. How can a dream feel so real?" My body pulled to his and our lips connected softly.

I wasn't sure why, but every time I tried to progress our affection, Luke always retreated slightly, as if that wasn't what he wanted. Sure, in real life, I wouldn't want that either, but it was a dream, after all, and as such, why *not* do whatever curiosity tempted you with?

At this thought, Luke rolled out of bed and went to the mouth of the cave. There was a heavy layer of mist and fog that impeded the view of the surrounding canyon. I climbed out too and tip-toed over to him, taking sharp notice of the cold air outside the comfort of the bed.

"It's so bleak, isn't it?" I said, noticing the greyness. "Spring is like this in Nova Scotia. I miss the colours of fall."

"Then let there be colour," Luke said, and with a wave of his hand, the clouds parted, trees with bright green foliage and vibrant purple, pink and yellow flowers sprouted up throughout the canyon and on various rock landings along the cliffs. Colourful birds soared through the air and one even landed next to us on a bush growing near the mouth of the cave.

"It's beautiful," I gasped. "How did you do that?"

Luke didn't answer, but instead sat down at the edge

of the cave and put his head in his hands.

"Are you okay?" I rested my hand on his back and took a seat next to him.

He nodded. "Just tired," he said before turning to smile at me. "It's easier to make bad things happen. This *colourful* stuff takes some energy."

I considered that odd comment. "Did you sleep last night?" I asked.

He looked at me for a second before answering. "Not much. I was too busy watching you sleep."

I laughed. "Again—creepy."

He smiled and pulled me into him so he could kiss my forehead. "Get used to it."

"Why don't you sleep now?" I suggested. "I'm not going anywhere."

"Not a chance," he said without hesitation. "Your alarm will go off again and you'll be gone before I know it."

"Fair enough." I was glad he wasn't going to sleep. I loved being with him. I knew it wasn't real, and who knew if I would ever have such a great dream again. I needed to enjoy it while it lasted.

Off in the distance, I heard a horse neigh. Luke propped his head up and looked around fervently.

"A horse?" I asked, feeling curious, but a little nervous at the same time.

"You're scared," Luke noticed.

"I'm not," I defended, but I wasn't fooling anyone. My hands were sweating, my heartbeat had quickened, and I felt too dizzy to stand up.

Luke closed his eyes and waved his hand in the direction of the neighing. It stopped at once.

"Thank you," I said, keeping my distance in the safety of the cave.

"You don't like horses," he guessed.

"I love horses," I corrected, "but I'm terrified of them. When I was thirteen, my foster parents put me in horseback riding lessons. I normally rode this beautiful chestnut horse who was so gentle and sweet, but one day she was sick so I had to ride this massive black horse named Gremlin." As I recounted the story, I could see the horse in my mind—his legs were almost taller than me, his hooves were as big as soccer balls, and his eyes were black as night with not a glimmer of kindness in them. "I was scared, but tried not to show it. I didn't want to disappoint my parents. Halfway through the lesson, the horse freaked. It reared up on its hind legs, let out a ferocious cry, and then bolted around the arena, leaving me to hold on with all my might, or be trampled. When the horse leaped over the fence, I fell off and landed on my arm, breaking it in two places." I shuddered at the memory.

He was in front of me now, his hands holding my arms in place. "Well, you're safe with me," he finally said.

He leaned down to kiss me, and I obliged more than willingly.

Suddenly a loud crashing noise came from all sides. We broke apart and Luke sighed heavily at the realization of something, then pulled me in tight and said, "You have to go. I'll see you around, princess."

DREW BURST THROUGH my bedroom door, startling both Lucia and I into a ridged upright position.

"What the hell, Drew!" I demanded as Luke's voice still bounced around as an echo inside my head.

"Sarah, it's nine thirty. When you didn't show up for school this morning, I was worried sick! What the hell are you doing?"

"Sleeping." I leaned over to adjust my alarm clock, and confirmed the late hour. "Dreaming, actually." My voice croaked with the distress of just being woken out of a deep sleep.

"Geez, Sarah. What the hell were you dreaming about that you couldn't hear your freaking alarm? Or your doorbell? Or me banging on your door for the last ten minutes?" Drew whipped open my closet and rummaged through for an outfit. "By the way, you really shouldn't leave your living room windows unlocked."

"You climbed through my windows?"

"I had to get in somehow, didn't I?" he snapped.

I threw back my blankets and let my feet hit the cold

floor. "I was dreaming about you," I said, wondering what kind of reaction I would get from him.

"No you weren't," he said, seemingly disgusted at the notion.

"How would you know?" I challenged.

"Trust me, I'd know if you were dreaming of me."

I shook my head and rolled my eyes. "Well, I *thought* it was you at one point because he was wearing a key like yours, but turns out it wasn't you."

Drew stopped and turned to face me. "He had a key?" His eyes darted the space around me.

"Yeah, but it wasn't you."

"It was *like* mine?" He was still fixated on the necklace.

"Yes, like yours." I went to him and pulled his necklace from his shirt. I ran my fingers down the body of the key and back up to the circular top. "But this part here was different. There was a different symbol in the circle."

"What was it? What was the symbol?"

"I don't remember." I took my clothes from Drew and motioned for him to turn around. I probably could remember if I tried, but I felt oddly protective over Luke and his key. "I didn't get a good look at it." I snickered. "It was just a dream after all." I whipped off my top and pulled on the shirt Drew had picked out for me. Not one of my favourites, but who was I to argue when I was this late for school.

"Well, if you didn't get a good look, how do you know it wasn't me?"

"Oh, I got a good look at *him*, but just not the necklace." I smiled, recalling Luke's handsome features and luscious lips, strong arms and—

"What did he look like?" Drew pressed.

"Tall, dark and handsome," I blurted, blushing slightly.

Drew paced the room. "How tall?" He stopped. "Taller than me?"

I stood next to Drew and measured myself against him. When I kissed Luke, I had to tilt my head up and he leaned down slightly. His chest was just about at my shoulder height. "Hmmm," I said as I touched Drew's chest with both hands. It seemed about the right height, but I wouldn't know for sure unless he kissed me, which I knew he wouldn't do.

"What the hell are you doing?!" he scolded. "Were you *this* close to him?!"

I held back my laughter as I could see he was genuinely upset about this. "Drew, it was a freaking *dream*!" *And you're not my boyfriend!*

Drew was pacing the floor again, muttering to himself, so I continued getting dressed. "Tall, but not taller than me. Dark, but that could mean anyone. *Handsome*," he said with disgust, "but really, it could still be Eli or his second. . . ."

I assumed he meant Eli from our Science class. Not at all tall, dark or handsome. In my opinion, anyway. Nice guy, but no Luke.

"It wasn't Eli," I said, sitting down to pull on a pair of pants.

"Why? Why do you say that?"

"Because his name was Luke."

Drew spun around. "WHAT?!"

"Drew!" I clutched my pants to my belly in an awkward attempt to hide my underwear. "Turn around!"

"Did you just say his name was *Luke*?"

"Yes, Drew, now turn around!" I said more forcefully, but he was back to pacing my room and completely ignoring me. He was obviously not interested in the fact that I was half naked, so I continued getting dressed.

"What is your problem?" I asked as I pulled on my pants.

"What did he do to you? What did he want?"

"Nothing," I laughed. "Are you really freaking out about this? You have seriously got to get over your freakish dream obsession. I don't even know anyone by the name of Luke in real life. This was just a dream. A nice dream, mind you, but just a dream."

"What do you mean *a nice dream*?" Drew challenged, now standing right in front of me, his face red with anger. "Do you actually *like* this guy?"

"Drew!" I gasped. "You can't possibly be jealous over

a dream!"

"Jealous? Nah. More *disgusted*."

Before I registered what I was doing, I reached up and let my open hand make contact with his face. *Slap!*

I gasped. "I am so sorry," I said, sitting back down on my bed, appalled at what I had just done. My hand stung from the impact. His cheek was now a rosy pink.

Drew clenched his jaw. "Get to school." He left my room, slamming the door behind him.

CHAPTER 7

The Nightmare

~ SARAH ~

MY PHONE HAD been set to vibrate for morning classes.
I kept pulling it from my pocket and checking it in case I
had missed something, but no texts or calls from Drew.
No explanation. Nothing. I texted twice and left a
voicemail: "Drew, I am so sorry that I slapped you. You
did not deserve that. I don't know what came over me.
Please talk to me. I'm sick about this. Call me back."

When the lunch bell rang, I sauntered down the hall
and out the back doors to the arboretum where Drew and
I always ate our lunches. Maddy and Caleb were already
there, feeding each other grapes and giggling at each
other's . . . salty fingertips? I erased the look of disgust
from my face and sat down across from them at the picnic

table, my back to the door. I wished I could trade places with them so I could watch the door while I ate. Maybe Drew just needed a few hours to calm down and he'd meet us here for lunch.

"Hey," I said as I pulled out my brown paper bag that was my lunch and set it on the table.

Maddy smiled her wide, beautiful smile, then looked past me. "Where's Drew?"

I shrugged. "Dunno."

Neither of them responded. Surely they, too, thought it was weird that Drew would just disappear. We could always be found together. Always.

"He's mad at me," I divulged.

"What the hell did you do?" Maddy said, wide-eyed, popping a grape into her own mouth and forgetting about Caleb.

"Slapped him." I kept my eyes on my lunch bag as my throat started constricting. I slapped him. I. Slapped. Drew. How could I have done that? I dropped my head into my hands. "I'm the worst friend in the world."

It took a few seconds, but then Maddy said, "No, no you're not, sweetie. I'm sure you had good reason. Right? What happened?"

"For the record," Caleb spoke up, "I'm not sure there's ever a good enough reason to hit your boyfriend."

Maddy glared at him. "First of all, he's not her boy-friend. Second of all, stay out of it." Caleb took a bite of his sandwich and looked down.

"He offended me, I think?" I said, trying to explain it the best I could without sounding completely insane. *He insulted my taste in fake boyfriends.*

"So he's avoiding you now?"

"Yeah. He won't answer my texts."

"That doesn't sound at all like Drew," Maddy acknowledged.

"Is he even here today?" Caleb asked.

"He wasn't in Geography," Maddy confirmed.

"He wasn't in Math, either," I said, feeling even sicker now that I knew it wasn't just me he was avoiding.

DREW DIDN'T SHOW up to school for the rest of the day and never returned any of my messages, or Caleb's, or Maddy's. Science was my last class of the day, but when all I could seem to focus on was Drew's empty seat next to me, I decided I couldn't stay any longer. I packed my books back in my bag and waited until Mr. Geddes paused long enough for me to interrupt with my hand in the air.

"Yes, Sarah?"

"I'm not feeling well. Could I be excused?" I was sure my face was a perfect reflection of how I felt on the inside—finished. Defeated. Miserable.

"Of course, of course," he said, waving me toward the door. "You look quite pale, Sarah. I hope you're feeling better tomorrow."

"Me, too." I left the classroom and headed straight for the back doors down the south corridor.

The cool spring air filled my lungs as I sucked it in deeply, letting it reach every part of me and calming my soul. Then I walked. And walked. Down the path to my neighbourhood, up Drew's street, down my street. I didn't want to go home. Darlene had worked backshift last night and would be getting up around now. It was wise to avoid her for a few hours during this period. Instead, I took the long path to the clearing in the woods with the big apple tree. The tree where Drew and I had first met.

It had been a sunny morning the day we met. I was perched high, writing in my leather-bound notebook, lost inside the ink of a love story that I created to escape my own misery. And Drew had been exploring the woods with his father, a dreamcatcher swinging from one hand as they walked together. His father was watching him with fondness, a look that stirred warm feelings, but no memories of my own. I had watched them for a while, but as I turned on the branch to get a better look, my notebook slipped from my lap and fell to the ground. They both looked up at me and his father had smiled large. "There she is, son," he had said. "Go on. Go introduce yourself." And he did. And that's how Drew and I began.

The tree was warm and inviting, and I climbed to the

branch with the dip near the trunk which provided a nice resting place. I saddled the branch and closed my eyes, listening to the wind wrestle with the leaves, and wondering where Drew was. Part of me had quietly hoped that I would find him here at this tree. The tree I liked to think was ours, although he probably didn't see it that way at all. I pulled out my phone and texted him again: "Where. Are. You???" and hit send. I called his phone, but again it went straight to voicemail. I wanted to throw my phone. I was so mad at myself for hitting him. It was so unlike me. Why did I feel so protective over this stupid Dream Guy, anyway?

Drew was never jealous. Not once in the five years that I had known him was he ever jealous over anything. A bit overprotective sometimes, maybe. Especially *any* time I ever considered going to a party, with or without him. If he couldn't go because of plans he had with his dad or something, then I was definitely *not* allowed to go on my own. Even if Maddy was going. He was also super overprotective whenever a guy asked me out. He had a hundred questions for the guy and acted like I was his little sister and his duty was to look out for me. But I didn't want his protection. All I ever wanted was for Drew to consider me more than just a friend.

The more I thought about Drew and how he was always controlling my life from the sidelines, the angrier I got. Why wouldn't he just answer his phone so I could apologize for hitting him and then yell at him for being so dramatic and ruining my whole day?

Soon I was too exhausted to feel angry anymore, and my eyes grew heavier and heavier. I focused on a knot in the tree branch in front of me. The knot faded in and out and I knew I was being pulled into a sleep. But I shouldn't have been tired. Why was I falling asleep? I fought against it, pinching myself to keep awake, but it was no use. The world around me was getting hazier and hazier. I laid my head back in the crook of the tree and let myself go, secretly hoping I would see Luke and forget about my problems with Drew.

I WAS FLOATING peacefully on a surfboard in the middle of a shoreless ocean. My legs dangled over the sides, pushing through the calm, warm water. The bright colours of the surfboard matching the darkening sky and lonely temperature.

"Luke?" I called out into the air, expecting him to just appear and join me on the surfboard.

It was different this time. Scarier. The water was dark and things lurked underneath my surfboard. I pulled my legs onto the board and tried hard to stay atop. The eerily calm water was now rippling, and in the distance I saw bigger swells of water emerging. I called for Luke again, but no one came. Soon the waves were too large to handle comfortably. I dipped my hands in the frigid water and paddled desperately away from the waves.

"Luke!" I screamed as another wave brought me up and then crashing down again. This time the surfboard flipped and I found myself beneath the surface, clinging desperately to the board above. I resurfaced and screamed Luke's name again through the thick, salty air as a huge wave came crashing down on me. My hands slipped from the board and I spun through the icy water, the current pulling me under as another wave crashed above.

I kicked and pushed away at the water as hard as I could, but didn't seem to be getting anywhere. My chest ached from the air that was caught inside.

It's just a dream! I told myself as I continued to fight. *I can still breathe.*

I sucked in deeply, expecting a sensation of air to fill my chest, but instead salt stung my insides as the water filled my lungs. The sea became darker and darker and the sound of the crashing waves became more distant. I was sinking. Drowning. This was it. What happened to people who died in their dreams?

In the distant blackness, someone dove into the water, causing bubbles to rise all around. He grabbed me around the waist, but the edges of my vision blackened and I lost consciousness before we reached the surface.

The next thing I knew, I was lying in the sand with a figure hovering over top of me. I coughed and water poured out of my mouth, stinging my throat as it came.

"You okay?" he asked as he finished emptying the contents of a bottle down my throat. Not that I had a choice with the purple liquid pouring down my throat, I swallowed the sweet, tangy juice. It tasted better than the sea water.

His face was darkened by the backdrop of the sun behind him and his voice muffled by the water in my ears.

"Yes," I coughed again, gasping for air.

"Good. You can't die yet. We're just getting started and I'm not done with you yet." He recapped the empty bottle and slid it into his pocket.

"Luke?"

He stood up, his silhouette lingering for a moment before he turned and disappeared.

Startled, I woke suddenly and found myself lying face down in the grass ten feet below the branch on which I had fallen asleep, my face and arm hurting uncomfortably so. I sat up quickly, clambered backward until the trunk of the tree was against me, and held there as I caught my breath, and my bearings.

I am by the tree. I am awake. I am dry. No broken bones. I am safe. Breathe.

Once the light fog in my head had dissipated and the heaviness in my chest lifted, I retrieved my backpack and headed for home, the remnants of my latest dream—or nightmare—lingering heavily in my mind, causing my senses to be heightened and fear exaggerated.

A dog barked as I walked passed a driveway, and it startled me so much that I nearly dropped my backpack. It was just a dog.

A car honked its horn, waiting for its passenger, and my heart nearly leaped from my chest. What was happening to me? Why had this dream affected me so badly?

When I got home, Drew was sitting on my front step, elbows resting on his knees and looking down at his folded hands. As I meandered up the front walk, he turned his face up, showing his black eye and fat lip.

I gasped and ran to him. "Drew!"

He shook his head, stood up and hugged me tight. "I'm sorry about this morning."

I pulled away and touched the bruise next to his eye. "I don't care about that right now. And I should be the one apologizing anyway. What happened? Who did this to you? Was this . . . did *I* do this??"

He laughed. "No, you didn't do this to me, Sarah." He seemed to think it was cute that I thought I could leave a mark like that.

"Well then who did?"

"Doesn't matter. I let my temper get the better of me, that's all."

"Geez, Drew. Come in. I'll get some ice and you can tell me what the hell happened to you."

"Really, it's fine. You should see the other guy."

I laughed with a snort. "Not funny. Who did this?" I couldn't think of one person that Drew had an issue with at school. Everyone liked him. He was calm, cool and collected all of the time. And he never bothered with anyone. Drew would only ever be involved in a fight to break it up.

He looked me in the eyes now and I could tell he saw something that he didn't like. His brow furrowed and he stepped back, taking in the rest of me. "What happened to you? What is this mark from?" He touched my forehead and a stinging sensation registered.

My fingers lifted to my head and I felt the bump just below my hairline near my temple.

"I fell," I said, shuddering from the memory of the dream.

"You fell," he repeated, suggesting his disbelief. "What do you mean you fell? Where? How?"

My palms began to sweat. I didn't want to tell him. For some reason, I knew it would upset him. But I had to. He would see through any lie I told, if ever I was able to lie to Drew.

"I . . . fell out of the tree," I said, watching his expression carefully. He knew what tree I was referring to. His eyes pinballed mine.

"What were you doing in the tree?" His jaw tensed.

"I left school. I was worried about you. I couldn't concentrate."

"You skipped school? Sarah!" he scolded.

"Well, you should've answered your texts," I countered. "And you're one to talk! You didn't go to *any* classes."

"So you went to the tree," he said, ignoring my last retort.

"I did," I confirmed, "and I fell asleep." I watched his face go through the changes from annoyed, to concerned, to angry. "And then I fell out of the tree."

"Did you dream?"

I tried to keep the crinkle from my brow. "Yes," I said slowly.

He craned his neck and I saw his jawbone protrude at the same time. His eyes narrowed and turned an emerald green. "About?"

"I was drowning," I said carefully, trying to keep the trauma from my voice. Somehow, saying it aloud brought the terror front and centre again.

Drew's chest started rising and falling quickly. He waited for me to finish.

"But I was pulled out by someone."

"Luke?"

"I think so, but I can't be sure. He said, 'You can't die yet. We're just getting started and I'm not done with you yet.'"

Drew closed his eyes. "Did he say or do anything else?"

"He gave me something to drink."

"What colour?"

"What?"

"What colour was the stuff he gave you to drink?" His eyes were still closed, his voice firm.

"I . . . I don't remember." I thought hard, and saw the small bottle flash before my eyes. "Purple," I said. "I think it was purple."

"A revival," Drew muttered to himself, seemingly confused by this.

It wasn't unusual for Drew to ask a hundred and one questions about a dream whenever Maddy shared hers with us, so that part was normal. He liked to decode the dreams and tell us what he thought they meant. But what I didn't understand was why he was getting so upset about my dreams.

"What does any of that matter?" I asked, gently.

Drew opened his eyes and smiled, pushing away the darkness surrounding him. "Just curious." He grinned and then stood up, gathering me in his arms. "It was probably my fault for putting you in such a bad mood."

"I'm so sorry for hitting you," I said, feeling tears well up in my eyes.

"I should be the one apologizing. I've been a jerk, and I'm sorry."

He let go and fiddled with his school ring, sliding it back and forth on his finger, then he twisted it off and held it out. "I want you to have this."

Confused, and slightly speechless, I took the ring from him. "But . . . we're just friends."

"I've realized that the thought of you with someone else makes me sick, Sarah. I may not be able to be what you want right now, but I want you to know that I would never be with anyone else either." He slid the ring onto my index finger—a little big, but still a perfect fit. A wave of guilt washed over me, as though I was somehow cheating on Luke. Two days ago, getting a ring from Drew would have sent me over the moon and back with excitement. But now, I felt oddly connected to Luke, even though I knew he wasn't real.

"Thank you," I managed to say. "It fits."

He hugged me again and held on, protectively tight.

"Are you sure you want me to wear this at school?" His answer would confirm that he was okay if others thought we were together.

"I hope you'll never take it off." And his words enveloped me with the comfort and security that I needed. "And I hope you'll never fall out of that tree again." He squeezed me tighter, but I could hear the concern in his voice.

I stayed for a few seconds longer in his embrace before answering. "Probably you should never leave me like that again."

"I won't. I promise."

CHAPTER 8

Dilemma

~ SARAH ~

AS MUCH AS I wanted to dream of Luke again (the good kind of dream; not the kind where he saves me from drowning), several nights passed without any dreams. His scent became a faded, distant memory. I couldn't remember what his voice even sounded like. It was deep and sultry, I remembered, but what did it sound like? How could I expect to remember all the details? It was probably best that I moved on and focused on "real world" stuff. Unfortunately, with things going back to normal, Drew was distancing himself a bit more, too. It was almost as if the whole thing had been a dream. If it weren't for the ring that I was still wearing, I would have to wonder if it was.

When my phone rang Monday morning, I jumped at it, expecting it to be Drew telling me he'd be by to pick me up or walk with me to school. But it wasn't.

"Hey Maddy," I answered, sounding a bit too disappointed.

"What's wrong? You sound bummed."

I took a deep breath, deciding I didn't need Maddy interrogating me on my feelings and putting Drew and me on the spot later during lunch.

"Nothing," I said, content with the revived perkiness of my voice. "What's up?"

"I'm taking the car to school today. Wanna drive?"

I laughed. "I literally live like a five minute walk from school."

"But it's raining," she pointed out. I squinted out my bedroom window and saw the rain pounding the sidewalk below.

I looked at the time. 8:45am. If Drew was going to drive me, he would've called by now. He liked being to school at least a half hour early. And we had Math together first thing, so we usually drove together and talked about our homework.

"Come on, Sarah. You drive with Drew sometimes," she pointed out, with a hint of pout in her tone.

"Yeah, but that's different. He lives like two seconds away. You'd have to go out of your way to come get me. I could probably be at the school faster than if you picked me up." I shoved my binder into my backpack. Why was I being so difficult? I supposed Maddy's offer made me realize that Drew hadn't called, and that upset me. Frustrated me. Angered me, really.

"So you want a drive or what?" Maddy said, feigning impatience.

"I'd love one," I said, resigning to the fact that if Drew hadn't called or shown up by now, he wasn't coming for me. "I'm ready when you are."

"Be there in less than ten."

MADDY, I SHOULD have known, was nearly twenty minutes getting to my house, which would make us late for first class. Normally this would annoy me, but with the empty feeling plaguing me from Drew's evasiveness, I didn't much care at the moment.

"Drew okay with you coming with me today?" Maddy asked as I climbed into her mother's little red Civic hatchback.

I shrugged. "Meh."

"What was that?"

"It was an 'I have no idea, nor do I care.'"

Maddy nodded slowly as she pulled out of my driveway. "Trouble in paradise?"

"Is that what you call this? Paradise? Maddy, I'm honestly at a complete loss as to what is going on with Drew and me. Or if there even is anything going on."

"Sarah, he gave you his ring. That says something."

I stole a quick glance at Drew's ring wrapped snugly around my finger, then turned my head and watched the houses as we crept past. "Why are you driving so slow? You realize we're already late for first, right?"

"Mmm," Maddy said, her eyes fixated on the road ahead.

"What's wrong with you?" I asked, realizing for the first time that something was on Maddy's mind, and I had been so self-involved to not have noticed that this was the reason she wanted to drive me to school.

"Caleb," she answered without hesitation.

"Caleb what?" My voice caught in my throat as I considered the possibilities. Did he break up with her? It would shock me to say the least. He seemed so into her. And he had just given her his ring.

Maddy's knuckles whitened as her hands gripped the steering wheel, her speed decelerating to a crawl, until finally she pulled over and shut the car off. The rain pounding on the windshield was the only sound now.

"Maddy, did he break up with you?" I pressed.

"No." She shook her head.

I inhaled sharply. "Did he *cheat* on you?" My own hands were gripping my phone tightly. All she had to do was nod 'yes' and I would have his number dialled and be tearing a strip off of him in less than a minute's time.

"No." Maddy shook her head even harder this time.

Relieved, I said, "Then what is it?"

"He wants more," she finally said, turning her ashen face to me. Her eyes were hollow with dark circles, a clear sign she had been up all night with this on her mind.

"What do you mean he wants more? He wants your necklace?" She knew how I felt about giving away our school necklaces. It was stupid and careless and not worth the risk. What if he lost it? What if they broke up and he threw it away out of spite? Those were keepsakes, an heirloom to be passed down to our children one day. Not to mention giving away a piece of herself to someone she had only been dating for less than three months.

She looked down at her necklace and rubbed it between her thumb and finger. "Maybe that would be enough," she said, as if to herself.

And this was why she was losing sleep—Caleb wanted to take their relationship to the next level, and she wasn't ready.

I looked down at my fingers now twisting the strap on my backpack around and around. "What did you say to him?"

"I wanted to think about it." She returned her gaze to the blurry windshield.

"That's fair," I said. "What are you thinking?"

"If I give him my necklace, will it be enough? Will he still want me?" Maddy's voice cracked at her last word and a tear spilled down her cheek.

"Oh, Maddy," I said, reaching over and pulling her into a hug. "If he doesn't want you for who you are and all your values, wants and wishes, he's not worth it."

Maddy let out a very wet laugh into my shirt. "I love him, Sarah."

"I know you do, Madz. But you can't possibly know already that you can put up with him for longer than a few months. I mean, it's only been three months, right?"

She nodded.

"You'll love lots of guys, no doubt, in your lifetime. It's okay to love. It's not okay to compromise your beliefs and your comforts in an effort to keep that love. If he's a decent guy, he'll understand."

Maddy tucked her necklace back into her jacket. "You're right." She sat up straight and wiped her tears from her face. "I look like crap now, right?"

"Right," I said with a grin.

Maddy pulled out her emergency make-up kit from her backpack and began fixing her face when my phone rang. It was Drew.

"Where are you?" he said before I had a chance to say hello.

"Almost to school. Why?" Maddy and I exchanged troubled looks.

"Uh, I don't know, 'cause you're like twenty minutes late for class and that's not like you."

"Well, thanks for your concern," I placated, "but

we're okay."

"Who's we?" Drew demanded, his tone severe.

"What the hell, Drew. I'm with Maddy. What is your problem?"

I heard him suck in a deep breath. "Just get to school, Sarah. Stop giving me a heart attack." And he hung up.

I held the phone out and stared at it for a minute, eyebrows hitched, waiting for an explanation. "Did you hear that?" I asked Maddy as she finished re-applying mascara.

"I did," she said. "Very odd."

"It sounds like he cares about me."

"It does," Maddy agreed.

"But then he ignores me, and he doesn't pick me up for school, or even call for that matter, or even answer my texts when I say goodnight. I am so freaking confused." I pressed my palms into my temples.

"Have you tried to talk to him about it?" Maddy started the car, and the windshield wipers took off at top speed again.

I huffed a sigh of annoyance. "I try, but he never returns my calls, or if he does, he can't talk long because he's helping his *dad* with something."

"Do you believe him?"

"I don't know," I resigned. "I can't imagine Drew ever lying to me, but it's just all so messed up."

"So corner him today at lunch. I'll take Caleb away so

you two can have some privacy. It'll actually be a good time for me to tell Caleb that I've decided to take things slow."

We exchanged smiles, instilling confidence into each other for what we both had to do at lunch hour.

WITH ONLY TWENTY minutes left of class, Maddy and I decided to sit in the parking lot until the bell rang. We hurried inside, out of the rain, and said our good-byes before heading off to second period in opposite directions.

"Sarah!" my name echoed through the east corridor just as I was about to head into Biology class.

I turned to see Drew pushing through the crowd. When he reached me he took my face in his hands and studied me, as if looking for something. Then he pulled me into his chest and held me there.

"You had me so sick," he said before releasing me and placing me neatly back by the wall.

Confused, I tried to play off like all of this was normal. "Sorry?"

"No, it's my fault," he said, shamefully. "I should've picked you up for school. I was just . . . I had things to do. I've been busy."

I smiled, but the corners of my mouth only widened; there was no arc of sincerity.

"I can drive with Maddy. Or I can walk. Doesn't matter," I said casually, focusing on the droves of people walking past us. "I don't need you." There was a bite to my words, which I could see had an effect on Drew.

He studied my face a little and then said, "Sure. Yeah. Of course you can."

"Your eye looks much better. Bruise is gone already," I noticed.

Drew touched his face. "Fast healer," he said, then averted his eyes as if this was embarrassing. I thought about asking again who he got into a brawl with, but decided to leave it. I had more pressing things on my mind, the first being our relationship status.

"Drew," I began, searching for the right words. I didn't want to sound desperate. Needy. Longing.

"Yes?"

"Are we . . . are we still going to prom?" It was the best I could do. Why couldn't I just ask him—are we together? Are you my boyfriend? Do you feel the same for me as I do for you? I tried not to notice the muscles in his jaw protruding. Why was he angry?

"To be honest, I don't really want to," he finally said. "It'll be lame, don't you think?"

Normally, at this, I would agree and suppress my feelings until I was alone with Lucia on my bed, at which point I would release it all and cry myself to sleep. But not this time. "No, I don't think it'll be lame. I actually want to go."

I watched his face as he processed my defiance. My independence. If I wasn't mistaken, he looked almost happy for me, like he didn't expect me to voice my opinion against his.

"I still don't want to go," he said, and with that, he squashed all my hopes.

Holly Haverstock was making her way through the hallway toward Biology. I rolled my eyes and looked away, adjusting my backpack as I shifted the weight higher onto my shoulder.

"Are you kidding me?" Holly said as she got closer, craning her neck and eyeballing something in the area of my shoulder. When she reached me she took my hand that was holding my backpack strap. "Sarah Marley is actually wearing an X ring." Her look of mock surprise confirmed that she didn't believe I was pretty or cool enough to earn one.

I pulled my hand back and returned it to my backpack strap.

"Okay, so which science loser gave it to you?" Holly laughed, looking to Drew for confirmation that she was right.

Drew didn't say anything, just kept his eyes on me. Holly looked from Drew, back to me, and back to Drew's left hand. Then his right hand, both of which were ring-free.

"It's your ring," she said, a dumbfounded look on her face.

Drew nodded, his eyes still glued to mine. This would have been the opportune time to kiss me. In front of Holly. In front of everyone. *Kiss me. Show the world, namely Holly Haverstock, that you want me. Show* me *that you want me!*

Holly gasped, her eyes darting to my chest. "Did you give him your necklace?" Even Holly knew giving away your school necklace was a bigger sign of commitment. The next step in a relationship.

I pulled my necklace from inside my shirt, proving I wasn't as easy as she thought I was.

Holly nodded slowly, as if deciding this made a little more sense.

Mr. Chase came to the door. "Sarah, Holly, find your seats, please."

Holly hurried into the room and I watched as her blonde ponytail swayed back and forth, begging me to yank it and pull her to the floor. Wait . . . where did that come from?

"I have to go," I said, turning to leave.

"See you at lunch?" Drew asked, reaching for my hand, but I let it slip and he didn't reach again.

"Sure." And I left him standing there. I didn't look back. It was my turn to make a statement.

I SLID QUIETLY into my seat, which was uncomfortably close to Holly's. Mr. Chase was writing notes on the board and instructing us to pay close attention as everything from here on out would be on the final exam.

"Seriously," Holly whispered over my shoulder. "How did *you* land a guy like Drew?"

"We're just friends," I muttered, although I secretly wished I could rub it in her face that we were madly in love and that he was taking me to prom. That I was better than her, prettier than her, more desirable than her. But in reality, I was too angry, too shafted to give Drew the credit of having my heart. We were just friends. That was it.

"Just friends," Holly repeated slowly. "So, what? You're just babysitting his ring?"

"Something like that." I bent low over my paper and began earnestly scribbling Mr. Chase's instructions into my notebook. What *was* I doing with Drew's ring?

CHAPTER 9

Distance

~ SARAH ~

BY THE END of class, it was all I could do to hold back the tears that threatened to leak at the mention of the X ring, relationships, love, or anything else Drew-related. I slid his ring off my finger and stuck it deep into my pocket while I wandered mindlessly through the crowded halls.

"Hey," Drew said as I sat down at our lunch table. As usual, his charm was on because he could sense my coldness.

"Hi," I said, keeping my eyes on the grey wood tabletop.

"How was Bio?"

"Oh, quit with the small talk, Drew," I burst, feeling my face hot with anger.

Drew put his sandwich down and sat back, as if waiting for a wrath of conviction that was duly his.

"I can't figure you out. I can't figure *this* out. *Us* out."

"What do you—"

"I'm not done," I interrupted. "You gave me your ring, with the song and dance that you couldn't give me what I wanted, but promising to always be there for me. But you're not. You are more emotionally distant than you've ever been. And I can't figure out why I am wearing your ring. Or why I even care."

"Where *is* my ring?" Drew said, noticing my bare fingers. Really? And that's what he had to say in return?

I shoved my hand into my pocket, pulled out his ring, and thrust it back at him. "I don't want it." My eyes stung and I didn't have enough care to stop the water from leaking through them.

"Sarah, please—"

"No." I stood up. "I can't do this, Drew. I'm just . . . so confused." I grabbed my backpack and swung it over my shoulder.

"I want you," he blurted. "I need you." And the world froze. Maddy, who had just entered the arboretum, stopped in her tracks. Then she turned and walked back out.

What did he just say? My back was burning with his stare. I pressed my eyes together and more tears cascaded. I quickly wiped my face with my sleeves. "What?"

I asked, wanting, needing to hear it again.

"I . . . please, Sarah. Please don't leave." He was right behind me now. His breath on the top of my head. "Please don't go."

My backpack fell to the ground and I turned into him, falling into his embrace. He held me for a long time, but he didn't seem to mind, while I cried into his chest. Why I was crying, I couldn't articulate. I was exhausted. Tired of being lonely. Tired of being confused. Tired of being unloved.

By the time he released me, the arboretum tables were full. I looked around, somewhat embarrassed, as most people tried to pretend they weren't tweeting about my meltdown.

Drew opened his palm and revealed his X ring. "Please wear it," he said. "It would mean a lot to me."

Still unsure of what it meant to wear his ring, I took it and slid it back onto my finger.

"Promise you'll keep it on this time?"

I nodded.

"Good," he said in approval, then looking back toward the doors, he said, "I think Maddy is waiting for you in the hall."

Maddy was pacing in front of the double glass doors. Caleb wasn't with her. Had they had their talk? Did it not go well?

"I'll be back," I said, hurrying off to my friend's aid.

As soon as I came through the doors, Maddy grabbed my arm and led me to the washroom down the hall. Once inside, she climbed up onto the sill of the large fogged window.

"Get cleaned up," she ordered, gesturing to the mirror.

I looked in the mirror and saw that my eyes were swollen and blotchy, my mascara was smudged down my left cheek and on my right eyelid.

"Geez," I groaned. "Drew saw me like this."

"You've looked worse," Maddy teased. Or maybe she wasn't teasing. Sometimes Maddy could be brutally honest. It was part of her charm.

"Did you talk to Caleb?" I asked as I scrubbed the mascara from my face.

"Didn't have to."

"What do you mean?"

"Well, when I didn't answer his texts this morning, and then didn't show up for first class, he apparently thought that he had scared me off." Maddy smiled as if this was part of an ingenious plan of hers. "So, when I left second period, he was at my classroom door with a bouquet of handpicked flowers from the school garden, asking me to forgive him for trying to rush things."

Maddy beamed as she pulled her necklace from her shirt and said, "So I guess I get to hang onto this for a little while longer."

"It's yours, Maddy. No one can *make* you give it to them."

"I know. And when the right time comes, I'll know."

"Assuming he's even the right guy."

"Oh, I think he is, Sarah."

"Really?" This was unusual for skeptical Maddy.

"I do. Especially after today."

I nodded approvingly. "Yes, he certainly has earned some brownie points, even if the flowers were just weeds from the school garden."

We both giggled.

"So," Maddy said, prying with her glaring eyes.

"So?"

"I heard him."

I applied another layer of mascara then stuck the bottle back into my backpack. "Heard who say what?"

"Heard Drew say he wants and needs you."

I took a deep breath and stared profoundly into the reflection of my own eyes. "Yeah, I heard that, too," I admitted.

"That's awesome, right?"

"Maddy," I said as I turned to face the one person I could whole-heartedly trust with this, "hearing him say those words was like hearing a chorus of angels singing. It was like . . . like seeing a ship sailing toward you after having been deserted on an island for three months. It was like—"

"I get it. It was awesome."

I closed my mouth in mid-sentence, puckered my eyebrows, then continued, "Yes, it was awesome. But, it doesn't solve anything."

"Sarah, what did you want him to say?"

"I want him to say he's my boyfriend. That I'm his girlfriend, and he wants to take me to prom. I want him to hold my hand in the hallways, to call me every night before he goes to sleep to say he loves me. I want him to—"

"I get it. You want to feel loved."

Again, I closed my mouth, somewhat taken aback by her continued rudeness. Although I wasn't sure why it still surprised me after all these years.

"But didn't you talk to him about that? Wasn't that your plan?"

"It was. I even gave his ring back to him but then he practically begged me to keep it. And after he said he wants me and needs me, I just couldn't talk anymore. It was like as soon as he said those words, it erased all of my doubts, all of my fears, all of my—"

"I get it. You—"

"Would you let me finish a freaking sentence for once?" I bellowed, startling her so much that she nearly slipped off the windowsill.

"Sorry," she quickly apologized.

"It's okay," I said, running my hands through my hair

and taking a deep breath. "Anyway, I don't know why I couldn't talk about it, I just couldn't. And now things aren't any clearer than they were. I think."

"Call him tonight," Maddy suggested. "Maybe he'll be able to talk about his feelings better over the phone when you can't see his face. Maybe he's one of those guys."

I shook my head. "He's never been one of those guys. He just . . . doesn't talk."

"You'll never know unless you—"

"I get it. Unless I try," I finished for her, smiling mischievously.

"Okay, okay, I hear ya," Maddy laughed. "I'll try to be a better listener." She hopped off the windowsill and hooked her arm into mine as we walked back to the arboretum together. "But to be honest? If he doesn't know how awesome you are, he's not worth waiting for."

I nodded and then rested my head against Maddy's. "Where's Caleb anyway?"

"Office," Maddy snorted. "He got in trouble for picking the flowers."

MADDY WAS SPRAWLED out on my bedroom floor piecing together our poster board project for English class, while I sat at my desk and printed off pages and pictures for her to organize.

"You can do the title across the top if you want." I

tossed a package of markers next to her.

"Okay. Do you care what colour?" Maddy dumped the markers out onto the poster board.

"All of them if you can."

"There are like" —Maddy counted on her fingers— "fourteen letters in Romeo and Juliet. I'll do my best."

"It's fine," I laughed. "Just use the colours of the rainbow."

"Yes, ma'am." Maddy pulled off the top to the red marker and then said, "Speaking of taking orders, how are you and Drew?"

Confused, I laughed a little, but then said, "What does that have to do with taking orders?"

"Isn't it obvious? You only have a *thing* because he told you to wear his ring."

I looked quickly down at Drew's ring dominating my finger. "That's not true."

"So you're not wearing his ring?" Maddy carefully traced the 'R' in Romeo as she spoke so simply.

"I am." My finger hovered over the print button as I waited for Maddy to explain her potentially hurtful accusation.

"Then what? You don't have a thing?"

"I don't think so."

"Sarah, for the love of Pete—just call him and ask him, would you?"

"No," I answered quickly. "We talked at school to-day."

"Did he ask you out?"

"No."

"Then I don't know why you wear his ring. I wouldn't. It tells all the other guys that you're taken, but yet he won't commit to it. Screw him."

"Maddy!" I laughed. "It's Drew."

"I know. And I like Drew. I really do. But I like you more, Sarah, and I'm sorry to have to say this, but I think you need to be firmer with him."

I stared at my phone, hoping it would ring, or a text would come through from Drew. Then, with a surge of confidence and petulance, I whipped it up off my desk and typed out a text to Drew.

DREW

Today at 9:23pm
Hey. What's up?

I stared at the screen, waiting patiently for his reply. Finally . . .

DREW

Today at 9:23pm
Hey. What's up?

Today at 9:26pm
Notta. You?

>**Today at 9:26pm**
>*Working on my R&J project
>with Maddy.*

Today at 9:27pm
Cool.

>**Today at 9:27pm**
>*Thanks for not freaking out
>when I had my meltdown to-
>day.*

Today at 9:27pm
*Haha. No prob. That's what
friends are for.*

I read his text three times before I got the nerve to
slowly read it out loud to Maddy.

"That's what *friends* are for?" Maddy said, sitting up
and meeting my gaze.

"What do I say to that?" I said, returning my eyes to
my phone screen.

"Just ask him. What's the worst that could happen?"

DREW

Today at 9:27pm
*Haha. No prob. That's what
friends are for.*

Today at 9:30pm
*What'd you mean earlier when
you said you need me?*

Today at 9:33pm
I don't know.

Today at 9:33pm
*So...it was just something you
said so I wouldn't walk away?*

Today at 9:34pm
I don't know.

I threw my phone on my bed and let out a howl of frustration.

"What'd he say?" Maddy asked as she hopped up and took my phone from my bed. She read the texts to herself while I buried my head in my arms on my desk.

"Just ignore him," Maddy said. "He doesn't deserve you." She tossed my phone in my bedside table and closed the drawer tight. "Now, let's get this project done before we both fail English."

With Lucia curled up at the bottom of my chair, keeping my feet cozy and warm, and Maddy sprawled out on my rug, I released my anger and hurt over Drew and willed myself to think about happy thoughts.

"Maddy, do you ever dream?" I asked as I fiddled with the scroll button on the mouse.

"Do I ever dream?" she repeated. "What kind of question is that? Of course I dream. Don't you?"

"Yeah," I answered, "sometimes. I just don't usually remember them, I guess."

"Yeah, I don't usually remember mine either." Maddy continued tracing the letters at the top of our poster board.

"Have you ever had a dream where you like totally fall for someone and you still have the feelings when you wake up? Like it was real?"

Maddy laughed. "Don't repeat this to anyone." She sat up. "Promise?"

"Repeat what?"

"Promise first!"

"I promise," I laughed.

"So you know Kevin from our English class?"

"Nose picker Kevin?"

Maddy shuddered. "Yes."

"He's a super nice guy. What about him?"

"I had this dream about him last year. We were making out on top of the teacher's desk and we . . . well, let's just say I gave him my school necklace."

"Oh my gosh. Are you serious?"

Maddy buried her face in her hands and fell over laughing. "I'm dead serious. In my dream he was so incredibly sexy, and I could not get the thought of him out of my head for *weeks!*"

"Oh man, I wish you'd told me. I could've had a lot of fun with that," I teased.

"Which is exactly why I didn't tell you. I had enough trouble keeping my composure around him, I didn't need encouragement from you."

"So do you still have feelings for him?"

"Hell, no!"

This gave me hope. Maybe she could give me some solid advice on how I could rid myself of the feelings I felt towards this fake dream guy. Maybe if I could forget about him, I could move on with Drew without any barriers.

"How'd you . . . how'd you get over him?" I asked, hopeful.

Maddy gagged. "He picked his nose and wiped it under his desk. Pretty much sealed his fate right there."

I burst out laughing. "Yeah, that would do it."

Maddy shook her head and retrieved the green marker from the floor. "What about you?"

I watched her for a minute before answering. "I've had steamy dreams, but not with anyone I know."

"Not even Drew?" She watched me doubtfully.

"I wish," I admitted.

"Well, you're lucky then. Sometimes dreaming about a guy can make it that much harder to forget about them. And if you ask me, you definitely need to forget about Drew. He's too much baggage for you right now. You're smart and beautiful and you could probably have any guy in the school if you wanted."

I rolled my eyes. She had me until that last part. "Thanks, Madz."

"Yeah, let's get back to our project. The last thing I need is to be thinking about Kevin when I fall asleep tonight. Can't have that train wreck again."

MY ALARM WENT off the next morning and I dug my phone out of my bedside table to silence it. Maddy stirred beside me and I nearly forgot that she had stayed the night.

"Ugh," she groaned before pulling the pillow over her head. "I'm not ready to get up."

"I'll wake you when I get out of the shower," I told her before falling out of bed and fumbling my way to the bathroom down the hall.

I turned the water on and waited for it to heat up while I checked my messages and updates. There was a new text from Drew.

DREW

Yesterday at 9:35pm
I agree.

Agree? Agree with what? I scrolled back up and read the

last few texts.

DREW

Yesterday at 9:27pm
*Haha. No prob. That's what
friends are for.*

> **Yesterday at 9:30pm**
> *What'd you mean earlier when
> you said you need me?*

Yesterday at 9:33pm
I don't know.

> **Yesterday at 9:33pm**
> *So…it was just something you
> said so I wouldn't walk away?*

Yesterday at 9:34pm
I don't know.

> **Yesterday at 9:35pm**
> *Doesn't matter. I'm too good
> for you anyway.*

Yesterday at 9:35pm
I agree.

"What the hell?" I said aloud, my voice bouncing off the bathroom walls. *I did not write that. I would not say I was too good for him . . . But . . . Maddy!* I frowned as I stared at the bathroom door. *She must have written that before she threw my phone in my bedside table.* As angry as I was, I had a hard time focusing on that fact, when the bigger pressing matter was that Drew *agreed* with her . . . agreed with me . . . whatever.

I decided the easiest thing to do was pretend that I didn't know any of it happened. The steam from the shower was filling the room now and my body ached for the comfort of it. I got in, let the water completely envelope me and melted in its heat.

CHAPTER 10

The New Guy

~ SARAH ~

WHEN MADDY AND I arrived at school, just in time for first period, Drew's car was nowhere in the parking lot. I had hoped he would be in Science class already, sitting, waiting, smiling . . . but he wasn't. Although the temptation to text him was great, I decided to let it be. Besides, he had plenty of opportunities to make it right with me. He could've told me last night that he loved me. He could've said something more than just "I agree" when Maddy said I was too good for him. And when I didn't respond, why hadn't he texted again? Or called me? Why was I wasting all of this time, energy and thought on him when he clearly didn't care?

Drew didn't show up during Science at all. Maddy

and I had English next and, against Maddy's better judgment, I couldn't resist texting Drew. Just once.

"You should be playing hard to get for once," Maddy warned.

"Just a quick one. It'd be rude if I didn't ask where he is," I pointed out. "There. Sent. No big deal. I just asked if he was coming to school today."

There was no answer from him for the rest of the period.

The bell rang and Maddy threw her books into her bag. "Let's go. I'm starving."

I carefully put my pens back in their case, tidied up my paper in my binder and then slid my binder into my backpack.

"Sarah, you are honestly the slowest person I've ever met."

I smiled with effort and followed her to the arboretum for lunch.

THE DOOR TO the arboretum opened and, although I couldn't see them, I could tell from their fragrance and the sound of their heels on the brick walkway, that it was Holly, Bria, and Karley. Not my three most favourite people.

"Oh my gosh, he is so hot! I call dibbs, okay girls? He's totally mine," Holly said as they sat down at a table next to us and pulled out her carrot sticks. "What are you looking at, Freak?" she snapped when she caught me looking in their direction.

"Nothing of interest," I said before turning back to roll my eyes at Maddy.

"Oh my gosh, Holly, here he comes," Karley said, blushing a deep pink.

Holly reached into her purse and pulled out a lipstick. She coated her lips then slowly turned in her seat toward whomever she now had her claws set on catching.

"Looking for a seat?" she said in a fake, sweet voice as she slid over and slapped Bria's leg, forcing her to move across the table next to Karley.

I made a snorting noise as Maddy giggled.

"No, I'm good. I'll just sit over here."

The voice was thick, rich, deep, sexy. It was calming, familiar, dream-like. It was . . . it was *his* voice. The voice from my dreams. Was it? Could it be? I froze, averting my eyes and face. Was it my imagination, or could I smell the ocean?

"Oh, don't be silly," Holly said, a little southern drawl in her voice that wasn't there before. "There's plenty of room over here. Are you new? I haven't seen you around before."

The guy approached their table, but didn't take a seat. I stole a sideways glance, studying in his strong profile, dark wind-swept hair, built physique. Was it him?

"Not new yet. Just scoping out the school," his rich

voice answered.

"Well, Xavier is an awesome school. You should totally come." She sat up straight, pushing her breasts as far out as she could manage. "I'm Holly. These are my friends Karley and Bria."

He nodded and then jerked his head toward our table. "And who are they?"

Holly pursed her lips and smiled forcefully. "No one of interest," she said, her tone suggesting that she was deliberately throwing my words of earlier back at me.

"Caleb," Caleb said as he stood up and shook the new guy's hand. "This is my girlfriend Maddy, and her best friend Sarah."

I slowly turned and met eyes with the new guy. I almost fell off my seat as I took in his facial features. Bright blue eyes, full lips, long lashes. This was the guy from my dreams! Xavier's newest recruit was the guy I had been dreaming about. Could it be that I had seen him around before, and that was the reason he showed up in my dreams? It would make the most sense. But what didn't make sense was why I still felt so connected with this guy. I didn't even know him. He was real now. Not just a dream, but my feelings were strong. Real. Intense.

"Sarah?" Maddy said quietly as she nudged me under the table. "Are you okay?"

My eyes were locked with his. I couldn't move. Neither of us spoke.

"And where's your boyfriend, Sarah?" Holly piped up. "Sarah has a boyfriend. His name is Drew. He should be along shortly."

The new guy's eyes shot down to my hand, which was clutching my water bottle. Drew's ring was still on my finger, and I could tell he noticed this. He nodded slowly, as if suddenly understanding something. His eyes narrowed for a second and I caught a small glimpse of a grin. What the hell was Holly doing, anyway?

"Drew's not her boyfriend!" Maddy retorted, coming to my rescue. "She's single."

"No one asked you, Bird Brain!" Holly snapped.

"It's Burbane!" Maddy shouted, becoming irate at the surname insult that I would've thought she'd be used to by now.

"You haven't told us your name yet," Karley said, interrupting the feud.

I couldn't help but notice that he glanced briefly at me before answering. "Luke."

I gasped, then turned my face to Maddy, eyes wide. *Did he just say Luke?* Maddy stared at me with a *what-the-hell-is-the-matter-with-you* look.

Holly stepped over the picnic bench and held out her hand. "Well, it's a pleasure to meet you, Luke." And her drawl was back.

The room was spinning slightly and my heart was pounding. *The guy from my dreams is here. At Xavier. Luke is here. But how is this possible? Had I seen him before in a magazine? Newspaper? Maybe I saw his picture at the office with his name and info beside it. Maybe my subconscious logged it, but I just couldn't remember it until now.*

While Luke was busy meeting the trio, I mouthed to Maddy, "I have to go." She nodded and I slowly got up and sneaked toward the arboretum doors.

"Wait," Luke called after me. I froze. "Where are you going?"

I couldn't look at him. I kept my eyes on the doors, willing for them to open. "I . . . I have to go."

"Can I come with you?"

Holly laughed. "Why would you want to? I mean seriously, Luke, if you're looking to make some friends around here, you'll need to associate with the right people."

"Sarah," Luke said, ignoring Holly to my greatest pleasure.

I slowly turned, but when my eyes found his, I couldn't breathe. I could feel him. I could smell him. My body ached for his.

"What do you want from me?" I heard myself say.

He smiled his perfect crooked smile. "Could you show me where the office is?"

Holly stepped forward. "Oh, is that what you're looking for? I'll take you. I'm heading there now."

"No," he said a bit too quickly. He looked at me, almost pleading for my agreement to help him. To be with him. But how could I? I could hardly speak around him. If I dreamed of him, did that mean he dreamed of me? Confusion mixed with an intense feeling of embarrassment would not allow me to walk with him to the office.

"I'm not going that way," I said. "Holly will show you." I turned and pulled the door open. "I'm sorry."

Once inside the nearest girls' washroom, I locked myself into a stall and pressed my back against the door. Drew was nowhere to be found, and the idea of seeing Luke again and losing my breath, tripping over my own feet, or not being able to talk again, was enough to send me over the edge. What if he decided to stay? What if he was going to be in my classes? I had to leave. I had to get out of there.

I was almost out of the school when my phone vibrated. *Drew!* I fumbled it out of my pocket and read the text. It wasn't Drew.

MADDY

Today at 12:45pm
*OMG, Sarah! Hot new guy
keeps asking about you. Holly
is so pissed. This is awesome!
Where are you??*

I pushed open the side doors and breathed in the cool, spring air. What was happening? None of this made any sense. He was just a figment of my imagination. Or he was real, but my dream was just that—a dream. I was imagining this real-life connection. I convinced myself of this as I made my way down the dirt path to the main road. My fingers trembled as I typed out a response to Maddy.

MADDY

Today at 12:45pm
OMG, Sarah! Hot new guy keeps asking about you. Holly is so pissed. This is awesome! Where are you??

Today at 12:47pm
He's not into me. I'm leaving for the day. Don't feel well.

Today at 12:47pm
Is this about Drew?

Today at 12:48pm
I think so.

Today at 12:48pm
?

Today at 12:48pm
?

Today at 12:50pm
*OMG! Luke just gave me a
note…to give to YOU!*

I stood frozen in the middle of the path, feeling completely sick about Drew, and more than nervous about Luke. But maybe I was excited. No, definitely nervous. Excited? What the hell??

I couldn't respond to Maddy. I just shoved my phone back in my pocket and ran.

CHAPTER 11

Blackout

~ SARAH ~

MADDY WAS AT my door only minutes after school ended. I was thankful for the absence of my parents as their wrath about me missing afternoon classes would have been an unneeded addition to my already bad day.

I opened the door wide and let Maddy in. She didn't hesitate before holding out the folded note.

"Read it. What's it say?" she prompted excitedly. "Oh, who am I kidding?" she laughed. "I already read it. He wants to meet up tonight!"

I unfolded the paper and read his scrawl carefully. "I need to see you. Please meet me at the school soccer field tonight. Anytime. I'll be there."

My breath became hard to regulate. It sucked in at erratic intervals and left in quick exhales.

"Sarah? Are you okay?" Maddy had her hand on my back and was leading me into the living room. She pulled me down onto the couch next to her. "Just breathe," she ordered.

"I'm okay," I said, finally able to control the regularity of the air going in and out of my lungs. I forced a smile and looked back down at the paper. How was this happening? Who was this guy? Why did he want to see me? Every fibre inside me wanted to go to him. To see if this was real, but I couldn't. I couldn't think when I was near him. I couldn't function, and that wasn't a normal response to have. It scared the hell out of me.

"What are you thinking?" Maddy pressed.

"I don't know," I lied. How could I possibly tell Maddy what was going through my head? How could I tell her that I had been dreaming about this guy? That I had already fallen for him? How could I explain any of this without sounding crazy?

"So will you go?" she pressed.

"Maddy, I don't even know who he is. I can't possibly meet a stranger after dark at an isolated location," I pointed out, even though he wasn't a stranger. I already knew him. Somehow.

"True," she assented. "I'll go with you. And Drew."

"Ha!" I said. "I don't think Drew would go."

"Why? You guys aren't together, right? He's made it clear that he just thinks of you as a friend."

"Yeah." It stung.

"Then shouldn't he be happy if you're happy?"

"I don't think Drew works like that."

"Sarah, come on. You've been single long enough. Isn't it time you started dating?"

My head was spinning. How could this be happening? Last week I was single, happy with my relationship with Drew—whatever it was—and not at all interested in anyone else. But now—now I could think of nothing else but this tall, dark, muscle-defined dream guy who I had somehow made come to life.

"Maybe," I said, knowing this would appease Maddy for now.

"Eek!" Maddy screeched. "Really? So you'll go?"

"I said *maybe*. But if I do, I'll go on my own."

Maddy huffed. "Why?" She didn't like this arrangement. "You said yourself that you don't even know him and it's an isolated location. Makes sense that I should go with you."

I looked at her sideways. "Sometimes, Maddy . . . sometimes you make it a little more awkward."

Maddy looked offended. "I do not!"

"You do."

Maddy shook her head as if ridding it of the last insult. "Fine, maybe I can be a little forward. But sometimes you're just too dumbstruck and can't speak."

I nodded. I knew that.

"Okay," Maddy sullenly agreed. "But call me before you go and the minute you get back."

I smiled and pushed her leg playfully. "You'll be the first to know. But don't be disappointed if I don't go. I'm sure we'll see him again."

"True. And it probably wouldn't hurt to play hard to get for once, either."

"Get out of my house," I teased.

"What? Why?" Maddy pouted as I stood up.

"Because I have homework and chores to do before my parents get home. And I have to take Lucia for a walk. Unless you wanted to come?" I smiled at her recoil. Maddy wasn't into exercise or fresh air, so combining the two things made her retreat.

"No, I'm good." She led the way to the front door. "I'll talk to you later?"

"Or see you tomorrow," I said, reminding her of my other option to play hard to get.

Maddy left and I leaned against the door, sighing heavily. I wasn't going to the school to meet Luke. I couldn't. It was far too strange, and I hadn't yet begun to wrap my head around it. Maybe if I could at least start to forget about the intense dreams I had had about him, then I could properly get to know him.

I dug my phone from my pocket and texted Drew.

DREW

Today at 4:18pm
I need to talk to you.

I waited for what seemed like forever.

DREW

Today at 4:18pm
I need to talk to you.

Today at 4:24pm
Please, Drew. I don't like when you disappear like this. You promised me you wouldn't do this to me anymore.

After a few more minutes, I slid my phone back into my pocket and went about my chores. If I got the kitchen cleaned, laundry done, garbage out, and floors swept now, I wouldn't have to deal with Darlene about it later tonight.

Before long, George was on his way in the front door home from work, marking the time of twenty after six or thereabouts.

"Hey, kiddo!" he called up the stairs as I carried a basket of freshly laundered clothes up to my room.

"Hey, George. How was work?"

"Same old thing different day," he said, more to himself.

"Dinner's in the fridge. I've got a lot of homework to do so going to work on that. If Drew comes by, let me know, though, please."

"Sure thing, kiddo."

I closed my bedroom door behind me and dumped the basket of warm clothes over my bed. Lucia curled up inside the clothes—her beloved spot. I uncovered my favourite yellow sweater from the pile and pulled it on over my head, the heat enveloping me like a hot summer's day.

I dumped the contents of my backpack onto my desk and sorted through my homework. Something from every subject. An English assignment, study notes for a math test tomorrow, lab results for Science, and chart labelling for Biology. I sighed heavily, wishing my phone would interrupt me with a text from Drew.

Three hours later, I was packing my books away. The only texts were from Maddy, asking if I had gone to meet Luke. I ignored them, not wanting to explain my reasons for having decided to leave it alone for now, until things made more sense. And for some reason, I felt like Drew, the reader of dreams, could make sense of it for me.

CALEB, MADDY AND Drew were already in the school parking lot, leaning against Drew's car, when I arrived the next morning. Drew hadn't returned any of my calls or texts from the night before and I hadn't heard from him this morning offering a drive.

"Oh, so you're alive," I said to Drew, giving him my best look of disapproval.

"Was busy with my dad."

"Whatever, Drew." I hoped he didn't think for one second that I believed him. "You broke a promise."

"So, what'd you do last night?" Maddy asked, eye-balling me curiously, and ignoring the tension between Drew and me.

I glared at her—a silent plea to back off. Since not having spoken to Drew in over twenty-four hours, I didn't think telling him about the new guy was the best way to start the day. But maybe he wouldn't care at all. Sure seemed that way lately.

"Tell me everything," Maddy said, ignoring my glare. "Did you end up meeting up with him?"

"I didn't," I said firmly, widening my eyes at her and wishing she'd stop talking.

"Who's this?" Drew asked casually.

"The potential new guy," Maddy squealed. "He is SO cute. *And* he happens to have a crush on Sarah already."

Drew looked down at me and chuckled. "Who is this new guy?"

"We met him yesterday when *you* were nowhere to be found. Again."

Drew raised his eyebrows and nodded. "Fair."

"Anyway," I said, turning back to Maddy, "I'm not interested right now."

"Are you kidding me?" Maddy said, a look of shock evident on her face. "He is like the hottest guy in the school." She turned to Caleb and then Drew. "No offence. Not hotter than you guys of course."

"I know. I won't lie, he is cute, but I'm just not interested right now."

Drew's ring seemed to be burning into my finger. We weren't together, and we weren't dating. And he admitted to not being able to be what I wanted. But he also admitted to wanting me. And needing me. And who was Luke anyway? Was he at all like the guy in my dreams? Could I actually have real feelings for him? It was all too much to think about, so I preferred to keep it all at a distance until I figured out what *I* wanted.

"But the chemistry," Maddy continued. "You two were like deep into each other. It was eerie. You don't think that's worth exploring?"

Drew's head tilted back and his eyes met with the sky. What was he thinking?

"Maddy, just give it up, okay?" I said forcefully.

Maddy followed my gaze to Drew. "Okay," she said. "Sorry."

Drew spoke next. "So maybe I should meet this new guy."

"Great idea," came a deep, familiar voice from behind us. Oh no. I froze.

Drew turned around. The two were identical in height, but that's where the similarities ended. Drew's hair was messy and blonde, and his eyes were a bright green, whereas Luke's hair was darker and shorter, and his eyes were the most mesmerizing blue I had ever seen.

Luke walked around the car and held out his hand to Drew. "Luke."

Drew hesitated, studying him for a moment, but then said, "Drew."

"I know who you are," Luke said, smiling.

"Oh?"

"Sarah's keeper." His voice was hard. Firm. The softness was gone.

Drew clenched his jaw as his eyes narrowed suspiciously, accusingly.

What was this? Some new term for boyfriend? Well, even if it was, I could guarantee I would *never* refer to my boyfriend as my *keeper*. "He's not my *keeper*," I laughed. "He's my . . . my . . ." I looked up at Drew who was still staring at Luke. What the hell was he to me? Friend? Best friend? Ring-giver?

"Boyfriend," Drew answered in a hard tone that matched Luke's.

Boyfriend!? Well, that was a first!

Luke smirked and nodded. I blushed, feeling a deep sense of regret. I wanted to tell him I was sorry. But why? For cheating on the dream version of him? For accepting Drew's ring when I didn't even know he was real? For the way Drew was treating him right now?

"I see," Luke said. "Well, I am sorry. I guess I didn't know that *you* were her boyfriend." He smiled weakly at me while Drew held his head high, puffing his chest like a peacock. "I'll . . . be on my way." He bowed slightly in my direction, which reminded me that he had called me princess in my dreams. But this was ridiculous. Probably my mind playing tricks on me.

Drew made a deliberate motion toward him, but thought better of it when Luke turned to leave.

"Wait," I called after him. What was I doing? Why did it hurt me so badly to see him walk away like this?

Luke turned around slowly and faced me. Drew grabbed my arm and pulled me back. "What are you doing?" he growled.

"Being friendly," I scorned. "Luke, why don't you meet us for lunch today?"

Drew turned away and rested his arms against the roof of his car. I knew he was pissed, but he really didn't have any right. Up until one minute ago I had no idea he considered himself my boyfriend. And did he really even mean that? Or was it his ridiculous idea that I should only have eyes for him?

"You sure?" Luke asked, his adorable smile spreading across his perfect face as his eyes lit up.

"Of course. We'll be in the arboretum again."

"Okay, cool. See you there, princess." He winked and then walked away.

Princess? Did he just say that out loud? Did I imagine that?

"What did he just call you?" Caleb laughed.

Okay, I'm not hearing things. He did just call me princess.

Drew threw his fist into his car door.

"Drew!" I gasped.

"Who the hell does he think he is?" He paced back and forth, fists clenched and face red with anger.

"Honestly, Drew. Maddy told him yesterday that I was single," I said. "So he probably doesn't believe that you and I are together. That you actually *want* to be my boyfriend. And to be honest, I'm not so sure I believe it either."

Drew kept pacing, ignoring my silent plea for him to confirm his commitment to me. When it was clear it wasn't coming, I slid his ring from my finger, my heart aching as I did, and set it on the hood of his car. He saw me do this, but made no effort to stop me. My chest squeezed with a pain that I couldn't justify or explain, so I turned and left him standing there.

Maddy caught up to me, leaving Caleb behind with

Drew. "What. Was. That?"

"I don't know," I said, my thoughts reeling.

"Are you and Drew together?"

"I don't know."

"Do you like Luke?"

"I don't know."

"This is freaking awesome." Maddy laughed hysterically.

"Huh?"

"Who would've thought my best friend would be caught in a love triangle with the two hottest guys in school?"

"I feel sick." My head was spinning.

"What?"

"I feel like I'm . . ." I stumbled to a bench and fell onto it, my bag falling to the ground before I could find stability.

"Sarah, are you okay?" I heard Maddy ask, although her voice echoed and her face was spinning along with my thoughts.

"Help," I tried to say, but I was sure the sound was only in my head.

Maddy's arms were around me. "Someone help!" I heard her scream. "Help!"

All I could see was sky. Blue sky and one large, white cloud flickering and spiralling. Then Drew.

"I got her. I got you, Sarah." Drew's face was the last

thing I saw before darkness took over.

IT WAS MORE difficult to clear the haze from my head this time. Blackness was closing in on me, and then lifting, as if a great struggle between my conscious and subconscious.

I groaned. Two figures stood over me, their faces blackened by the light behind them.

"Is it really her?" a female voice asked.

"The one and only."

She scoffed. "What the hell does Luke see in her?"

"Now, now, no time to be jealous."

"I'm not jealous. She has nothing on me," the woman spat. "Besides, when we get what we need, we can kill her and Luke will—"

"Exactly. No need to rush things," the man mused.

"What have you found out so far?"

"Nothing. This is the first time I've checked in." The man reached his hand toward my face. He clutched the air as if he was going to squeeze my face, and then an excruciating pain ripped through my whole body and everything went black.

When my conscious started to come back around, I kept quiet and still. I was on a cold, hard surface and the man and woman were standing further into the shadows of the room, talking to a black figure. I could only make out some of their questions for the figure, and I wasn't sure how they understand any of his answers because they came in the form of hisses and high-pitch whispers. Maybe I had hit my head when I fell. This didn't seem to make any sense.

"Okay," said the man. "You know what you have to do." His footsteps came toward me and as his hand came down to my face, I tried to move out of the way, but I was frozen; paralyzed by whatever spell he had on me. The shadow of his hand covered my face and then everything was black again.

"HERE." DREW HAD me in his arms, sitting next to me on a low cot and feeding me a purple liquid from a small bottle. "Drink. Quickly."

I swallowed and closed my eyes again as fatigue settled back in. He laid me back on the bed as the door opened. Where were we?

"How is she?" a woman's voice asked as Drew stood up and slid the bottle into his back pocket. My eyes lingered on his pocket as I tried to focus and rid my head of the confusion and fog.

"She's coming around a little bit," Drew answered. "You should probably send her home, though. Apparently she's not safe *here* anymore." This last part was muttered under his breath.

"Yes, well, I'll keep her here for observation for a bit and see how she is. You're welcome to stay with her."

Drew didn't answer and I couldn't keep my eyes open

long enough to tell if he nodded or smiled or what.

I groaned. "Where am I?" The room swayed slightly as I spoke.

"Nurse's office," Drew answered, then he turned to the nurse. "Looks like she's uncomfortable. Could she have a couple of aspirins?"

"Sure, I'll be right back." She left the room.

"My head," I groaned as my fingers touched the back of my head. The pain seared through to my forehead.

"What's wrong with your head? You didn't fall. I caught you."

"I must've hit my head," I recalled as the painful memory of my head bouncing off the stone flashed before my eyes.

Drew knelt down beside me. "Sarah, listen to me. You need to tell me everything you remember from when you blacked out?"

I shook my head slowly. "I was with Maddy and then I got dizzy and—"

"Not that part," Drew interrupted. "When you were out. Did you . . . did anything happen? Did you have a bad dream or anything?"

I tried to roll my eyes, but it was difficult. I still didn't have complete control over my body apparently. Why was it always all about dreams with him? Why did he always only seem to care about . . . ? But wait . . . an image fleeted through my brain—a man and woman hovered over me, having an odd conversation.

"Two people were talking about me," I said, knowing I should be alarmed by this, feeling the danger in it and knowing that it was all wrong.

I watched the recognition and panic hit his face. "What did they say?" he pressed.

"They said something about needing something from me and then they would kill me." There was also something about Luke, but everything inside of me told me not to divulge this part. It would just make things worse. It wasn't relevant anyway. And besides, it was just a dream and there was no point in creating any more animosity between him and the new guy over a stupid dream. "It's not real, right, Drew?"

Drew slammed his fist into the wall at the head of my cot. "What did they look like?" he demanded.

"I don't know. I couldn't see them."

Drew stared at me, and I couldn't read just one emotion from him. He was angry. Frustrated. Worried. Afraid.

"How long was I out?"

"Seven minutes." He pushed a strand of hair from my face. As attentive as he was, I could see distance in his eyes. His mind was elsewhere.

It had only felt like a minute or two, but I supposed I was unconscious for most of it. Then when I woke, they were talking to that strange black hissing figure. I wondered if I should tell Drew that part.

"What is it?" he pressed.

"There was a third person," I said. "I was unconscious for most of it, but they were talking to him and asking questions. He talked weird, like how I imagine a snake would sound if it could talk."

"Geezus." Drew's head fell back and he stared at the ceiling.

"What?"

"Did they say what they want you to get for them?"

"No, I told you. I don't remember anything else after that."

His intensity was unsettling. I knew he wholeheartedly believed in dreams. But was it the symbolism of the dreams that he believed in? Or was he actually convinced that this dream happened? Maybe I was still unconscious. Maybe this strange exchange was still part of my dream.

"What happened to me?" I asked quietly.

"You fainted," Drew said through clenched teeth.

"But how? I never faint."

"I have an idea of how. I just have to be sure before I cause a war."

"Drew, please don't do this." I reached for him but he moved out of my way and my hand fell. "Is this about Luke? For some stupid reason, I feel like it is. But why?"

"Sarah, there are things you just don't understand, okay? Things that you can't fix with a bat of your eyelashes or a flash of your smile."

I wasn't sure whether to be offended or flattered. I was leaning toward offended.

"You'll just have to trust me," he finished.

"Tell me, then," I said. "Help me understand."

He paused. "Not yet."

I rolled my eyes and turned my head away from him. Then I felt his warm hand on mine. He slid his fingers between mine and kissed my hand gently.

"Stay here. I'll be back soon," he whispered.

He was almost at the door when I said, "Drew, please stay! I need you here. I may fall asleep. What if I fall asleep?" I wasn't sure why this would be a bad thing, but I knew Drew would think it would be, and I was desperate to keep him there. To stop him from going. He was angry and vengeful and I didn't want him getting hurt.

The nurse came back into the room, passing Drew at the door. He broke eye contact with me and then addressed the nurse. "I have to go. Make sure she doesn't go to sleep. She's showing signs of a concussion." He turned to the door and swung it open before turning back to the nurse. "And *don't* let her out of this room." And he left. The door closed behind him, trapping me in the small, cold room with no one to love me. No one to take care of me.

After swallowing the two white pills from the nurse, I stood up and struggled to get my arm into the sleeve of my coat, which was when I noticed Drew's ring on my finger. Hadn't I given that back to him? Maybe he did care about me after all, although I couldn't think about that right now. His mind games were exhausting.

"Oh no, dear, please come have a sit, I don't think you should be up and about just yet." The nurse took my arm and led me back to the cot.

"I'm fine." I politely maneuvered my arm from her grasp. "I just want to get to class."

"Well, I can respect that, Sarah, but I think I should give your parents a call to—"

"No!" I said quickly. "Really, I'm fine. I . . . I promise I will either come back to see you, or go straight home if I feel at all dizzy."

She looked displeased, but her rebuttal was interrupted by a knock at the door.

"Yes?" she said as she opened the door a crack. I took the opportunity to finish putting on my coat and gathering my backpack.

"I, uh, was just checking on Sarah. Is she . . . is she okay?" It was the unmistakeable, dreamy voice of Luke.

The nurse looked back at me and I nodded, trying to keep my composure. She opened the door wider and gave me a disapproving look.

"Remember, Sarah, if you feel at all nauseous or

dizzy, or out of sorts at all, come see me straight away."

"I'll take care of her, Ms."—Luke read the name on her lapel—"Ms. Tarves. We have the same class right now so I'll walk her there and keep an eye on her."

My eyebrows came together in a display of puzzlement. How did he know what class I had next?

"Sarah?" The nurse turned to me for my consensus.

"Yes, that's okay."

Luke took my backpack from me as soon as we left the office.

"So what class are you supposed to be in right now?" I asked as we walked slowly down the hall, not convinced that he had been telling the truth.

"I'm not," he answered plainly.

"Then why are you here?"

He looked at me, and I felt like he was holding back what he really wanted to say, but instead chose to say, "I'm still checking the school out. Principal said I could sit in on some classes to get a feel for the school and teachers."

"So where are you taking me then?"

"To your class—Biology."

I looked up at him swiftly. "How do you know what class I have?"

He smirked, and although I should have felt uneasy about this, I only felt comfort. "Curious about you, I guess. It's not hard to get info from your friend Maddy."

He winked.

"Aah," I said, full comprehension washing over me. "Good ol' Maddy."

"So what happened to you anyway? Maddy said you fainted."

I shook my head and shrugged. "Yeah, I guess so."

"That happen often?"

"Never."

He nodded slowly and then reached in his schoolbag for something. He pulled out a half a bottle of water and handed it to me. "Here, why don't you drink this?"

"I'm okay, really. I had a drink in the nurse's office. I'm not thirsty. Really." I pushed the water bottle back toward him. He hesitated, looked regretful, but then slid the bottle back into his bag.

"What did you have to drink in the nurse's office?"

"Water, I think. Drew gave it to me."

He nodded as if he expected this. "So he was with you?"

"He was," I confirmed.

"Where'd he go?"

I sighed heavily. "To be honest, I have no idea. He just said he had something to take care of and left."

"Weird," Luke said, but I could tell he thought more of it, too.

"I'm sure it's fine," I lied.

Drew and I both had Math after my Biology class, but

I wasn't sure I could wait that long to find out what was going on with him.

DREW DIDN'T SHOW up for Math class and Ms. Kerr made a point to make a public note of it.

"Drew is absent again, I see. Looks like he's on his way to setting a fine path for his future." She stared at me over the rim of her thick, boxy glasses. "Any excuse for him today, Sarah?"

"No," I muttered as I leafed through my textbook, pretending to be too busy to care that she was somehow blaming me for his tardiness.

I kept my phone on my desk during class, watching it closely for a text or call from Drew. But nothing. The longer I waited for him to show up to class, the angrier I got. Somehow I knew he was okay, and that thought allowed me to let my anger brew. Why would he keep me in the dark? What did he make me drink? What was he keeping from me?

CHAPTER 12

Truth

~ SARAH ~

THE LUNCH BELL rang and the classroom emptied quickly. I threw the rest of my things into my schoolbag in an uncharacteristic, haphazard manner, then caught up with the other students in the hall who were eager to get out of the building for the next hour.

"Hey you!" Maddy called as I headed for the arboretum.

I turned around and braced myself in case she leveraged herself off of my shoulders as she oftentimes did. This time she didn't.

"How are you feeling?" she asked as she studied my face and put her hand to my forehead.

I grinned. "I'm fine, Maddy."

"Where's Drew?" she asked, looking around.

"M.I.A."

"Again?"

"Again."

"What'd you do, hit him?"

I glared at her. "No."

"Then what? He's off sulking about Luke?"

"Maybe."

"Did I hear my name?" Luke said as he approached from behind. My heart started beating wildly in my chest.

I smiled weakly. "You did. Thanks again for walking me to class this morning."

Maddy turned to me with wide eyes, impressively high eyebrows, and a huge smile. I tried to ignore her but could feel my face flushing slightly.

Luke grinned. "Shall we?" He held out his arm for me to take and gestured toward the arboretum. At my hesitation, he said, "Doctor's orders."

A smile played on my lips. "Nurse's orders, actually," I smartly corrected, then awkwardly took his arm and allowed him to lead me to our lunch table, which I was impressed he remembered.

A few minutes into lunch, the arboretum doors burst open. Luke, with his back to the door, stood up slowly and sucked in a deep breath before turning around to face Drew. How had he known the bold entrance was meant for him?

"Drew!" I said. "What the hell! Where have you—"

"Sarah," Drew said, pointing to me but not taking his eyes from Luke's, "get away from him."

Luke grinned but didn't say a word.

"What the hell is going on?" I demanded.

Drew ignored me and rounded back on Luke. "Tried to pay a little visit to you today, but turns out your brother's been acting on your behalf."

"It's the only way I could see her," Luke said, matching Drew's glare.

"Not anymore. Get away from her. Now."

"Oh my gosh, are you kidding me?" Holly stood up from her table, hands on her hips. "Are you two seriously fighting over *her*?"

"Sit down!" both Drew and Luke shouted, which made my heart smile if only for a second.

Drew was in Luke's face now. "Why are you here?" he growled, his voice low, tense, but sure.

"For her."

"But *why*?"

"You wouldn't let her come back to me, so I had to come to her."

"Why?" Drew hissed. "You want her necklace? You'll never get it."

"No," Luke said without hesitation. A little hesitation would have been nice. And was Drew freaking serious? My school necklace—the very one that symbolized deep commitment to another? Didn't he know me by now? Or was he just worried that Luke wanted a relationship with me? And if that was the reason—what right did he have to stand in the way? He had his chance. Too many of them!

"Then tell me this—who isn't done with her yet?" Drew growled.

"I don't know what the hell you're talking about."

Drew's voice was lower now, barely audible. "She had a dream. Someone told her she couldn't die until he was done with her."

You have got to be kidding me! Does Drew honestly think my dream is Luke's fault?

"When did that happen?" Luke asked, his eyes darting back and forth as if in deep thought.

Wait . . . what? "It didn't happen," I interjected. "It was a dream. Thus, not real."

"First time was a week ago," Drew continued, both of them ignoring my interruption. "And then you show up and it happens again."

"How? Didn't you give her your ring?"

"Not soon enough."

What was going on? Luke was actually buying into this dream stuff? And why did Drew's ring have anything to do with this?

Drew grabbed Luke by his shirt. "If you so much as lay one effing finger on her, you'll be sorry, Luke."

Luke chuckled. "That's a little dark for you, isn't it, Drew?"

"You wanna talk about dark, do you?" Drew challenged.

"Don't say anything you'll regret," Luke warned.

"Drew, back off *right* now," I said, pushing Drew back and wedging my way between the two.

"I'll back off when he leaves." Drew looked down at me and clenched his jaw.

Luke was watching me now, too. He wasn't answering, but I could tell he was considering Drew's threat. Finally, he exhaled and returned his gaze to Drew. "Don't screw this up," he said. His eyes narrowed on him before he addressed me. "'Till we meet again." He winked and then his eyes fell to my lips before he turned and left the arboretum.

When he was out of sight and everyone returned to their lunches, Drew reached for my hand. "Sarah—"

"Don't," I said, pulling my arms into my chest. "I . . . I don't understand."

"Everything's fine."

I covered my ears. *How can any of this be real? They talked about my dreams. They talked about each other as if they know each other. As if Luke knows me. I dreamed of Luke and now he's real. How is any of this possible?*

I felt my feet carrying me away as Drew tried to call me back. I ran. I ran as fast and as far as I could. I didn't know where I was running. But the wind in my face was real. It made sense, and I needed that.

Before I knew it, I was at the old apple tree. Another constant that made sense with its branches in the same shape and position that I had left them. I climbed high and pulled my legs into my chest as I cradled myself on a large branch, back resting against the trunk.

"Sarah?" I heard Drew call as he came through the woods into the clearing.

I didn't answer.

He walked to the base of the tree and looked up at me. I kept my head turned, tears streaming down my face as I locked my gaze at the thick row of trees ahead of me. Trees that made sense. Trees that swayed when the wind blew. Foliage that changed with the seasons.

"How did I know you'd come here?" Drew said as he pulled himself up to sit in front of me on the same branch.

I pinched my eyes closed, letting the tears fall down my face. I didn't care anymore. I didn't care if Drew Spencer saw me cry. I didn't care if he didn't like what he saw. What did it all matter anyway? I was crazy. The world was crazy.

"Talk to me, Sarah."

"What do you want me to say, Drew? That I'm losing my mind?"

"You're not losing your mind."

"Then who is he?" I said with my head in my hands.

"Explain to me why I've been dreaming of a guy I had never met, but you apparently know quite well."

"He's no one," Drew grumbled.

"Then I'm going crazy. This is impossible, Drew." I let out a sob and Drew put his arms around me.

"You're not going crazy." He pushed hair from my face.

"The dreams that seem so real, the keys—I saw it on him today—the words he said, his voice. It was definitely him in my dreams, Drew. But why?"

Drew was quiet for a minute, then finally took in a deep breath and said, "He's a keeper."

I waited for him to explain, but when he didn't, I gave him an agitated look, letting him know I couldn't handle any nonsense right now. I needed things to make sense.

"From a dream world called Etak," he continued. He wasn't lifting his eyes to mine, but he wasn't biting his lip either, so I listened. Whether it was true or not, Drew believed what he was saying.

"Drew, what the hell are you talking about?"

"Earth is not the only world in our universe," he began. "There are . . . other worlds. And when someone dreams, they visit these other worlds." He looked up. His eyes were sorrowful as if telling me this was physically hurting him. "You following so far?"

"What's not to follow? You think there are other worlds you can visit through dreaming."

"Yes," he confirmed. "And some of those worlds are good worlds, but some are . . . quite the opposite." When I didn't reply, he said, "Can I show you something?" He held out his hand for me. I hesitantly took it, and then he took his key in his other hand and whispered, "Take us to Nevaeh."

A few seconds later, after a swirling vortex of time and space, we were standing in the middle of a garden, the canopy of apples no longer above us. The sky was a bright blue and the grass was a vibrant green. A pond was to our right with crystal clear water, and if I wasn't mistaken, the bottom was lined in shimmering gold.

"Where are we?" I gasped, my hand clutching his tighter.

"This is one of the light worlds. Nevaeh."

There was a sensation of warmth that enveloped me and my heart was bursting with joy. Suddenly nothing else mattered. We were in a place of happiness and I couldn't even remember what Drew and I had been arguing about. All I knew was that we were together and holding hands, and I never felt more certain or more in love than I did at that moment. I flung my arms around Drew. "I love you so much!" I cried.

It took a few seconds, and I imagined he was caught by surprise, but his arms found their way around me and squeezed. He breathed out, and a tiny moan slipped with it. He loved me, too. He didn't have to say it. I knew.

A second later we were back under the canopy of the apple tree, standing at the base with a grey sky above. I was still clinging to Drew, but suddenly doubt and fear lingered, seeping back into my consciousness, and I released him. "I'm sorry," I said, feeling embarrassed.

"Don't be," he said. "Nevaeh is a very powerful world. Its light helps to restore and heal."

I sat down on the grass, still processing what I had just seen. "So this is real. You're not lying."

"It's real. Some of the worlds are light worlds and some are dark. Good dreams happen in the light worlds; nightmares happen in the dark worlds."

I nodded along, determined now for him to tell me everything. "What are the names of these worlds?"

"Nevaeh," he said, nodding his head toward the past, "Leviathan, Lorendale, Nitsua and Etak." He looked down. "There was another light world, but it's gone now. The dark worlds created a ruthless, immortal beast and sent it to destroy the light world and everyone in it."

I cringed. "Sorry to hear that."

His face softened and I knew it was a relief for him to be able to finally share this with me. "For each world there is a keeper," he continued. "One who governs the world and protects the portal or gateway, into their world. Luke is Etak's keeper. I am Earth's keeper."

"Wait—why does Earth need a keeper, too?"

"Earth is the heart of the dream worlds. She keeps the

other worlds alive." He smirked before his next words. "That's where Earth got her name. Same letters as the word heart, just rearranged slightly."

E-a-r-t-h . . . H-e-a-r-t. Hmph. I never noticed.

"I want to show you something. Take off your shoes," Drew said, his voice soft.

I rested against the tree as I slid my shoes off. No questions asked.

"And your socks," he added. When I had completed that task, he said, "Now feel the Earth on your feet."

I sunk my feet into the grass and moved my toes, feeling the cold lumps and brittle blades beneath my soles.

"Can you feel that?" he asked.

"The grass?"

"No, deeper than that. Think past what you can see."

I closed my eyes and let my thoughts travel past the layer of cool grass, into the thawing dirt, down through the rocks and right to the core of the Earth. I saw the blazing ball of heat in the centre, beating and breathing as if it were alive. Heat embodied my feet and a rhythmic drumming vibrated from the Earth's centre right up through the ground and into my body.

I fell back, hopping on the ground until the sensation was gone. "What was that?" I gasped.

Drew looked impressed. "You felt it? Not many people do. That was Earth's heartbeat." He smiled proudly. "She's an orb of energy and we can feel that energy best when we're connected with her. But we can't connect with her unless we touch her with our bare skin. Then she'll give us all the energy and help we need."

Slightly freaked out, I slid my shoes back on and stuffed my socks into my backpack.

"We always have shoes on when we're outside, but when we take off the layers between ourselves and the Earth, that's when we feel . . . Earth's magic. And that's why being barefoot at the beach is the best soul food for people."

I stared at the patch of grass that was hot and throbbing only seconds ago. Part of me wanted to remove my shoes and try it again, but the hammering in my heart prevented me. I would try it later.

"So," I began, returning my attention to our earlier conversation, "you said a keeper's job is to protect the portal. What does that mean?"

"Each world has a portal. It's like a hub for dreamers. It's how they travel in and out of each world." Drew looked around at our surroundings. "Have you ever wondered why you keep coming here? Why this place brings you peace?"

"Because it's the only place I can shoot some arrows in peace. It's quiet and no one else knows about it." *Duh.*

Drew chuckled. "This place is full of life, Sarah. It's where the souls come and go." He stepped forward and ran his hand down the tree's trunk. "It's Earth's portal."

"What do you mean—it's where souls come and go?"

"When people die, their souls transfer to one of these other worlds. Depending on how much light or dark energy is in them when they die, they'll either live out eternity in one of the light worlds, or one of the dark worlds."

"What? Like heaven and hell?"

"Yeah, except there are more than just the two options. And we call them by different names." I was quiet so he continued, "That's how people can sometimes see deceased loved ones when they dream."

"Their souls travel through this tree?" I touched the bark of the huge apple tree, tentatively.

Drew nodded. "The tree of life."

The meadow had always felt like a special place. Like a place where my worries and fears could disappear. But I had always thought it was because it was so quiet, so untouched, and the only place, this close to the city, where I never ran into another human being.

Drew cleared his throat. "This place is shielded from mortal eyes."

"What do you mean?" I shook my head. "I'm here. I can see it."

"Yeah," he said, avoiding my eyes. "I guess some people can."

Maybe I'm special, I let myself think. Or maybe Drew gave me special access because he liked our time alone here. Whatever the reason, I loved this place even more now. Now, it not only *felt* like our special place, it *was* our special place.

Now that I had a flurry of complicated information that confused but enlightened me, I still had one burning question on my mind—Luke. Why had he come to Earth? And how did he get here? Okay, two burning questions. But Drew's openness about all of this made me hesitant to ask about Luke—the one topic I knew would turn his mood.

Drew pulled his necklace from his shirt, displaying his gold key at the end. "This key can take me to any world at any time."

I studied the key in his hand. "What is your job as keeper?"

"I have a few responsibilities, but mostly my job is to protect the portal from unwanted visitors."

"What do you mean—unwanted visitors?" A shiver crawled up my spine as I awaited his answer.

"If there's ever an invasion, this is where the monsters will come out."

"The monsters?" My body moved closer to Drew's.

"From the dark worlds," he confirmed. "Like Luke's." The last part must've tasted bitter.

"What would the monsters do?"

"Cause mass destruction."

"Has that ever happened?"

"A few times. Remember dinosaurs?"

I chuckled, but stopped quickly when I realized he wasn't joking. "Are you serious?"

"Yeah, and a few other monsters that impersonated actual people. Remember Hitler?"

His eyes were focused at thoughts in the distance. The lines in his face were firm and his eyebrows were tight. He was serious.

"Okay," I began slowly, "so your job is to stop these things from happening. Did we not have a keeper back then or something?"

"A keeper's job is to *try* to stop these things from happening. It's not as easy as it sounds. The dark worlds are constantly trying to drown Earth in darkness. That's what keeps my father and me so busy."

"So your father knows about all of this?"

Drew nodded. "He was Earth's keeper before me."

I let this resonate for a minute, bringing comfort in the fact that if I had any doubt after this conversation, then I could always go ask Mr. Spencer if his son was going crazy. "So the dark worlds try to destroy Earth by sending monsters."

"And viruses."

"Viruses?"

He paused and turned his eyes to mine. "Have you ever thought it was strange how one day you're alive and well, and the next day you wake up and you're sick and dying?"

"You catch colds . . . viruses. That's normal, Drew."

"Those viruses have to start somewhere. The dark

worlds send them in. The Black Plague of the 1300's that took out half of Europe's population? The Ebola Virus, Malaria, Small Pox? . . . They all started somewhere."

"And what? You think the dark worlds sent them in?"

"They did, Sarah. Dad and I work closely with the World Health Organization. We help them find cures."

I nodded, realizing the magnitude of what he was saying. Had he not brought me to Nevaeh to experience a dream world myself, or showed me Earth's heartbeat, then I probably would've thought he was crazy by now.

I shook my head. "This is too much information, Drew."

"You're right, I'm sorry. Really, all you need to know is that there are good dream worlds and bad dream worlds. I'm trying to protect you from the bad ones."

"So when someone has good dreams, they are visiting a good dream world, and when they have nightmares, they're in a bad dream world?" I shuddered at the memory of my one and only nightmare that took place in this very tree.

"Typically," he said. "Most people dream several times a night. They slip in and out of these dream worlds. They might visit one of the light worlds and have a good dream, and then they might find themselves in a dark world having a nightmare."

I felt stupid for asking, but I figured the conversation

was already beyond normal, and given my last night-mare, I thought it was justified. "Can you die in a dream world?"

"It's happened, yes. When people die in their sleep, or slip into comas, it means they're trapped in one of the dark worlds. Sometimes I'm able to help pull them out, but . . . sometimes I can't."

"So let's pretend all this is true," I began. "If I am vis-iting Luke's world when I dream, why does this bother you so much?"

"Because Etak is one of the dark worlds, Sarah. Luke is the keeper of a dark world. It's not safe. He's up to something."

"But I don't have nightmares when I'm there."

"Thanks to your dreamcatcher," he mumbled.

"What did you just say?" I thought I heard him, but I wasn't sure I wanted to believe him.

"The dreamcatcher I gave you when we met. It helps filter the bad dreams."

I shook my head. "Did you know that when you gave it to me?"

"Of course I did," he answered. "It's my job to protect dreamers."

I had always believed Drew gave me the dream-catcher because he liked me. I thought we had a special connection and he gave me something that was im-portant to him. But now I find out it was only because of duty. Responsibility. And that hurt.

"If it weren't for your dreamcatcher, you probably wouldn't even *like* that guy. He would've probably tortured you, or at the very least, made you ride a black horse." He stiffened when he said it, expecting me to lash out at him for using my fear against me in this argument.

"Why did he come here then?" I challenged. "If Luke is such a bad guy, why did he come here to see me?"

"I don't know. After you told me you were dreaming about a guy with a key like mine and his name was Luke, I went straight to Etak to find out what he was up to. That's where I got that black eye. I thought I was dealing with Luke, but apparently it was his brother. So when you introduced me to Luke this morning, I didn't recognize him. Then he called me your keeper, and I just assumed he was working for Luke, ordered to come here to get more info on you. I couldn't make a scene there so I let him walk away, prepared to deal with him later. And then you fainted and you were able to be cured with the elixir, so I figured he had been sent here on a mission to drug you."

"What are you talking about? You think Luke drugged me?"

"I think he infected you with a virus from Etak. When I left the nurse's office, I went back to Etak, and that's when I found out Luke's brother has been playing Prince of Etak while Luke's been here drugging you."

I slowly shook my head as pieces of this gigantic puzzle tried to find their way into place. "Luke's not bad, Drew," I said, my head still shaking.

Drew let his head fall back and sighed heavily. "I think I'd know more than you. Etak is a dark world, therefore, Luke is a dark lord. He's a master of deception. I'm not lying to you, Sarah."

Drew was hardly wrong about things, but I could tell he was too upset about this to think rationally. He was too bitter to get the facts straight. Besides, none of this made any sense. Luke liked me, I was sure of it. He had even mentioned Drew's ring and seemed unnerved by the fact that I had it . . . or *didn't* have it on when I had the nightmare. Why had he asked Drew about the ring? Did he care that Drew was claiming me?

"Why were you guys talking about my . . . your ring? Why did he seem to think that me wearing your ring would make a difference with that nightmare I had?"

Drew inhaled slowly and closed his eyes. "Emerald is Earth's stone. Each world has a stone, a colour associated with it—the darkest and lightest worlds are black and white, and the other worlds are red, yellow, green, blue and purple—the colours of the rainbow. Earth is the centre of the worlds, so green, the middle colour of the rainbow, is Earth's colour. Emeralds are Earth's stone. And an emerald protects you from dreaming." He watched me tentatively. "My ring," he added quietly. "The emerald in the centre was always there to protect you in case you needed it."

"Your ring?" I gasped and looked down at his school ring. "You gave me this so I wouldn't dream anymore? So I couldn't see Luke?"

He nodded.

My heart squeezed, pushing the breath from my lungs. His ring wasn't given as a symbol of his love for me. It was only to prevent me from being happy with someone else. My eyes stung with this realization. He never cared about me; he only cared that I didn't dream. Then a thought struck me. "Before you gave me your ring, what stopped me from dreaming all these years?"

Drew tensed, and hesitated, but finally answered, "Your Daughter's Pride ring."

I felt my jaw go slack as his words registered. My Daughter's Pride ring. The ring George and Darlene gave me for my twelfth birthday, three months after they took me in—it was only given to protect me? But why would they do that? Did they know about the dream worlds, too? Was I the last to find out?

"No one else knows about the dream worlds," Drew said, as if in answer to my thoughts. "Just you, me and my father."

"Then why did my foster parents give me that ring?"

"My father had it made for you. He sold it to George

one day, pretending to be a jewellery salesman."

"Why?" I said, and it came out louder than I had intended. "Why would you do that? You didn't even know me then!"

"Sarah, the dream worlds are much more dangerous for some dreamers than others."

"How so?"

"Some dreamers . . . attract the attention of the wrong people. They are irresistible, so to speak, and the dark lords will do just about anything to either keep the dreamer for themselves, or destroy them. . . . And you are one of those dreamers. We needed to protect you."

"What makes you think I'm one of those dreamers?"

"It's a keeper's business to know these things and before I was Earth's keeper, my father was. He was the one who decided you were one of those rare dreamers who would need extra protection."

Did he just say this because he knew I'd have a harder time being mad at Mr. Spencer?

"That might've been okay when I was twelve, Drew, but I'm seventeen now. Don't I have a right to know this stuff?"

"I'm telling you now, aren't I?"

"Only because Luke came! What if he hadn't? Would you ever have told me? Or would you have kept me in the dark forever?"

He didn't answer.

"What gave you the right to stop me from dreaming? What gave you the right to forbid me from leaving this awful world? You kept me as a prisoner in this world! Why? Why would you do that, Drew?" Tears were flowing now and I knew Drew was shocked at my outburst, but not hurt. He didn't feel shame for what he had done.

"Sarah, please. I know what's best for you."

"Drew," I said firmly, "you put a ring on my finger to prevent me from dreaming. Think about that for a second. You wanted to protect me from what? Your dad's hunch that I might attract danger? Well, all you did was block my happiness! You had no right to do that."

"I care about you," he blurted. "That's why I did it, Sarah. I know what's out there and the harm that can come to people who dream. I didn't want that for you."

"Are you listening to yourself right now? Dreams don't kill people, Drew."

"They can," he said. "And I've never been willing to take that chance with you."

I shook his hands from my waist and pulled away from him. "This is twisted. I don't know what to believe, but I know it's messed up."

"Sarah, wait!" Drew called after me and he hurried to catch up as I was already decidedly on my way home. He grabbed a hold of my arm.

"Leave me alone, Drew!"

He pulled me into him and our bodies connected.

Pushing his lips into mine, he held my body firm against his.

I let the shock of his kiss catch me for a few seconds, but then I pushed away from him. "Stop it! Stop manipulating me! Giving me this ring meant nothing to you. You just don't want me with Luke, because for some reason it messes with your responsibilities as a dream keeper."

"No," Drew interrupted. "It means everything to me. I gave you that ring to protect you from all of the bad stuff that goes on in those worlds. You have no idea what they're capable of. Luke is dangerous. And I have to protect you. I *have* to."

I shook my head repeatedly. "First of all, he's not dangerous. He cares about me." I realized how naïve that sounded the second it came from my lips. "But anyway, what do you care? You just don't want me to be happy. That's clear now."

"You're being unreasonable, Sarah," he said, much to my astonishment. How could he say that? How would *any* response be unreasonable at this point? I just found out that I had been lied to for the last five years by the one person I trusted most.

"I won't be needing this anymore." I pulled off his ring and pushed it into his hand.

"Sarah, wait, you don't understand."

"I understand, Drew. I understand that I was stupid

to think that you actually cared about me." I looked down at his hands that were reaching for mine. "If you cared about me, you would let me live. I've always loved you, Drew . . . but I'm realizing now that it was all one-sided, and I was stupid to ever trust you."

His silence cut deep like a knife. It hurt. It hurt to breathe. It hurt to stand there with his eyes burning into mine. I had to run, and my feet carried me home. Home to the comfort of Lucia.

CHAPTER 13

Ultimatum

~ SARAH ~

"YOU'RE HOME EARLY," Darlene said as I walked through the door and kicked off my shoes. It wasn't a pleasant greeting, and I knew she hadn't meant it as a good thing. I had interrupted her routine and the sight of me bothered her.

I couldn't even bring myself to acknowledge her. My heart was hurting so badly and the last thing I needed was more rejection. I needed Lucia. I needed the one creature that could make my hurt fade.

"Sarah, don't leave your shoes lying in front of the door like that. Come back and pick them up," she shouted up the stairs after me.

"Leave me alone!" I yelled, adrenaline coursing

through my body. I had never, ever dared to speak to her that way and I wasn't quite sure how this would affect me in the long run, but at the moment, I didn't care. I could not possibly be more miserable.

I slammed my door and threw myself onto my bed. The beads from my dreamcatcher tinkered against my headboard, reminding me that I had never been in control of my own dreams, I had always been played by Drew. I yanked the decoration from my headboard and whipped it across my room, hearing its metal—no, *platinum*—frame hit the wall with a clink. I slung my arms around Lucia as she licked my face. I hadn't seen her there when I flung my door open, but she was here now. And I cried. I let it all out. My hurt over Drew, my confusion over Luke, my resentment toward my foster mother. Everything came crashing down on me in that one moment. Lucia snuggled in next to me and kept her nose next to my ear. It took a long time, but eventually my tears ran dry. My head pounded, my nose was stuffed, and my pillow was soaked. I rolled onto my back and let Lucia rest her head on my neck.

"I love you, girl," I whispered.

And as if she understood and wanted to say it back, she nuzzled in closer and groaned. I smiled and ran my fingers through her hair.

"Grab me a Tylenol?" I asked, amused with myself as if she could understand.

When it was clear she wasn't complying, I rolled out of bed and sauntered down the hall toward the medicine closet, but whispers coming from downstairs caught my attention and steered me toward the top landing instead.

". . . I was just worried and wanted to make sure she was okay," I heard Drew say in a hushed tone.

"She sounded pretty upset when she came in," Darlene murmured.

"Did she?" A hint of regret, maybe?

"Well, I can tell her you're here and see if she'll come down."

"Probably best to leave her be. I'm probably the last person she wants to see right now anyway."

"Well, it sounds like she's done wailing anyway," Darlene said, much to my complete embarrassment. "Maybe she's fallen asleep."

"Asleep?" Drew's voice was noticeably louder. "Maybe I will go check on her." Of course he would. Of course he wouldn't want me to sleep. When he thought I was awake and in my room sulking, he was fine with leaving me alone. He didn't actually care about me at all, he just didn't want me to die on his watch.

Darlene paused before answering, "Sure, whatever."

Drew's footsteps came down the hallway toward the stairs as I tiptoed back to my room, closed the door quietly and climbed back into my bed, burying my face between my pillow and Lucia's fur.

By the time my bedroom door opened, I was breathing heavily. Much to my amusement, Lucia didn't move from my side, but instead pretended to be sleeping, too.

"Sarah?" Drew whispered as he pulled the chair from my desk and sat down beside my bed. He listened to me breathe for a few minutes, and I focused on making it deep, slow and even. His finger brushed against my cheek as he moved a strand of hair from my face. A minute later he stood up and quietly put the chair back. His footsteps carried him to the door and then stopped. He picked something up from the floor and came back to my bed. I could have guessed what it was, but when I heard the beads hit my headboard, I knew—he was fastening my dreamcatcher back in place. His footsteps softened and then he said from the doorway so that I could barely hear him, "I'm sorry."

There was a small trace of regret and agony in his voice and I wondered how difficult it was for him to let me dream. He didn't try to wake me. He didn't try to slide the ring back on my finger while I slept. He trusted me. . . . Or maybe it was that he just didn't care anymore. I let this thought carry me away as I drifted off to sleep.

I COULD FEEL Luke. He was waiting for me on the other side of reality. I would see him soon and this thought filled me with a nervous excitement. He was real. This was real. But then the haze was lifting and a new feeling swept over my body—a feeling of despair and frustration as my body was being pulled into another direction.

"Luke?" my voice echoed as I struggled to get back to him. I could feel him drifting away, but knew he felt an urgency about it, so I fought harder to get to him. The harder I fought, the stronger the pull was in the other direction.

Then I heard Drew's soft, soothing voice: "Sarah, come to me."

I turned away from Luke and saw Drew standing by the apple tree surrounded by mist and light and holding his hand out to me.

"Drew?" How could I be dreaming of Drew?

"Sarah, please stay with me," Drew pleaded.

And then I knew—Drew, the keeper of Earth, was interfering with my dream. His job was to protect the portal from things coming in, but instead he was preventing me from going out. The *one* thing that was supposed to be all mine—my own dreams—and he was trying to control those, too.

"No!" I shouted, feeling anger course through my body. "You can't do this to me, Drew! You've toyed with me long enough." I flung my body away from him with such force and certainty that in a flash, it was just me and Luke.

We stood in the middle of a forest that was scattered with ribbons of light filtering through the canopy of trees above. Luke was leaning against a tree, looking exhausted and worn like he had just fought a battle that left no visible wounds. Instinctively, I ran to him and he held me, pressing and holding his lips to the top of my head as he breathed heavily.

"What was that all about?" I asked after a moment of enjoying his embrace.

He stepped back and I saw that he looked much better already. "Drew was pulling you back," Luke said. "He was trying to make sure you didn't come here." He wore a look of respect on his face, which managed to confuse me.

"Well, it didn't work," I said.

"You're stronger than he gives you credit for."

"I just wanted to see you again."

He smiled. "You don't know how happy that makes me to hear you say that."

He cupped my chin and gently brought his mouth to mine. With my heart racing, I was much more aware of our kiss this time. This time I knew it was real. That it would be carried over into the real world and I couldn't hide my insecurities behind a veil of fog at the end of my dream. I let his lips linger on mine for a few seconds, but then my embarrassment slowly pulled me away.

His eyes penetrated mine. "What's wrong?"

"You're real," I said quietly, my face feeling flush and my eyes falling to his chest.

"I was real before, too."

"You were whatever I wanted you to be before. You didn't tell me you were a *prince*. You didn't tell me you knew Drew—"

"In my defence, I don't *know* Drew. It wasn't until after you left that I figured out your friend Drew was one and the same as Earth's keeper." When I didn't respond, he took my hand and continued, "Sarah, I never meant to keep this from you. But it wasn't my job to tell you about the dream worlds, either. As Earth's keeper, it's Drew's job to keep you from finding out about them. And even more so with you, I can tell he wants to keep you safe from them. And I have to agree with him—I think there's a lot of stuff in these worlds that could hurt you. Especially given your connection to Earth's keeper."

I still didn't respond. I couldn't make eye contact with him. Even though being in this dream world gave me more courage than I had on Earth, I still felt embarrassed over my less than ladylike actions during previous dreams.

"I'm very drawn to you, Sarah," he continued, "but I've never felt these feelings before so I'm not sure what to do with them."

My heart fluttered and I allowed myself to smile. "You've really never cared about anyone before?"

"I've been attracted to people before," he admitted, much to my chagrin, "but I've never felt quite like this. I don't know what it is, but I know I don't want to lose it."

Although this was a completely foreign circumstance, I did find myself similarly confused. What did social protocol have to say about dating someone from another world? Someone you've already made out with, but only when you thought they were a figment of your imagination?

His hand was holding mine, delicate but deliberate, and the warmth from his fingers made me nervous. I didn't want to move my hand, in fact, I wanted the rest of his body to touch me in the same way, but I didn't know how to say that. Now that this was real, I was much more aware of my insecurities.

"I'm not that girl," I said.

"What do you mean?" He was right in front of me now, tilting my chin up so I would make eye contact.

"That adventurous, spontaneous, carefree girl that you were drawn to—that's not me. I'm . . . I'm insecure and I care what people think. I'm scared of a lot of things."

He smiled. "Trust me, you are far more like that carefree, adventurous girl than you think."

I rolled my eyes. "I wish that were true."

"Okay," he tried, "then let's just start over. Let me get to know the so-called *real* Sarah."

"You wouldn't like her."

"Let me be the judge of that."

I nodded. "Fine." His lips were moist and I wanted to kiss them, but instead I studied their curve and then gradually found his eyes. His deep blue eyes. "So that was you at my school today," I said, ignoring the combat of feelings inside.

"It was," he confirmed. His fingers trailed up my arm until they reached my neck where they lingered, provoking a series of shivers down my spine. "I needed to see you. To know you were okay."

"Drew gave me a ring that prevented me from dreaming," I told him, reminding myself that I was angry with Drew.

"I figured as much." Again, I could see that he respected that.

"I gave it back to him today. He can't stop me from seeing you."

Luke didn't respond. Instead he took my hand and we began walking through the forest together.

"He thinks you're dangerous and that someone is after me and I could die in your world or something stupid like that."

Again, Luke was silent.

I waited eagerly for his response. For his assurance that all was okay. That he wasn't dangerous. That his world wasn't dark. That everything could still be perfect.

"Luke?" I stopped walking, and turned to study his reluctant face. "This is not a dark world here, right?

You're not dangerous, right?"

"I'm not," he said quickly. "I would *never* hurt you."

"Why were you silent?"

"Because . . . because Etak *is* a dark world, Sarah."

I stiffened and I knew he felt it.

"But I would never hurt you. And I would never let anything hurt you while you are here."

"So this is a dangerous place?"

"No," he said, but then he added, "not when you're with me."

"So there's no problem then."

"I don't disagree with Drew. I think someone *could* hurt you, and I can't always guarantee you'll come to me when you dream."

"Where else would I go?"

"Any other world," he said, too quickly. "This isn't the only dark world, and the other worlds don't have a keeper hell bent on protecting you."

"You think other keepers would want to hurt me?"

He studied me for a second as if deciding how he should answer that. "I think that's where you had your nightmare. One of the dark lords is after you for some reason."

"But why?"

"Hard to say. Earth is the heart of the dream worlds. It possesses most of the power that keeps the other worlds alive, and dark lords are greedy. They figure if they can possess Earth, they'll gain its power, then overturn the light worlds, gaining their powers, too."

"But how does threatening me have anything to do with overturning Earth?"

He grinned. "Drew is Earth's keeper. And you are Drew's weakness."

"Weakness," I repeated. "What are you talking about?"

"You're cute."

"What?"

His eyebrows pulled down. "Do you really not think Drew would do anything for you? Give anything to get you back if you disappeared?"

I shook my head and turned away. "He wouldn't. Yes, we're friends, but it doesn't go any further than that."

"I think you're wrong." He watched me with curious interest. Amused, for some reason, at my assumption of the situation. "Nonetheless, if you ever do get pulled into another dream world, you should know that, as a dreamer, you have powers, too. There are seven powers associated with the seven worlds, and dreamers have access to them all."

He had my attention. "Like what kind of powers?"

"You could fly," he said, a sly grin on his face, "but don't go jumping off any ledges anytime soon." He winked. "You could alter the ground, air, water and fire. You could change shape. . . . You just need to believe it."

Alter the ground, I thought, as I studied the dirt at my feet. I narrowed my eyes on a pebble and focused my thoughts, trying to make the pebble jump.

Suddenly there was a gust of wind and a man appeared in the woods not far from us. Luke grabbed my arm and pulled me behind him, putting himself between me and the visitor.

"Devon," Luke said, a trace of concern in his voice.

Devon looked to be about as tall as Luke and had a similar physique. He wore black pants and a fitted blue t-shirt with two swords sheathed and at his sides. His black hair had a fresh-out-of-bed look to it, but it worked well framing his rather good-looking face. There was a hardness about him, but he didn't scare me, although when our eyes met, they narrowed on me, accusingly.

"What's wrong, Devon?" Luke pressed.

"Earth's keeper is here for you," he said, his voice low and sure.

I tried to step out, but Luke held me behind him.

"Where is he?" Luke asked.

"At the portal. He wanted me to bring him to you, but I told him I would find you first."

Luke nodded. "Did he say what he wants?"

Devon shook his head. "No, but I assume it has something to do with a dreamer." He craned his neck until our eyes met next to Luke's shoulder.

"I'm not going anywhere," I protested, pushing

Luke's arm down and stepping out. Devon's hand hovered over the hilt of his sword.

"Watch yourself, Devon," Luke growled.

"Luke, what the hell are you doing?" Devon hissed. "You want to start a war over a human?"

"Drew doesn't want a war," Luke clarified. "I'm not hurting her."

"He wants her back and you have no jurisdiction over her."

Luke's jaw clenched.

"Devon, hi," I said, stepping forward. Devon's eyes flickered to Luke's. "I promise I'm here on my own free will. I don't want to go back to Earth right now. Please tell Drew I'll go back when I'm ready."

"Who are you?" Devon said, his stare burning into me.

"I'm Sarah," I said. "Sarah Mar—"

"Devon," Luke cut me off, "if you know what's good for you, you'll go tell Drew she's in good hands, and then you'll keep quiet about this until I fill you in later."

Devon lowered his head slightly. "At your command." He disappeared a second later, but not before our eyes connected and he gave a menacing grin that failed to sit well.

"Who was that?" I asked the moment he was gone.

"Devon's my advisor." Luke was pacing now, his hands caressing each other.

"Like your right hand man?"

"Sort of," he said. "My brother's the second-in-command, but I gave Devon special permission so he can port to me when we're in Etak. He can't leave Etak, though."

"Why do I have a feeling he hates me already?"

"He doesn't hate you," he said. "We've been best friends since we were kids. He's just . . . protective, I guess. He doesn't want me to screw up."

"Are you screwing up right now? Is keeping me here against the rules?"

He shook his head. "Not really. I'm not keeping you against your will. Earth's keeper has never personally come looking for anyone before, so Devon just didn't know what to do."

I went to him and stopped him in mid-pace. "Relax," I said, "even if you let him take me back, I still wouldn't put his ring on. I'd be back again."

"Do you still think he doesn't care about you?"

"So he comes looking for me once. Big deal. The only other show of concern he's ever done is give me his ring, which he's admitted before means nothing to him."

"He thinks this is the best way to ensure your safety, Sarah. And I think he's right."

"Wait," I said, stepping back until I found a rock to sit on while Luke watched me carefully. "What are you saying?"

"I want you to be safe, too. Clearly someone has it out

for you, and I don't want to be the reason something happens to you."

"What are you saying?" I repeated, my eyes stinging with the anticipation of his next words.

"I want you to go back and wear the ring." He looked away and I knew it hurt him to say it as much as it hurt me to hear it.

"No!" I protested. "I will not. I would rather risk my life in another dimension than live one day without . . . you." My chest thudded with my hammering heart and I was no longer sitting, but pacing back and forth. "You can't make me, Luke. If you send me back, I will not wear his ring."

Luke took his turn sitting on the rock now, his head in his hands.

"I won't do it, Luke," I repeated, as if drilling this idea into his head was the only way to make him change his mind, but I could see that he wasn't wavering. Something in the firmness of his face told me that he wasn't backing down, either. He wanted to keep me out of the dream worlds, and he would make sure of it. Somehow.

Then I had an idea. I knelt down in front of him and took his hands in mine. He was still gorgeous, even with his tired, red eyes and firm, sad mouth. "I'll make you a deal," I began. "I will wear the stupid ring . . . *if* you come back to Earth."

His eyebrows creased as he contemplated my suggestion.

"I'm not done getting to know you. Come back as a student at Xavier. And I will wear the ring and never take it off." My heart was racing. It was bold of me to ask, and stupid of me to assume he cared enough to do it. But I had nothing to lose. As keeper of Etak, he could probably lock me out of his world. I couldn't risk losing this. This exhilarating feeling of . . . love.

"Drew would never go for that," Luke finally said, as if all the other pieces of the puzzle would fit but that one.

"Leave him to me. If he wants me to wear the ring so badly, then he'll have to be okay with it, won't he?" A part of me doubted Drew would go for it. His distrust for Luke was probably greater than his desire to protect me from whatever he feared would happen if I dreamed.

"Okay," Luke said after a moment. "I'll do it. If you *promise* you will wear his ring and will never, not even for a minute, take it off." This last part was said through clenched teeth.

"I promise."

"Until I get you a ring to wear," he added, as if another term to the agreement. "You can give Drew's ring back to him as soon as I get a ring for you."

My bubbling of excitement stirred in my heart. For some reason it was much more exciting to get a ring from a guy who actually cared for me. A guy who actually wanted to be with me. Although his purpose for giving it to me was still the same as Drew's, but that didn't matter.

I flung myself into his arms. "Thank you!"

"I'll have to get some things in place here before I go. I'll have to get my brother to take over while I'm with you."

"He did it today," I pointed out.

"Yes," he said, "but it wasn't meant to be a long term thing. I had just wanted to check to make sure you were really okay."

I blushed. "I'm better now."

"I see that." His crooked smile begged me to kiss him.

"So do you think your brother will mind taking over for a little while longer? I mean, I don't know for how long. I assume eventually Drew will figure out who is threatening me and once we deal with that, we can go back to me visiting your world if you really must go back."

Luke watched me curiously. "I'm sure he won't mind. He's been pining for this job ever since I was born."

"If he's older, why didn't he get to be keeper?"

"It's not about birth order. The key chooses the keeper. And my brother was never chosen. He tried it every day of his life, but it never illuminated for him. When I turned twelve, the key chose me."

"Lucky you," I said, smiling and feeling a sense of pride.

He kind of laughed in a way that I didn't like. "Some may think so," he said. "Others may disagree."

"So if he hasn't been chosen, will he be able to do the job while you're gone?"

"As keeper, I can appoint him." His thoughts were somewhere else. "I'll have to go talk to him about this. It will take time to set up."

"How much time? I'm not taking Drew's ring back until you're with me on Earth."

He nodded as if thinking it through.

"Can we go talk to your brother now? I'll go with you."

"No," he said too quickly. "He can't know why I'm doing this."

Although the reason for this wasn't obvious, I trusted the firmness of his face and knew he had good reason.

"Then go and I'll wait here for you."

"I can't do that, either. You'll wake up just before dawn and then I'll go talk to him. And I'll meet you at school. What time?"

"Eight forty-five," I said. "At the main office."

"But you need to promise me that you won't go back to sleep once you wake up." He was beginning to sound like Drew.

"Yes, I promise. I'll be too excited to sleep, anyway." I let him pull me into him. "So we have a few hours. I was thinking we could go back to the beach and you could teach me how to surf."

"Surf," he laughed. "Now that you know Etak is dark world, I feel comfortable telling you that that will *never* happen. It would take every single bit of power in me to prevent you from drowning or getting eaten by sharks."

I cringed. "Okay, that's fair. How about a picnic then?"

"That I can do."

CHAPTER 14

Losing Her

~ DREW ~

WHAT THE HELL did she see in that world? It was dark, bleak, and even had a smell to it that was in complete contrast to the sweet smell of lilies she was so fond of. I would be surprised if there was even a single daisy in that entire world. I snickered at the thought. She was crushing on a keeper of a world without flowers.

I was aware of my pacing, but standing still only made the time go slower. What in the hell was taking Devon so long? I gritted my teeth at our earlier exchange. He wasn't even Luke's second-in-command and he was arrogant enough to forbid me to go looking for one of my own. Of course he didn't know that was my reason for being there. I couldn't very well tell him. Someone was out to get Sarah, and it was no coincidence that it happened right after she met Luke. I could trust no one.

The air changed and Devon reappeared in front of me. Luke wasn't with him, which wasn't a complete surprise. He'd have been a fool to leave her alone. But part of me did expect them to show up together. She'd have fought him every step, of course, but she was no match for him, especially in this world. He could've made her do whatever he wanted.

"Well?" I pressed. "Where is he?"

"He's busy," Devon said, his voice threateningly low.

I threw my hands in my hair, desperately trying to keep my cool. "I'm here on keeper business, Devon. I demand to see him."

"Your little *friend* is fine," he said. "And she's made it clear that she doesn't want to go back with you."

We stared at each other while I decided how I was supposed to respond to that. He knew Sarah was there. He saw her. But did he know who she was? Did he know she was *my* Sarah? Not just a dreamer—but the only person on Earth I would fight to death for.

"Damnit, Devon!" I shouted. "Bring me to them NOW!" My sword was drawn and it quivered with the shake of my firm grip.

"You're gonna want to put that away, Drew," he growled. "You may be Earth's keeper, but there's no way in hell you're getting past me." He drew his own sword and took three steps toward me until our blades were touching.

"Well, well, well," a new voice chided. "What do we have here?"

Devon's upper lip curled in disgust. "Riley, I got this."

"Sure, Devon. Looks like you're handling this just great." Riley circled around Devon until he was standing between us. He lowered our swords with his bare hand. "What brings you back to Etak, Drew? Looking for another fight?"

"I'm here for—"

"Luke," Devon said, cutting me off. "He's here for Luke." Our eyes met and his softened. Did he know that protecting Sarah's identity was important, too? Maybe Luke had told him to keep quiet. Whatever the reason, I was grateful for the unlikely alliance.

Riley's brow furrowed as he looked from Devon, to me, and back to Devon. "Looking for Luke," he said slowly. "What do you want with my brother? Is he harassing another dreamer, is he? Did he cause some trouble when he was on Earth earlier today?"

I glared at him, unwilling to answer his questions.

"Oh, do tell, Drew. Luke can be so secretive sometimes. It's really quite annoying."

"Drew has an issue with the severity of the nightmares humans are having in Etak lately," Devon said. "I was just telling him that Luke doesn't care what he thinks and he needs to go home now." Devon nodded to me as if that was my cue to leave.

"I'll go," I said, "but tell Luke if so much as a hair on any dreamer's head is out of place when they wake, I'll be back."

Riley scoffed, and Devon watched him for further reaction. I took my key and ported back to Earth before either could respond.

I went to Sarah's bedroom instead of my own. I took the risk that no one would be in her room to witness my arrival. Although it wasn't much of a risk. George and Darlene weren't the type of parents to check in on Sarah, even when they knew she was upset.

She slept soundly, curled up with Lucia, who didn't think too much of my sudden appearance. She gave me one glance, then closed her eyes again.

At least I knew that as long as she was with Luke, she would be safe. He had seemed genuinely surprised by Sarah's nightmare and the fact that someone could be after her. It didn't matter, there was nothing I could do about it now.

The dreamcatcher still hung valiantly above her. Maybe I was reading into things too much. The dreamcatcher would've caught any shadow that tried to get through to her head. Although her description of the snake-like figure did sound an awful lot like a shadow.

And that was something she couldn't make up on her own.

My stomach twisted into knots. I had failed her. She was essentially in a coma, completely at the mercy of a dark lord. I held onto Luke's last words to me: "Don't screw this up." It didn't seem like a threat. It felt more like a plea. There was determination in his voice and concern in his eyes. As much as I hated the thought of him anywhere near Sarah, it was too late to hide her from him now, and at least I knew he didn't want her dead. But it was clear someone did.

I sat with her for most of the night, making sure she still breathed. I hated when she smiled and moaned, but at least that meant she was still alive. Eventually I left for home and tried to get some sleep. It would be a long night otherwise because if I knew Sarah, she was determined to teach me a lesson on this one. And as much as it killed me to admit, I was beginning to second guess my protection strategy. Should I have told her about the dream worlds sooner? Should I have given her the option to explore them with me first so she saw their real dangers? Or should I have given her my school ring two years ago? What was I afraid of?

I knew what I was afraid of—This. Losing her.

CHAPTER 15

The New Student

~ SARAH ~

IN THE EARLY morning, Luke kissed me goodbye and I slowly disappeared into a fog that pulled me from my sleep. I rolled over in my bed and picked up my cell phone. It was exactly five o'clock. And I had five new texts from Drew.

DREW

Yesterday at 3:33pm
You awake yet?

Yesterday at 5:48pm
Hey.

Yesterday at 7:10pm
*Called your house. Darlene
said you're still sleeping. She
wouldn't let me wake you. Call
me the second you wake up.*

Yesterday at 9:23pm
*What the hell, Sarah? I know
you're with Luke and if he so
much as lays one finger on
you…*

Yesterday at 11:02pm
*Just call me when you wake
up. I hate this.*

Had I really fallen asleep in the afternoon and slept right through until morning? Very early morning, mind you, but still.

DREW

Today at 5:03am
*I'm awake. And *gasp* I'm
alive, too! Told you he wasn't
dangerous.*

Drew read it right away and was typing back before I could blink.

DREW

Yesterday at 11:02pm
Just call me when you wake up. I hate this.

Today at 5:03am
I'm awake. And *gasp* I'm alive, too! Told you he wasn't dangerous.

Today at 5:03am
Calling...

My phone rang before I had a chance to silence it.

"Hey," I whispered.

"You're killing me. You know that, right?"

"Sorry," I said quietly.

There was a pause before he muttered, "I'm glad you're okay."

"Of course I'm okay, Drew. But while we're on the subject, what you did yesterday—trying to pull me back to Earth—that wasn't cool. Don't do that again."

"Sorry," he mumbled, much to my surprise.

"S'okay." This would've been a good time to tell him that Luke was coming back to school, but the words just failed to form.

"Were you with Luke that whole time?" Drew asked after a moment of silence.

"I was."

"I went there looking for you," he said, a note of bitterness in his voice.

"I know. That wasn't cool, either."

Silence.

"Did you sleep at all?" I asked, trying to break the uncomfortable silence.

"No. How could I? I was busy searching for you and pacing my bedroom floor all night."

"That's not my fault."

He sighed heavily as if resigning to the fact that I was going to be stubborn and this could go on all day.

"I should go," I said. "I have homework to do from yesterday, and I want to get to school early today." I still couldn't bring myself to tell him about Luke's impending arrival.

"What time did you want me to pick you up?"

"I don't, actually," I said quickly. "I think I'll walk today. I need the fresh air."

"Can I walk with you?"

"Drew, just give me this, okay? A lot has happened lately and I just need time to think."

"Sure," he said. "So you're getting up now?"

I rolled my eyes. "Yes, Drew, I'm getting up. I won't

go back to sleep."

He was silent, but then said, "You're special, Sarah."

"I know," I answered. "Luke tells me all the time."

I could hear him exhaling slowly and knew I had struck a nerve. "I bet he does," he said bitterly. "See you at school."

"See you at school." I hung up and threw myself back onto my pillow. This was *not* going to be an easy day.

"OKAY, MR. ANDERSON, you're all set to go," our principal, Mr. Jackson, said as Luke scrawled his signature on the last piece of paper and slid it back to him. "Glad you decided to join us for the remainder of your high school experience."

"Well, it's supposed to be the best school in the area," Luke said politely, much to Mr. Jackson's delight.

"I see you've met Sarah Marley." Mr. Jackson smiled and nodded at me.

I stepped forward, allowing myself into their conversation. "Yes, we met . . . a few days ago." I looked at Luke and his eyes twinkled.

"Very good. Well, Sarah, I trust you'll help Luke find his way around."

"Of course I will."

"Luke, Sarah is one of our best students here. Just let her know if there's anything you need."

Luke looked at me with a mischievous grin. "Oh, I

will, sir. Thank you." Then he gestured toward the paper now in Mr. Jackson's possession. "So, when do you think my school ring will arrive?"

"Oh, yes. Well, I have your payment so once I fax off this order form, the ring should arrive within a week. I'll page you to the office the moment it arrives." Mr. Jackson chuckled. It was clear that he took pride in the popularity of the school rings and necklaces.

"Okay, cool. Thanks."

"Oh, wait now." Mr. Jackson's eyes scanned the order form. "I see here that you put emerald down for the stone in the middle of the X, but your birthday is actually in July. I believe the birthstone for July is ruby."

Luke shot a quick glance in my direction. "Uh, yes, but I do still want an emerald centre. It . . . was my mother's birthstone."

"Oh, of course." Mr. Jackson looked down regretfully. "I'm sorry about that, Luke."

"It's not a problem. Just the sooner I get that ring, the better."

"Of course. I'll put a rush on it for you."

Mr. Jackson left us and Luke turned to me, leaning against the secretary's credenza. He reached for my hand and pulled me closer.

"Luke, we have to act as though we've just met," I reminded him, although there was nothing more I wanted at that moment than his touch.

He stepped away, holding onto my fingers for a few seconds longer.

"So you have your ring ordered," I said as we slowly left the office.

"I just wish it would come sooner."

"It's not a big deal."

"It is to me."

"I will wear Drew's ring until then."

"I know," he said with bite, confirming his problem.

I nudged him with my shoulder. "Is emerald really your mother's birthstone?"

"What? Oh. No, I don't think so."

I giggled.

"What was I supposed to say? I couldn't really tell him I needed an emerald so that my girlfriend wouldn't be able to dream anymore."

"True," I smiled. "He might think you're a little nuts."

"Maybe a little."

I liked the way the word 'girlfriend' sounded coming from his lips. I let it play a few more times in my head while we sauntered down the hall together, our fingers brushing every few steps.

"I want to hold your hand," he whispered in a tone of agony.

My lungs filled quickly at his need. "Me, too."

The hall was busy with students making their way to the section of the school for their first period.

"Come outside with me." I pushed through the crowd and led him down a corridor and out the large metal doors until the sun was on us.

"It's no less crowded out here," Luke noticed.

I shook my head. "It's not that. I can breathe easier out here." I sat down on a bench and let my backpack fall beside me. Luke sat down next to me.

"It's going to be really hard pretending we just met," he said after a minute.

"I know."

"But it might be kind of fun, too."

I smirked. "I know."

Just then I saw a familiar blonde head rounding the corner to the front entrance.

"Drew," I said.

Luke followed my stare until he found him. "He doesn't look happy."

"No, he doesn't."

"What the hell is this?" Drew said when he got near enough. He shoved Luke with one hand and pulled me away from him with the other.

Luke stepped back and held up his hands. "Didn't you tell him?"

"I didn't get a chance to yet."

Drew turned on me. "Well, now's your chance. Why is this asshole here at our school, carrying a backpack, and pretending he goes here?"

"I asked him to come, Drew."

"I don't want him here, Sarah."

"And you don't want me in Etak, but I want to see him. Drew, you both claim to care about me and only want to keep me safe. If he comes here, you can both have what you want. I will wear your stupid ring."

Drew looked at Luke and then back to me. "So you're saying if I let him stay, you'll wear the ring and never take it off?"

"Yes. Luke made me promise."

"Luke made you promise," he repeated as if considering this to be truth or not, and if it were true, what ulterior motive there could be.

"I want the same thing you do, Drew," Luke said.

Drew's eyes narrowed. "You think I want her necklace?" he hissed.

Really? My necklace? Why couldn't Drew get past this? No one was getting my necklace!

"No," Luke said. "I want to keep her safe. I don't know who is after her, but I can't protect her while I'm in Etak and she's here. Especially if she's taking off her ring every night in order to see me."

"And who's going to protect your portal while you're here?" Drew tested.

"Riley," Luke said. "My brother is next in line for keeper. He's keen on helping."

"Of course he is," Drew growled. "Yeah, tell your

brother thanks for the shiner."

"Drew, you know the rules—you go to a world uninvited, causing trouble, anything's game."

"Are those the rules, yeah? Because it looks like
you're in *my* world now, uninvited and looking for trouble." Drew's jaw throbbed and his fists clenched.

I stepped in front of Luke before Drew could take a
swing. "Drew, please." He continued to glare at Luke.
"Drew, I'm not doing this without him anymore. Either
he stays, or I go back to Etak with him."

Drew turned and threw his fist into the side of the
school. I heard a crunching noise as blood splattered from
his knuckles.

"Drew!" I gasped. "Oh my gosh! Are you alright?"

"He's fine," Luke answered, holding me in place and
preventing me from running to Drew's side. "A keeper
can't feel pain in his own world."

My heart raced as Drew retracted his hand from the
brick, covered in blood and misshapen. Clearly broken,
though it didn't seem to bother him at all.

"That doesn't hurt?"

He shook his head and held up his hand. It already
looked better. He flexed his fingers and his hand took a
regular shape again. It was still stained with blood, but
appeared to work without limitation.

"So, are you like invincible or something?" I asked.

Luke and Drew chuckled at the same time, which was

so nice to hear even if they were laughing at my naivety.

"Not invincible, just immune to pain . . . for the most part." He said this last part while glaring at me. Was I causing him pain? "And only here. I feel pain in other worlds." And that part was meant for Luke.

I hung my head, suddenly very aware that Luke's fingers were wrapped tightly around mine.

"So?" I finally asked, reaching for Drew's hand, too. "Will you give this to me? Can I have this one request?"

His eyes fell to his hand in mine. He made no effort to keep it there; it was all me. He drew in a deep breath and held it as he watched my thumb caress his X ring.

"If it makes you feel any better," Luke began, "you can hang out with us whenever—"

"Oh, I will," Drew growled before Luke could finish.

"So that's a yes?" I squealed.

Drew looked at me and his eyes were sorrowful. He hated this. For whatever reason, this tore him apart.

"We'll need to double date so I don't look like a third wheel," he said through clenched teeth. "I'll need a girlfriend, too."

The world stopped when I heard those words. "Why?" I snapped. Never once did he have a girlfriend in all the time I knew him, and he certainly never advanced on me, but suddenly now he needed one?

His eyes lit up as he caught mine. "It's only fair," he said with a smirk. Oh, he was enjoying this now.

"Fine. How about Lauren?" I said, offering up one of our mutual friends.

"Nah, I'm thinking Holly." A wicked smile swept across his face.

"Haverstock," I said, realizing the game he was playing. He thought if he chose the girl I disliked most, that I would call the whole thing off.

He nodded. "Holly Haverstock."

"Fine," I said, pitching my eyebrows in an effort to show that two could play his game.

"Thanks, Drew," Luke said.

"I didn't do it for you." He pulled his ring off his finger and handed it to me. "You don't take it off."

"I promise." I took the ring and slid it onto my finger. Drew kept his eyes on my hand, then turned and left us standing outside in the light rain that had started. The sweet, warm rain that held just the two of us. Luke picked me up and swung me around.

"Put me down." I slapped his shoulder and he quickly put me back down. I looked around to confirm that no one saw. "Okay, we're good."

He smiled and shook his head. "Let's get these next few days over with so we can finally stop pretending to be strangers."

THE BELL RANG, signalling the end of second period and the start of lunch hour. Drew slid his books off of his desk and into his bag next to him while I carefully loaded mine into my backpack. This was our routine. He was ready and standing by my desk, hurrying me along, while I neatly organized my belongings so they weren't a mess when I took them back out.

"You ready?" he asked, predictably, as he hovered.

"Do I look ready?" And this was my usual sarcastic response.

"I thought you'd be faster today for some reason," he said, matching my sarcasm.

"Yeah?"

"Thought you'd be in a hurry to see Luke." He said the name as if it tasted sour.

I zipped up my pencil case and looked up at him. "Drew, you know we have to pretend that we just met Luke, right?"

"So?"

"So, no one can know he and I have anything going on. Even Maddy."

Drew stretched his neck, then nodded. "Yup."

He wasn't looking at me so I finished packing my backpack. I knew he didn't want anyone suspecting Luke was up to something. My secret was his secret, too.

"You ready?"

"Do I look ready?" I smirked as I stood up and threw my backpack over my shoulder.

"Never fails," he chuckled. "We're always the last

ones out of here."

WHEN DREW AND I arrived at the lunch room, Holly Haverstock was leaning over our picnic table where Luke was sitting with Caleb and Maddy.

Drew sniggered. "Uh-oh, Sarah. Looks like you've got competition."

I scoffed as if the idea was ridiculous, but as I watched Holly flip her silky blonde hair and bat her long eyelashes at Luke, my stomach lurched.

"I was kidding," Drew said, putting his hand on my back. "She's got nothing on you. Go on."

Luke stood up when he saw us. "Hey, there you are." He took my backpack and set it under the table next to his.

Maddy beamed at me and I, too, tried to refrain from smiling too broadly.

Holly was about to finally walk away when Luke reached for her. "Why don't you join us?"

My heart sank. Drew was wrong—she did have something on me.

Holly smirked at me and then answered, "Sure, I'll be right back."

When she was gone, Luke slid his hand on my knee and squeezed. "It's for Drew," he whispered.

Holly was back with her bag seconds later. She looked at me sitting between Luke and Drew and curled her lip, flipped her hair, then took a place next to Caleb, opposite Luke.

"So," Holly said, using a flirtatious girly voice that begged me to slap her, "you're back. I was beginning to think Sarah scared you away for good."

Maddy kicked me under the table. "You gonna take that?" she mouthed, jerking her head toward the beast.

I shook my head and took another bite of my sandwich.

"Is there a reason you're at our table, Holly?" Maddy said, clearly deciding that *someone* ought to stick up for me.

"I'm sorry, Bird Brain, did you not hear Luke invite me?" Holly said.

"Yeah, I heard him being polite. Didn't know you were stupid enough to think that the *rest* of us wanted you here, too."

I gasped. Holly's eyes widened. She opened her mouth to say something, but then shut it promptly. She looked at Luke, then me, then Drew, then back to Luke.

"Okay, then. See you later, Luke. Drew." Holly stood up and turned to leave.

I squeezed Luke's hand under the table. He looked down at me and I nodded, giving him permission to call her back. He opened his mouth, but before he could say anything, Drew spoke.

"Holly, come back. I wanted you here, too."

I froze. Hearing Drew say the words was like nails down a chalkboard. He said them so softly, so genuinely, that I had to wonder if he didn't actually mean them.

Maddy's mouth fell open.

"I'll explain later," I whispered to her.

She just shook her head. "I'm out of here." Maddy threw her lunch bag into her backpack and stood up. "Come on, Caleb."

Caleb hurried to gather his things too, then nodded at the three of us still sitting in awkward silence at the table. "Later."

Drew and Luke nodded. I smiled.

"Well, I guess I'll join you again now that *she's* gone."

"Don't push your luck, Holly," I warned.

She looked at me warily for a moment, but chose not to retaliate.

"So Luke, how are you enjoying Xavier?" Holly said, tilting her head sideways as she popped a lollipop into her mouth.

"It's good," Luke answered. "Nice school."

"Did you get your school ring ordered?" she asked.

"Yes, we . . . I did it this morning."

"I bet it'll look hot on you."

What the hell was that? Every muscle in me tensed. I wanted to reach across the table and . . .

"Where's your ring, Drew?" Holly asked, knowing that I was wearing it.

"Sarah's holding it hostage," Drew joked. I flushed.

I slid it off my finger. "Here, you can have it back now if you want."

He glared at me and I smiled sweetly. He reached for it slowly, and I could see that he was deciding whether he should take it and save face, or demand that I put it back on. Luke's grip was firmer on my leg now, too.

I chuckled and pulled it away from him at the last second. "Kidding. I like it too much to give it back just yet."

A look of relief washed over him, mixed with a warning. "S'okay, you can keep it for now. I know where you live. And when I have someone I want to give it to, I'll come get it," he said, smiling devilishly as he cocked a smile at Holly, causing her to blush and my stomach to turn.

"Well, on that note," I said, standing up, "I have to go to Mr. Chase's room to pick up my lab notes. Luke, I'll make a copy for you if you want to come with."

"Yeah, that'd be great, thanks." He followed me out of the arboretum, neither of us bothering to say good-bye.

When we were out of sight and down another corridor, I turned into an empty classroom.

"What's the rush?" Luke asked, finally catching up.

I shut the door behind us and pushed Luke up against it. My fingers grasped his hair and held his face to mine as I pressed my lips into his. He moaned and slid his hands down to my waist, pulling me closer. My body was full of electricity, pulsating with the current in his. Then he stopped.

"What are you doing?" I breathed heavily. "Why'd you stop?"

"Now's not the time for the new guy to be found making out with the girl he just met."

I smiled half-heartedly.

"Besides, I'm still trying to figure out if it's me you want, or revenge on Drew."

"What?" I said, frustrated. "Luke, you *know* I want you."

"I know." He smiled as he nodded. "But right now. This. What was *this* about?"

"Uh, this was a day's worth of pent-up frustration and desire. Not being able to touch you. Not being able to tell everyone that you're mine. Watching Holly flaunt herself all over you, and you not telling her to get lost. All that really takes a toll on a girl."

He gathered me in his arms and kissed my head. "You have absolutely nothing to worry about with Holly." He smelled so good, and his arms around me were like the warmest, coziest blanket. "In a few days we'll be able to tell everyone that we're together. It just has to be believable, you know?" His voice vibrated inside his chest.

"I guess we should go on a date or two."

"How about you show me your favourite places," he suggested.

The bell rang and I pulled away. "Okay," I said. "After school. I'll take you to Peggy's Cove."

"Who's cove?"

"Peggy's Cove. It's a great place right by the ocean with huge rocks and cliffs."

"Uh, no thanks. Sounds a little too dangerous for you."

"Oh, please. I've been there like a hundred times. It's totally safe as long as you don't go on the black rocks, which I would never do."

"What happens on the black rocks?"

"It's where the water can touch. One big wave comes along and you're gone."

Luke's face paled. "And you've gone here before? Drew lets you go there?"

"Drew doesn't *let* me do anything. I can go wherever I choose."

Luke nodded. "Right, then. Okay, well, I guess we'll give Penny's Cove a try."

I giggled as I pushed him out the door. "*Peggy's* Cove."

CHAPTER 16

Agony

~ DREW ~

THE BELL RANG, signalling the end of lunch hour. When was the last time I was thankful for the end of lunch period? Sarah hadn't returned and I knew she was off somewhere with Luke, probably holding hands or . . . *kissing*. My stomach lurched at that thought, but I held the disgusted look from my face.

"So I'll see ya?" Holly said as she lingered by the table.

"Yeah," I said. "Where are you off to now?"

"Biology," she groaned, which reminded me that Sarah, too, had Biology.

"I'll walk you there," I offered, feeling a surge of eagerness.

She smiled and hooked her arm into mine. We walked down the corridor together, gathering lots of looks from other students. The guys all nodded with cheeky grins, confirming their acknowledgement that I had just landed the hottest girl in school, and the girls didn't hide their giggles from each other; their approval of the match evident, as well.

"Here I am," Holly said as we reached the classroom door. A quick look inside confirmed Sarah was there, unpacking her books. When she sat down, I saw Luke sitting next to her and my jaw clenched.

"What's wrong?" Holly asked, following my eyes into the classroom. "Sarah?" she said, a bitter sound to her voice.

"Nah, it's all good," I lied.

"Good." She adjusted the strings on my hoodie. "'Cause I think you are too good for her."

I found her eyes and tried to focus on the way they were painted perfectly so, and how her eyelashes were long and thick and her lips were glossy and plump. I knew any other guy would find this extremely attractive, and I wasn't denying that she wasn't, I just had a hard time allowing myself to think about anything other than Luke and Sarah.

"I'll . . . uh, see you later?" I managed to say.

She frowned, but quickly recovered with a flirty smile. "I hope so." She turned on her heel and headed into the classroom. I couldn't help but notice she gave Sarah a dirty look as she passed. Sarah, however, didn't notice as she was too interested in whatever bullshit Luke was saying.

Mr. Chase closed the classroom door, giving a nod to me as he did. I backed away, but couldn't bring myself to leave. How could I go to my class when every fibre in me was pulling me back to Sarah?

Her eyes were forward now, paying attention to whatever it was Mr. Chase was saying. A smile remained on her lips, though, and she stole glances at Luke too often for my liking.

"Whatcha lookin' at?"

I quickly ducked away from the doorway. "You scared me," I admitted when it was clear I wasn't going to be able to hide the fact.

Maddy giggled. "I don't think I've *ever* seen you startle before."

I continued down the hall, hoping she wouldn't ask any more questions, but it was Maddy, and I knew she was too clever to just let it go.

"Spying on Sarah and Luke?" she guessed.

I huffed. "Just checking in on her."

"Why?" She took my hand and pulled me down onto the bench that lined the stretch of the hallway.

I shrugged as I sat down. "Guess I don't have the best feeling about the guy."

"It's called jealousy," she said.

I frowned. "Doubt it."

"So you're trying to tell me that it doesn't bother you at all that he swoops in and she's all head over heels for him?"

I watched her small features, calculating my response. I couldn't help but smirk. "You think you have all the answers, don't you?"

"I *do* have all the answers," she teased.

"Is that right?" I shook my head and leaned forward, resting my forearms on my knees. "So how are things with Caleb?"

She harrumphed. "Meh."

"What? Does Maddy not have *all* the answers?"

She smacked me. "Not fair. No one ever has all the answers when it comes to their own love life."

"Love life," I mused. "Does that mean it's love?"

She shrugged. "I really like him."

I nodded, waiting for more, but she said nothing else. My eyes fell to her necklace and I was surprised, and relieved, to see it still hanging proudly against her chest.

"Yes, I still have it," she said, and I turned my eyes away immediately.

"I'm glad," I admitted. "Just make sure he's the one before you start giving pieces of yourself away, alright?"

Maddy blushed and lowered her head so that a strand of blonde hair fell over her eyes. She made no effort to move it away and so I turned my head, allowing her to conceal her embarrassment.

"Why did you call Holly back to the lunch table after I shooed her away earlier?" she asked after a quiet moment.

How was I supposed to answer that? With the truth—since Sarah's dating my nemesis, I'm going to move in on hers? Or with the story—I'm dating someone too so the four of us can double date and I can keep an eye on Luke and Sarah?

"Drew?" she prompted.

I shrugged. "I don't know."

Maddy cringed. "She's pure evil."

"She's not that bad."

"I'm going to pretend you didn't just say that." She leaned back onto the bench. "Why'd you let her go?"

"What do you mean?"

"Sarah. Why'd you let Sarah go? She's always cared about you, and I know you care about her, too. And I think if you said the right words, she would still choose you over him."

I shook my head. "She wouldn't," I said. "I see the way she looks at him."

"Well, have you seen him?" Maddy laughed. "I'm pretty sure every girl looks at him that way." When I didn't reply, she continued, "She used to look at you that way too, you know."

I chuckled. "I'm not sure if that's comforting or hurtful."

"Take it however you want," she said.

I shook my head. "Well, as long as she's happy." I stretched and stood up, pretending to be uninterested and ready to head back to class.

Maddy groaned. "You sure you don't want to talk some more?"

"Nah, I'm good."

"Fine, leave me for education. See if I care. I'm going to hide out in the washroom for a little while. I really don't want to go back to Geography."

I shuffled my hand through her hair. "You need all the education you can get. Looks won't get you far in life these days."

She laughed as she departed down the hall in the opposite direction. "I'm not sure if that was a compliment or an insult."

"Take it however you want." I smirked, knowing she would be grinning, too.

I was glad I ran into Maddy. Her carefree approach to life was refreshing and somehow made me a little less sick about Sarah being in class with Luke.

Besides, next period Sarah had Math with me.

CHAPTER 17

Peggy's Cove

~ SARAH ~

THE ROAD DOTTED with quaint, colourful cottages meandered through the deserted seaside village as we made our way to the empty parking lot. Peggy's Cove wasn't a destination of choice when the winds were high and sky was darkened with rain clouds.

Drew was driving, and although he hadn't said much in the forty minutes it took to get there, he was much more relaxed than I had expected. At my urging, Luke took the front passenger seat, and I sat in the middle of the back seat, content with seeing them both up front together. As we drove along the cliff, Luke craned his neck to peer over the edge, taking in the thrashing, untamed ocean below.

"Okay, so Sarah tells me this isn't her first time here," Luke said, and it was clear he didn't approve of the location.

"She's fine," Drew assured him.

"And what makes you so sure?" Luke pressed. "I mean, do you even know what your world is capable of?"

"Earth is not a dark world, Luke," Drew growled, and I could tell that Luke had suggested something that they strongly disagreed on.

"Dark things still happen here, Drew, whether you like it or not. And this looks like the perfect place for an *accident* to happen."

Drew watched Luke wrestle with his discomfort, and then Drew's face did something I hadn't seen in a long time. It softened. "It's okay, man. Nothing will happen to her here."

Luke nodded and took a deep breath, then turned back to face me. "Okay, princess, show me your favourite place."

THE PATH TO the lighthouse was sodden with the spring rains. We took a hard left just after the path ended on the massive rocks and I led the two across the mountain-like terrain to a quiet place at the bottom of a rock face on a private inlet of a landing. We were alone here in this sheltered haven. The wind no longer ripped at our clothes or whipped my hair into my face, although the waves still wreaked havoc on the rocks below us and we could feel the spray of the water every now and then.

"So this is it," I said after a few minutes of stillness. "I like to come here and sit, think, have a picnic, or whatever."

"I never knew you came here by yourself," Drew said as he watched the water below.

"I used to come with George and Darlene when I was younger, and then I came a couple times last summer on my own after I got my licence."

"Why?" Drew asked. "Where was I?"

"Uh, probably with your dad. Where you always were when I needed or wanted you." He heard the sarcasm, the hardness that was once frustration.

"Don't be hard on him, Sarah," Luke said, bringing his eyes to the ground. "Being keeper isn't an easy job."

Ouch. I felt the sting in his words as he stuck up for Drew. Like brothers in a sense. Both keepers. Both understanding the struggles and responsibilities that went along with that title. Drew didn't look at Luke, but his mouth was in a tight smile. He appreciated the comradery.

"Why did you come up here on your own?" Luke asked, reminding me that this had been Drew's first question before I spat hurt at him.

"To think about things," I answered. "Sometimes this world confuses the hell out of me. And things make more sense when I'm alone." I shivered as a gust of wind ripped around the rocks.

Luke slid his coat off and draped it over my shoulders. He still wore a sweater, having come better prepared than me.

Drew cleared his throat. "I'm gonna go for a walk. I won't be far. Holler if you need anything." I knew that last part was meant for me more so than Luke.

I studied him with curious skepticism. Was he really going to leave us here? He trusted Luke with me?

Luke spoke first. "Thanks, man. I got this."

"I know you do." Drew glanced quickly at me and then pulled himself up the rock and vanished out of sight.

I sat dumbfounded for a moment while Luke got comfortable against the rock wall. "Did that just really happen?"

"Yeah," Luke said. "I think he finally realizes I'm not here to hurt you." He motioned for me to come closer. "Plus, I'm sure he's putting a ring of protection around you right now."

"What do you mean?"

"The same as how I am able to alter and change things in my world, he's able to do the same here." Luke nodded toward the water. "I bet if you tried to jump off this cliff right now, you couldn't do it."

I cautiously peered over the ledge at the savage ocean below. "Seriously?"

"*Don't* try it," he warned. He pulled me closer to him and I cozied up between his legs, pressing my back into his warm chest. He wrapped his arms around me and I relaxed in his embrace.

"So, this is one of your favourite spots."

"It is." I lifted my chin and took in a slow breath of the warm, salty air. "There's almost something magical about it, you know?"

"It's quite awesome," Luke agreed.

"Told you." I nudged him while I settled back into his embrace. "Hey, what were you and Drew talking about earlier when you asked if he knew what his world is capable of, and he told you it wasn't dark?"

I felt him nodding, but it took a few seconds longer for him to answer.

"Earth is neither light nor dark. It hangs in the balance. For now."

"What do you mean—for now?"

"I guess, you know, it's one of those things—when the dark worlds are always attacking it, people start to lose faith in the good. They start to shut out the light. And without light, there's only darkness."

"You think Earth is darker than light, but he disagrees? Was that your argument?"

"I think Drew's trying his best, but given the current state of Earth . . . I just think . . . ."

"You think what?"

226

"I just think that there's not enough good left in this world to resist the darkness."

"Why? Why would you say that?"

He sighed heavily as if I was dragging words from him that he didn't want to speak. "Humans are greedy, selfish, jealous, full of hate for each other, and rarely ever put the welfare of someone else above their own." It came out as a big rush, as if he had been holding it back for a while. He was quiet now, no doubt waiting for my defensive response.

"That's quite the generalization."

"It is. I'm sorry," he said. "Not every human is that way." He squeezed me gently. "Some are very kind, loving and thoughtful."

Sure I was kind to people, but I still thought hateful things about people I didn't like—namely, Holly Haverstock. And when was the last time I did something for someone else that didn't affect me in some positive way? When was the last time I did a random act of kindness? When had I ever volunteered my time to help people I would never know? My heart was racing faster and faster. I may be one of the better humans left in this world, but was I even good enough? If everyone else on this planet was like me, would it be enough? And even if all this were true, what proof did Luke have that this was our demise?

"How do you know that Earth will go dark because

of the way we are?" I asked.

"I can already see signs and patterns proving that the light in this world is slowly diminishing."

"What signs? Patterns?"

"Wars, hate crimes, suicide bombings, murders, crimes against children, random acts of violence—"

"Okay, I get it," I said, cutting him off before he could remind me of any more reasons why I sometimes wished I wasn't a part of this world.

"Sorry," he whispered in my ear, "but those are all things that happen in dark worlds."

"Suppose it's true. Can we stop it?"

He shrugged. "Earth is the heart of the dream worlds, which means it gives and receives energy from the dream worlds. There used to be three dark dream worlds and three light dream worlds, which balanced Earth. One of the light worlds was destroyed a long time ago, and Earth has been on a steady decline ever since."

"How did they destroy the light world?" I felt a shiver crawl up my spine as I asked the question.

"The three dark worlds joined forces to ambush one of the light worlds, because without it, Earth would surely plunge itself into darkness. They sent in creatures, dragons, and . . . a revised version of the Black Plague." He looked down at this, as if he personally mourned for the losses of the light world.

"You said the *three* dark worlds. Does that mean . . .

was your world involved?"

It took him a few seconds to respond. "Yes," he said. "It happened about fifteen years ago. I was too young to do anything about it . . . but old enough to remember."

"What's done is done," I said. "At least Etak's in better hands now that you're keeper."

He gave a partial grin and nodded once.

"How can we beat this? How can we ensure Earth doesn't die?"

His arms tightened around me. "I don't know."

A wave of nausea flowed through my body followed by an unexplained dizziness. No wonder Drew was always so pre-occupied and stressed. If Earth was on a steady decline, and it was his job to save it, he had bigger things to worry about than taking me to prom.

"Don't worry," Luke whispered as his hold tightened around me. "I won't let you go down with this world."

Although his sentiments were touching, how could I find comfort in this? I believed him—he wouldn't let me go down with this world. He would take me to his own world, no matter what Drew said. And maybe he would even take Drew, too, but then what? What about Maddy? And our other friends? And their families? And what about Lucia?

Luke's hands were massaging my arms. "Sarah, honestly, though, this could take hundreds of years to happen. Don't fret about it."

Maybe he was right. There was nothing I could do about it in this moment anyway. I couldn't worry about something that I had no control over. Plus, I wasn't convinced that Earth was dark enough to be all that bad. Sure there was a lot of negative energy, but there were some positive things, too. Somewhere. Sometimes.

He brought his lips to my ear. "Can you kiss me now?"

I nearly choked on my laughter, fueled by my surprise. "Done talking about this, are we?"

He snickered. "Kind of."

I turned my body around and draped my legs over top of his, holding them close to his sides. My hands went straight for his thick, dark hair. At first I was content to just sit on his lap, play with his hair and exchange coy smiles and glances, but an eruption of desires began mounting quickly, coupled with urges that I couldn't explain, and before I knew it, I was pulling his face to mine, needing to feel the softness of his full lips, taste the sweetness of his kiss, smell the coconut on his skin.

Luke groaned as I knelt above him, our lips still attached, but his neck craning now to keep it that way. My heart was beating out of my chest, calling for him. Our bodies reacted explosively to each other as my fingers fumbled for the buttons down the front of my shirt.

"Stop," Luke mumbled through my heavy kisses.

"No," I said, pulling his head back and sinking my

teeth into his neck. "I . . . need you."

"And I love that," he panted heavily, "but not here. Not like this. Not yet."

I pulled away from him, adrenaline coursing through my body at unparalleled speeds. As my breath steadied and I became more aware of my body, I felt the redness creep up my neck and betray my face.

"It's okay," he said, noticing, no doubt, my embarrassment.

"I'm sorry," I said quickly. "Guess I just got carried away."

"Me, too." His fingers curled around the back of my neck and he pulled me back in gently for a softer kiss. "And don't get me wrong," he said between kisses, "it takes a lot of willpower to stop with you."

I blushed. "You're kind of perfect, you know that?"

"Yeah, I've been told a few times," he teased.

I smacked his arm and he gasped, feigning injury.

"Should we go check on Drew?" Luke suggested. "I think he's been generous to give us this much alone time—ring of protection or not. We probably shouldn't push our luck."

Luke was right. This took a lot from Drew and it was probably best to play it safe and obey his rules nicely.

Plus, I didn't really want him retaliating with Holly.

WHEN WE ROUNDED the corner, Drew was sitting on a

rock with his back to us, seemingly off in thought.

I put my finger to my lips and signalled for Luke to be quiet. He smirked and just shook his head. I tiptoed toward Drew, preparing to launch myself at him. As I got closer, I crouched, not making a single noise, and then—

Drew spun around and threw his hands at me. "RAAR!"

"AGGHHH!" I screamed, falling back into Luke's expecting arms.

Drew did a horrible job at hiding his laughter, while Luke stood me upright. "Babe, you're not quiet," he said, kissing my forehead.

"But—"

"No," Drew interrupted. "No buts. You're really not quiet at all."

"But I'm a good scarer!" I protested, trying to recall a single time that I had actually succeeded at scaring Drew.

"You're really not, though," Drew countered.

I pouted.

Luke wrapped his arms around me. "If it's any consolation, you scared me when you screamed."

I nudged him while Drew laughed.

"So," Drew said, smile fading from his lips, "what did you think of Peggy's Cove?"

Luke looked at him with respect and nodded. "Nice place."

"Pretty wild, right?"

They exchanged a knowing look and Luke nodded.

"Can we walk and talk?" I asked. "I have to use the washroom." A row of porta potties lined the parking lot ahead.

Luke took my hand in his and we walked quietly down the path with Drew trailing closely behind. I felt his stare burning into our hands. I wondered if it hurt him as much to see me holding Luke's hand as it would hurt me to witness Drew holding Holly's.

"I'll be right back." I let go of Luke's hand and left him and Drew at a nearby picnic table while I hurried off to the toilet.

"Careful," they called simultaneously.

I smiled and shook my head, waving my hand dismissively over my shoulder, although if I had to be honest with myself, I loved that they both cared.

The washrooms were locked so I headed back to where the guys were sitting, deep in conversation at the picnic table, their backs toward me. They were both bent over with their forearms resting on their knees. They hadn't seen me yet, so I made a wide loop and came up behind them, trying my hardest not to make a single sound. I would show them how sneaky I could be.

When I was about to pounce, I heard my name. I froze then ducked, keeping low behind a bush as I listened.

"Why Sarah? What made her stick out to you?" Drew had said.

"She was different from everyone else. She looked at my world with hope. She wasn't afraid."

"Because she has a dreamcatcher."

"A real one?"

"Yeah. I made it for her as extra protection. She always wore a ring, but I worried that she might one day take it off and I knew the dreamcatcher would help keep her from the dark worlds."

"But she still came to Etak."

"I know. She shouldn't have. But that's probably why her dream wasn't a nightmare."

"Well, I won't pretend there wasn't still a good amount of strength used to ward off the things that were still after her."

"What things?"

"She's afraid of horses," Luke said.

Drew nodded. "She was thrown from one when she was younger."

"And she wanted to go surfing, but I—"

"You wouldn't let her, right?"

"Of course not. I wouldn't let her out of my sight. I was literally drawn to her the minute she arrived. Whenever she came, I was pulled from whatever I was doing. It was like I needed to be there to protect her. I knew she was special the minute I saw her, but I didn't know why. Then she told me she never dreamed before and that you were her best friend, and I knew I couldn't be the only one who thought she was special."

"How did you find that out?"

"I wasn't a hundred percent sure it was you until you showed up to challenge me . . . or Riley, I guess. Up until then I had only speculated. She had said that her best friend Drew had a key like mine, so naturally I was curious."

Drew hung his head, showing his regret, perhaps for a mistake he felt he had made.

"But even so, I was already falling for her."

Drew nodded. "I believe you. She's easy to fall for."

They were both quiet for a few seconds.

"How did you get her to keep going back to your world? How did you control her like that?" Drew asked, an air of accusation back in his voice.

"Honestly, I never did. I was surprised too when she came back. I didn't lure her at all."

"Maybe something or someone else kept luring her back."

"It crossed my mind, I won't lie. And therein lies another reason why I wanted to come find her. When she didn't come back for five nights in a row, I was worried something had happened to her. I was a mess without her. Every day I didn't see her, I was worse than the day before. I had to make sure she was safe."

"That's my job."

"It's not just up to you anymore, Drew."

Drew was quiet for a few seconds. "Someone's after her, you know."

"Because she fainted?"

"She never faints," Drew said, "and when she was unconscious, she heard three people talking. She said one sounded like a snake."

"A shadow."

"I think so."

"But she doesn't show any signs."

Drew shrugged.

"I'll watch out for it," Luke promised.

"Thanks, but you know, you don't have to stay here. I can look out for her. You're a keeper, Luke, you shouldn't leave your world for this long."

"My brother's got it covered. I can't leave her now, Drew. I promised her. And I . . . I think I love her."

Drew coughed hard, which I was thankful for as it concealed my own gasp of surprise.

He thinks he loves me? Did he really just say that?

"I love her, too," I heard Drew say.

Their words echoed in my head—first Luke's "I think I love her" and then Drew's "I love her, too." Over and over they repeated as if there were no other sounds in any of the worlds.

"I know," Luke said, bringing me from my trance. And they both sat there together staring off into the distance.

I stood up slowly and took a step backward. And another. And another. I turned and kept walking toward the water, my feet carrying me up and over boulders, across gullies of water and down over the side of a weather-worn, enormous rock. The edge of the rock was suspended a dozen feet or more above the thrashing ocean below. Not quite close enough to be blackened with water, but close enough that I heard nothing else but the waves and my heart battering around inside my chest.

Luke thinks he loves me. They both do. Me. Unlovable as I have always been. The two guys that I love most in this whole universe just admitted to loving me back.

My breath was as erratic as the waves below — in, out, in, in, out. This was happening too fast. I didn't know how to be loved. What if I got hurt? What if I let them both love me and I ended up getting crushed? Abandoned? Forgotten? How was I supposed to allow them to love me? This was what I wanted, no? For Drew to love me? But now that he had said it, affirmed it, the very idea made me sick with anxiety.

And Luke — he was supposed to be something unreal. Someone I could spend time with, be a regular teenager with, but he could never love me because he didn't know what love was. He was a dark lord of a loveless world. But he had said he thought he loved me. Could he have just said it to gain Drew's trust? Or to express the foreign feelings he felt. Maybe he was wrong.

My name echoed off the surrounding rock faces, but I couldn't pry my eyes from the small rock pool below filling and emptying of water as the waves came in and sucked back out. I was that rock pool. Love and excitement rushing in, worry and despair sucking back out.

Again, my name carried through the air. This time, the sound of Luke's voice brought me out of my stupor. *Luke.*

I stood up and found him frantically scanning the surface of the rocks. "SARAH!"

"I'm here!" I called to him and when he saw me, he broke into a run.

"What the hell, Sarah!" he yelled as he closed the gap between us. He pulled me up over the ledge as he whipped out his phone with his other hand, punched in some numbers and spoke into it. "I found her. We'll be back in a minute. . . . No, she's fine. . . . I don't know. I'm about to find out." He shot me an angry look as he put the phone back in his pocket. "What the hell were you doing?"

I was so overcome with emotion when I saw him running to me, when I felt his arms around me as he lectured me, that all I could do was cry.

"Sarah?" Luke pulled my hands from my face and bent down to inspect my tears.

I shook my head and buried it in his chest. "I'm sorry."

"What happened?"

"Nothing," I reassured him. I couldn't bring myself to share my innermost thoughts and fears. What if he thought I was crazy? What if my confession reminded him that he didn't, in fact, love me?

"So you just walked off? You can't do that."

"I'm sorry," I sobbed.

"It's okay. It's okay." He lifted my chin with his finger, his dark blue eyes sinking into mine. He closed his eyes as brought his mouth to mine and I, once again, melted into him.

WHAT THE HELL was that?" Drew demanded as Luke and I rejoined him in the parking lot where he was busy pacing.

"I'm sorry," I said. "I just went for a walk."

Drew's eyebrows raised and he jerked his head back. "Oh, okay. And that seemed like a good idea, did it?"

"I—"

"When Luke and I are sitting here waiting for you to come back from the washroom."

"Drew, I—"

"And then we go out looking for you for ten freaking minutes, Sarah!" His voice was getting louder, his anger more clear. "Worried *sick!*"

"I said I was sorry!" I tried.

"Sarah, you have no idea what—"

"Okay, man, she gets it," Luke said, interrupting Drew's rant. Drew looked at him, closed his mouth and nodded.

"Don't let it happen again," Drew finished.

"I won't," I promised.

CHAPTER 18

Unwanted

~ SARAH ~

LUKE WAS WAITING at my front door when I skipped out the next morning. He caught me in his arms and squeezed me until I coughed.

"Sorry," he said with a laugh and put me back on the ground. "I missed you."

"I see that." I straightened my top and then kissed his firm, salty lips.

"So," Luke began as we started walking down the front path to the sidewalk, "my brother seems to have everything under control back at home."

"Good," I said. I had forgotten that Luke had another world to deal with. I guess I took for granted that, after he said goodbye to me last night, he hadn't gone home to bed—he still had to go home to another world and live another life, fulfill other duties. Guilt washed over me.

"Sarah!" My name rang through the air from a distance behind us.

Luke took my hand in his and we both turned quickly to see whose panicked voice was calling out to me.

Drew! It hadn't sounded at all like calm, cool and collected Drew. Luke must have sensed it, too—he stepped forward and held his arm across the front of me.

"Sarah!" Drew was only five feet away when he slowed down. "Are you okay?"

"I'm fine," I said, puzzled. "What's wrong with *you*?"

Drew looked from Luke to me, then at my house. His concern was evident, but when his eyes reached my face again, he relaxed.

"What is it?" Luke pressed.

"My house," Drew said. "My house was ransacked last night."

"What?!" I gasped, pushing Luke's arm away. "Were you home? Are you and your dad okay?"

"Yeah, yeah," Drew said, shaking his head and dismissing my concern for their safety. "We're fine."

"What did they take?"

"Nothing."

Drew and Luke exchanged a meaningful look. One that I knew they would never explain to me. Their worry was too deep. Their apparent anger too fresh.

"Then . . . why?" I pressed.

"You're okay, though?" Drew asked, ignoring my in-quisition.

"I'm fine, Drew. Why wouldn't I be?"

"Where were you?" Luke asked Drew. "When this happened. Where were you?"

Drew shot him a glare. "Working."

"Well," Luke said, sucking in a deep breath, "if no one was hurt, and nothing was taken, then I'd say we've got nothing to worry about."

I shook my head. "Wait—"

"He's right," Drew said. "It's nothing for you to worry about."

"But—"

Luke swooped down and kissed my forehead, eras-ing my last argument. "Drew and I will figure it out. Don't worry."

My face softened. "Okay," I said as Drew averted his eyes. "But *you're* okay?" I asked Drew as I looped my arm in his and we began walking again.

Our eyes met and he smiled. "I'm okay if you're okay."

And the rest of the walk to school was silent.

SARAH LOVES LUKE
Sarah Marley + Luke Anderson
Sarah Anderson

I hadn't noticed that I was professing my love through calligraphy until I heard Drew's fist slam into his desk, which startled me from my reverie.

His eyes were burning a hole into the letters scrawled neatly over the front of my pink binder.

"Sorry," I said, and flipped the binder open, hiding the words against my desk.

He shook his head and smiled. "It's not that." He laughed as if I was so naïve to think it was.

"Then what?" I flipped through my textbook, pretending not to be hurt by that.

"I forgot to call Holly back last night. Was supposed to make plans for tonight."

It wasn't deliberate, but my binder was closed again and I was now tracing the letters I had just inked.

"She called while we were at Peggy's Cove. It went straight to voice mail."

"Reception's terrible there," I muttered.

"Yeah, I shouldn't have gone." His words stung, and my pencil broke between my fingers. "You okay?" he asked smugly.

"Oh, shut-up, Drew!" I snapped. "Why the hell do you have to act like that?"

His grimace faded, being replaced with shock. "I—"

"And don't pretend you don't know what you're doing. You're trying to make me jealous," I spat. "And you know what?"

"What?"

"It's not working!"

Drew raised his eyebrows as if his opinion might differ from mine. "Good, then you won't mind if we don't include you on that date tonight, then."

I could feel my face heating up, and my heart was racing wildly. "Oh no you don't. You tagged along on my date yesterday, Luke and I are going on your date tonight. Where are we going?" My voice was louder than it should have been. Ms. Kerr was standing between or desks now. Drew was eagerly amused by my outburst and the fact that Ms. Kerr was glaring down at me.

"I am *not* jealous," I repeated for good measure.

"Of course not," he said, shaking his head. "You don't sound like a crazy, jealous girlfriend at all."

We both stared at each other as Ms. Kerr shook her head and walked away.

"I didn't mean girlfriend. I meant—"

"I know."

"Okay, good."

We returned to our textbooks and I was aware of his pencil working steadily on his math problems. I moved mine back and forth, but the lead didn't touch the paper.

"Sushi," he said after a minute.

"Huh?"

"We'll go for sushi tonight."

My pencil stopped moving, but I kept my eyes fixated

on the place where it had stopped. "Does she like sushi?"

Drew shrugged. "Don't know. . . . But you do."

My heart smiled. A piece of Drew was still mine.

THE BELL RANG at the end of next period at the same time my stomach growled signalling it was time for lunch. I slid my biology books into my backpack as Luke patiently waited for me.

"Sorry," I said. "I'm usually the last one out of class. I like to pack things away properly so it's not a mess later."

"I get it. I'm in no rush."

"Drew can't stand it. It annoys him."

Luke didn't respond and I wondered why I needed to say that. Finally I zipped up my backpack and hauled it up from the floor.

"So," I said as we sauntered slowly down the hallway, our fingers playing with each other as we walked, "I guess we're double dating tonight."

Luke nodded. "Drew and Holly?"

I watched the tiles pass beneath us. "Yeah."

"How do you feel about that?"

"It's fine. I mean she's annoying as hell, but if that's what it takes to keep you here, then I'm all for it." I stopped and turned to Luke. He turned too and his eyes smiled as they bore into mine. I touched his face and ran my thumb over his bottom lip. "Have I told you how happy you make me?"

He licked his lower lip and then bit it gently. "You haven't actually." He looked up and down the hall and then slid his hands around my waist and pulled me into him. "But I'd love to hear you say it."

Confirming no one was in the corridor, I placed my hands on his stomach, felt the ripples under his t-shirt and gently trailed my fingers down and around his torso. "When I'm with you, I feel like I'm floating. Like nothing else in the world matters. Like I could take on the world and any problem it throws at me."

He winced as if I touched a sore spot. My hands retreated slightly as I studied his face.

"There are a lot of problems this world could throw at you," he said.

"I know," I said, grinning. "But because of you, I'm not afraid anymore."

"You're not invincible," he challenged, and I sensed his anxiety over the direction of this conversation.

"I'm not saying I am, I'm just saying that I am more relaxed and—"

"But you shouldn't be. You should always be prepared—"

"Okay, well, I didn't mean for it to turn into a lecture, Luke. I just wanted to tell you I love being with you. And you make me happy." It sounded a bit weird, spitting those last words out when they were meant to have a more gentle effect.

His hands, which had been gripping my sides, were now loosening. He closed his eyes and sighed heavily. "I am so sorry."

I reached up and touched his lips with mine. "Don't apologize. All I heard was that you love being with me, too."

He opened his eyes and smiled. "I'm so glad that's what you heard—that's totally what I meant to say."

We both laughed as I pulled him down the hallway toward the arboretum, his grip on my hand a little tighter than usual.

MADDY, CALEB, HOLLY and Drew were already at our table when Luke and I arrived. Drew didn't raise his eyes to us—he was deep in conversation with Holly as she was showing him something on her phone. They laughed to-gether—hers genuinely annoying; his genuinely fake. Or at least that's what I let myself believe.

"So," Maddy muttered as I sat down next to her, "apparently Horrible Holly has decided she can sit here now."

Luke stifled a laugh at Maddy's nickname for Holly.

"Yeah, I think Drew has a thing for her," I said. Luke squeezed my hand.

"Shut-*up*," Maddy whispered viciously. "He does *not*! Sarah, tell me Drew has not stooped that low."

I raised my eyebrows and shrugged.

"Has he lost his freaking mind?"

"You know I can hear you, right?" Holly said casually without taking her eyes from her phone.

"You know I don't care, right?" Maddy replied.

I pinched Maddy's leg and she slapped my hand. "What has gotten into you?" she hissed.

"Come to the washroom with me," I said, dragging her out of her seat.

When we were in the hall, Maddy unleashed her fury. "Honestly, Sarah! Why are you putting up with this? Holly is evil! She has been awful to the both of us for as long as we've known her. She does not deserve to have Drew, and why the hell are you letting her get away with this?! You know if you said the word, Drew would banish her. Why aren't you? What the hell is going on?"

"Okay, okay." I raised my hands and waited until Maddy was breathing normally again before I explained. "I am crazy about Luke."

Maddy went from angry to elated in a split second. "That's awesome, Sarah! When did this happen?"

"I don't know. It just sort of did. We went to Peggy's Cove yesterday and I got to know him and he's so awesome." It felt wrong deceiving her, but the truth was too much to take on at the moment.

"So you're over Drew?"

"Well, that's the thing. I will always care about Drew, but I think he's having a hard time accepting the fact that

I want to be with Luke."

"So he's sort of rebounding?"

"Sort of, I guess. But I think it's good. If he can get his mind off of me and Luke by dating Holly, then it'll be worth it. He's so miserable when he's unhappy."

"He is," Maddy agreed. "So we *want* him with Holly?"

"Yes. We have to support it."

"Can't another girl do?"

"I would rather that, too, but he picked Holly."

"Probably trying to get under your skin," Maddy grumbled. "It's sure working for me."

I nodded. "Could very well be, but if that's what it takes for me to be happy with Luke, I have to go along with it."

"Fine," Maddy complained. "I'll be nice."

"Thank you!" I threw my arms around her tiny frame and hugged her hard. "I owe you one."

"You owe me like *fifty*."

"Oh, and I think we're going to double date with Drew and Holly tonight, and I would really, really, really like for you and Caleb to come. I need support."

Maddy sighed heavily. "*Fine.*"

"You're the best."

"I know." Maddy hooked her arm through mine and we headed back into the lunch room. "I want all the details about you and Luke, though. Have you kissed?"

I couldn't keep the smile from spreading wide.

"You did!" Maddy squealed.

"Yes," I admitted. "Maddy, honestly, he is so freaking amazing."

"Oh, Sarah, I'm so happy for you. You so deserve this. I bet Drew's kicking himself for not making a move sooner."

We both stopped and watched Holly with one arm draped around Drew's back and her face in his ear whispering something that made him shiver.

"I think he'll be fine," I said, feeling my heart crush a little. I turned my eyes to Luke who was watching me. He smiled and I forgot about Drew.

"So, Sarah," Holly chirped as I took my place next to Maddy and across from Luke, "Drew and I are going for dinner tonight," she paused, giving effect to her words, "and *Drew* was thinking it'd be fun to have you and Luke tag along."

Drew looked down, but I could see his smirk. He was enjoying how Holly was twisting his words.

"I said we'd go," Luke said, pulling my eyes to him. "If that's okay with you."

"Ummm, I'll have to check what's on. Weren't you and I going to do something tonight, Maddy?"

Drew snapped his head up and looked from me to Maddy.

"Oh, yeah," Maddy played along, "we were.

Hmmmm."

"Sorry, Drew, I have plans with Maddy tonight. Maybe next time. Have fun, though."

I caught Luke's mildly amused expression as he watched how this would play out. Drew was frantic. Perhaps he didn't want to be left alone with Holly after all.

"No problem," Holly said. "Next time maybe." She was happy.

"You know what?" Maddy added, having way too much fun with this. "Caleb and I are due for a date night, so how about we all go?"

Drew relaxed a little and caught my eyes. He narrowed his—a warning to stop playing games. I smirked.

"Oh," Holly said. "Well, sounds fun and all, but maybe we could do that another time."

"No, I'm pretty sure I'd like to do that tonight, actually," Maddy said.

"Yeah, you know what?" I added. "Let's do it. Luke?"

"Hmmmm," Luke said, turning my game on me. "I'm not sure, actually. I just remembered that I have a thing."

"You're coming," I cut him off before he could concoct a story.

"How could I say no to you?" He grinned. So handsome.

"Great," Drew said, interrupting our romantic wordless exchange. "So I'll make a reservation at Sushinami for the six of us at eight o'clock."

"Sushinami? Like real sushi?" Holly asked, looking thoroughly disgusted.

"Well, there's more than just raw fish there," Drew explained.

"Yeah, you can get vegetable rolls," I said.

"Or chicken or beef dishes," Drew added.

"It's so good," I said, trying to convince her, but watching her expression move from disgusted to unconvinced.

"I don't know," Holly said. "Maybe we could go someplace that we *all* like."

"It's going to be hard finding a place that we all like," added Maddy. "Caleb and I like sushi, too. I think we should go, and you should give it a try."

Now I knew Maddy wasn't a sushi fan, so for her to say this meant that she didn't care if we ate out of garbage cans in the back alley, as long as Holly didn't get her way.

"Okay," Holly said. "I'll give it a try." She turned to Drew. "If you think I'll like it." She batted her eyelashes and I rolled my eyes. Maddy kicked me under the table while Drew just smiled at Holly, unsure whether to make the promise or not.

"Anyway," Maddy said, "I've got the car tonight so Sarah, if you and Luke want to come with me, I'll pick you up."

"Sure," I said, reaching across the table to take Luke's hand. "You can pick us both up at my place."

Holly was looking at my hand in Luke's. "Sarah," she said, "is that Drew's ring?"

"Uh, yes," I said, catching eyes with Drew for a split second and feeling Luke's grip tighten around my fingers.

"Don't you think it's kind of . . . *odd* that you're wearing Drew's ring when you're clearly not even dating him."

"You're not technically dating him yet, either," Maddy pointed out sourly.

Holly shot her an evil look.

"No, you're right," I said quickly. "I just . . . I just like it, I guess." I looked to Drew for assistance, but he just stared back at me, putting all trust in me. But in doing so, he was leaving me out to dry. "Do you . . . Do you want it back, Drew?" I tried to send him a subliminal message – *would it be okay for me to not wear it during the day? Maybe you could just give it back to me after the date?* I knew the ring not only protected me from dreaming in my sleep, but it also protected me from being lured into sleep during the day when I wasn't even tired, but if I were with Luke, he could keep me awake or help me, couldn't he?

Drew was quiet, probably deciding on how he should answer. How he should deal with it. Could he tell Holly that he wanted me to wear it? That it didn't fit his finger so he gave it to me? Why else would I keep it? I looked selfish. Greedy.

I twisted his ring, watching him carefully for any indication that this was not okay, but he didn't object. I would just get it back from him after the date. All would be okay. If he wasn't prepared to defend my honour and tell Holly he wanted me to wear it, then what right did I have to keep it? The ring came loose and I slowly slid it from my finger.

"I don't see the big deal in wearing it," Luke said, catching the ring before it came off my finger. He pushed it back on. "You like it, I get it. I'm not insecure about you wearing it and I don't think Holly is, either. As soon as my school ring gets in, I hope you'll wear mine, and then you can give Drew's back."

Drew looked grateful to Luke for rescuing the situation. He shrugged. "Yeah, it doesn't mean anything to me. If I wanted to be with Sarah, I would've been with her. I've just never liked her like that."

Ouch.

That.

Hurt.

"Well, that's only if she'd have you, Drew," Luke said, "and I'm not so sure you're her type."

Maddy gave a little gasp next to me. She liked drama just as much as the next person, but even to this, she looked more alarmed than inspired. I studied Luke's face. It was firm. Angry, maybe? A touch of pink in his cheeks. He broke the staring contest between him and

Drew and returned his gaze to mine, his face softening.

"At least that's what I like to think," Luke added before kissing my fingers.

I blushed and melted as his lips touched my skin. "You're my type," I said quietly, as if just to him. He winked and I felt myself fall a little further.

"QUESTION FOR YOU," Luke said as he sat on my bed, petting Lucia. I flipped through the hangers in my closet looking for something decent to wear to dinner. I was starving, having skipped supper with my parents so I wouldn't be too full to eat sushi with my friends . . . and Holly. And when I was hungry, I was edgy. Some would even say cranky.

"Yes?" I said, throwing down another top to the floor—too plain.

"At lunch earlier, would you really have given Drew's ring back to him?"

"I don't know," I said, as I held up two tops, comparing them.

"What do you mean you don't know?"

I dropped my arms in exasperation. "I don't know, Luke. I. Don't. Know." How else could I have said that?

Luke grinned and dropped his eyes to the floor. "But you promised Drew and me both that you'd wear it and wouldn't take it off."

I rolled my eyes. "I realize that. But now Drew's dating Holly and how messed up is it that I'm still wearing his ring? I look so pathetic!" I threw the blue top on the floor and decided, frustratingly, on the yellow one.

"You don't look pathetic," Luke said, leaning over to pick up the blue top that landed near his feet.

"Besides," I added as I whipped off my shirt and pulled on the new yellow one, "I was planning on getting it back from him before I went to bed."

"But you could still be lured to sleep, or unconsciousness, during the day."

"I know that," I snapped, "which is why I would've made sure you were with me so that wouldn't have happened."

"But what if—"

"I didn't give it back to him, Luke, okay?"

"No!" Luke stood up, startling both Lucia and me. "No, it's not okay, Sarah!" He closed the distance between us. "You made a promise. I am giving up a lot to be here with you, and I'm only doing it because you promised you would wear that ring and not take it off. You have no idea what your little games do to Drew and me both. Can't you see how sick that made him today?"

My lips were moving, but words weren't coming out. Luke had *never* raised his voice to me before.

"Remember how he said if he wanted you, he could

have you, but that he just never liked you that way? Remember how that hurt?"

Thanks for the reminder. "Uh . . . yes?"

"Well, that was his intention. He wanted to hurt you. It was a warning to stop playing games. He was angry about the ring. He trusted you and you promised you'd wear it."

"But I—"

"Yeah, you got put in an awkward situation. I get it. We all get put in those situations sometimes and we have to deal with it. You don't back out of promises and you don't get scared off when someone challenges you."

"She's just going to keep harassing me about the ring. You know that, right?"

"Let her," Luke said, throwing his arms up as if he didn't see the problem.

"And without looking like a desperate fool, how do I tell her she can't have it? It's Drew's ring—shouldn't he be the one to tell her?"

Luke stepped back and nodded, as if something just dawned on him.

"What?" I said.

"You want Drew to tell her that he *wants* you to wear his ring."

"No," I said, alarmed at how childish that sounded.

"You want him to admit that it's because of *him* that you're wearing it. That *he* wants it and not you. You're

258

afraid if you take blame for wanting to wear the ring, then she'll believe Drew. She'll believe that he never wanted you."

"No!" I said again, more forcefully this time.

"Then what, Sarah? What are you afraid of?"

"I . . . I . . ." Tears stung my eyes and threatened to pour out.

He had his hands on my shoulders now and nudged me softly until my eyes met his. "What are you afraid of, Sarah? I need to know. You need to tell me." His eyes burned into mine with a fiery intensity. "What are you afraid of?"

And then the words burst from me like a river dam. "I just want to know I'm not alone in this," I cried. *I don't want to be alone. I can't do this on my own. It doesn't make enough sense. It's bigger than me. I can't figure it out. I don't know what's happening and how I can control it.*

Before I knew it, I was on my knees with my face in my hands, gasping for breath as sobs poured out of me. *Why is this happening? Why am I losing control? Why was I never good enough for Drew? Why does Luke, the only one who really cares about me, have to be from another world? Why do people want to kill me? What is happening to me?*

Maybe these words were just in my head, maybe I was sobbing them, I didn't know. But Luke was now crouched in front of me trying to pull me to my feet.

"You're not alone, Sarah," he whispered as he closed

his arms around me and I buried my face into his neatly pressed shirt. "You'll never be alone. I promise." Then he chuckled. "And *I* don't break promises like some people." He smiled, but it was another reminder that I had broken my promise to wear Drew's ring.

"Here," he said, pulling a Kleenex from the box on my nightstand. "I'm sorry I made you cry."

I shook my head as I blew my nose into the tissue.

"I know this has been hard for you," he continued, "and it kills me that I can't fix everything right now and put things back to normal for you."

I shook my head harder. "I don't want normal. Normal is without you."

He took my face in his hands and kissed my forehead. "Normal is safe."

CHAPTER 19

Abnormal is Unsafe

~ SARAH ~

DREW AND HOLLY were already seated when we arrived fashionably late. Maddy led the way to the table and I held tight to Luke's arm as nausea settled in.

"You okay?" Luke whispered over his shoulder as I trailed slightly behind.

"Uh-huh."

He stopped half way to the table and turned to look at me. "Sarah, we don't have to do this. If you want to go home, that's totally fine. You don't owe Drew this."

"I do owe him. I need to show him that this doesn't bother me."

"But it does."

"Because she's evil."

Luke nodded. "Just so you know, he's only doing this to make you jealous."

I shook my head. "No, he's not. Drew doesn't play games like that. He likes her."

Luke pressed his lips into the shape of a smile and raised his eyebrows. "If you say so."

"Anyway, it doesn't matter. I am crazy about you." I stood on my tiptoes and reached his lips with mine.

"Then shall we stay?"

"Yes." I sucked in a deep breath. "How do my eyes look?" I had spent the better part of the last hour trying to make myself look like I hadn't been sobbing my eyes out. When Maddy picked us up, I had hidden my face in the dark shadows of the evening, and avoided her eyes in the rear-view mirror. But now we were at a restaurant, dimly-lit, yes, but we would all be sitting across from each other.

"They're fine," Luke said. "You're beautiful."

"What's wrong?" Drew asked as soon as we sat down. He was studying my face and I could tell my efforts to cover my red, puffy eyes hadn't worked on Drew.

"Nothing," I said, dismissively. "Why would there be?"

Drew didn't answer, but he looked hard at Luke, accusation or inquisition plaguing his face. Was he accusing Luke of making me cry? Or enquiring about what it was that made me cry? Either way, he knew that I had been crying. Luke nodded to him in a way that Drew settled and I understood it to be a silent understanding between the two.

"We're starving," Luke said, picking up a menu and opening it up.

"Aah, that's her problem," Drew teased. "Sarah can get a little *cranky* without regular food injections."

"Ain't that the truth," Maddy said. "What'd you have a little meltdown over what outfit to wear?"

Luke nearly spit out his water. "Yes, actually. Yes, that's exactly what happened. How did you know?"

Drew and Maddy both laughed, then Maddy said, "I've known Sarah long enough. I keep a bag of almonds in my bag for when she starts to get a little edgy."

Drew laughed harder. "Do you? That's awesome. I keep a granola bar in my car for that same reason."

Luke was finding this all too funny. "I'll have to start carrying some food on me, too, I guess. Didn't realize how vicious she can get on an empty stomach." He squeezed my knee under the table.

"Ha. Ha. Ha," I said sarcastically. "Glad you're all having a good laugh at my expense."

Maddy reached into her purse and tossed a bag of almonds across the table. "Here. Should tide you over."

Luke chuckled before handing his menu to me. "Sorry, babe."

I softened. "I'm kidding. I'm fine, really."

"So," Holly said excitedly, "Drew's convinced me to try smoked salmon. Eek!"

I refrained from wincing, and instead said, "You'll love it. It's really good."

We placed our orders and the menus were taken away. Now, the six of us had to participate in conversation with no menus to hide behind.

Luke spoke first, "So what's the deal with prom? I keep seeing posters for it. When is it?"

"It's next Friday," Holly answered excitedly. "Are you two going?"

Luke looked at me and I gave a quick glance in Drew's direction. He was carefully opening his chopsticks, listening but not engaging.

"I don't know," I answered. "I haven't bought a dress or anything. I don't know if I really want to go." I looked at Luke. "What do you think?"

"If you want to go and you don't already have a date, I'd love to take you. It's your grade twelve prom. I think you should go."

I shrugged and looked down.

Holly turned to Drew. "What about you? Do you have a date yet?"

"Yeah, I don't think I'm going."

Holly pouted. "Really? I thought for sure you'd go."

"Nah, proms aren't really my thing."

I could've mouthed the words as he said them, but

instead, I just took a sip of water.

"Proms are fun if you go with the right people," Holly said, trailing her fingers down his chest.

Drew smiled at her, then bit his lower lip playfully. "Is that so?"

"Well, Caleb and I are going," Maddy said, interrupting the foreplay going on between Drew and Holly.

"Are you?" I asked, not surprised at all, but pretending to be.

"Yeah, but I don't have a dress yet. I have to go shopping tomorrow. Wanna come?"

"Oh my gosh!" Holly said. "That gives me an idea! How about the three of us go shopping for dresses tomorrow?"

"That's not an idea." Maddy scowled. "That's literally what I just said, minus the part where you were invited."

I hid my laughter. Luke nudged me and said, "Yeah, and maybe while you're out you'll find a dress and decide to go to prom, too." His eyes studied me. His deep, delicious, blue eyes encased in long, thick eyelashes.

"Maybe," I said, doubtfully. "But regardless, I do want to spend the evening with you. Whether it's at the school prom, or somewhere else." I puckered my lips and Luke brought his to mine. I revelled in the softness of them, my eyes closing to block out every other sight.

"Do *you* have a date yet?" Drew asked Holly, returning his attention to her, and reminding me that Luke and

I weren't alone.

"Well, I've had plenty of offers, but I am still waiting for the right one." She batted her eyelashes.

"I'd hate to be just another name in your rejection pile." I couldn't be sure, but it did sound as though Drew was flirting with Holly, and worse, asking her to prom.

"I promise that if you ask, I'll say yes."

Drew blushed. Maddy, Caleb, Luke and I all waited for Drew's next move. He leaned into Holly, bypassed her mouth and whispered something into her ear. She licked her lips and smiled. "I'd love to go with you," she whispered, a little louder so we could all hear, and her eyes connected with mine for a fraction of a second so that I knew she was pleased to have me witness the exchange.

Luke ran his thumb up and down my shoulder, a comforting gesture as he no doubt knew how hard this was for me to endure. Maddy's eyes were narrowed on Holly's and her cheeks throbbed with every clench of her jaw.

"So does that change anything for you, Sarah?" Maddy said through gritted teeth. "Can you come *now*?"

I forced a smile but couldn't answer.

"Yes, Sarah," Holly inserted. "I'd love for you to come help me pick out another dress. I had one, but I don't think it will go with Drew's eyes, so I'd like to get another one. And since you and Drew are such good friends, I'd love your input." She was softer now. Maybe she no longer saw me as a hurdle in the way of her goal. Maybe Drew was finally able to convince her that he never had a thing for me and he was only interested in her.

Luke's fingers pressed into my shoulder. Holding me steady, maybe? Whatever his intention, it was a welcomed distraction.

I smiled at Holly, keeping my eyes from Drew's smug face next to hers. "I'll go shopping," I said, "but really, Holly, you'll look beautiful in anything you try on."

Maddy made a small gagging noise, and it honestly took a lot out of me to say it, but I knew the smartness in that comment would catch Drew off guard. He'd wonder what my motive was, and maybe he'd just see that there was no use in trying to make me miserable—that was the story of my life before Luke came along, and I was able to play the game better than he was.

"I'll be back in a minute," I said to Luke who was watching me with curious wonder. "I have to go to the washroom."

"Oh, me too," Holly said, and I almost sat back down. What was the point in going to the washroom when my only intention was to get away from her for just one minute? "I'll go with you, Sarah."

Maddy enlarged her eyes, indicating she was on standby to accompany me if needed, but I shook my head and let her relax. Being around Holly this much was enough kryptonite for her, too. At least I was able to give *her* a break.

When the washroom door closed behind Holly, she came to stand beside me at the mirror. I was reapplying my lipstick, and she just watched. I raised my eyebrows to her and smiled. *Yes?*

"Thanks for that out there."

"For what?" I asked, feigning ignorance.

"For the compliment."

"That was nothing. It's true."

Holly smiled and looked down at her purse. "And I'm sorry," she said, her voice more hushed than before.

"For?"

"I haven't always been *nice* to you."

I winked at her. "I hadn't noticed."

She laughed and then took a deep breath. "I think Drew actually likes me."

"Of course he does."

"I was worried that he was only paying attention to me to make you jealous."

I shook my head. "No. Drew's not like that."

"Yeah, he's pretty great, huh?"

"He's one of the best."

"Luke's pretty awesome, too." She rummaged through her purse and pulled out her lipstick.

"Yes, he is." I couldn't help but smile at the mention of his name.

"Sarah," Holly said as we were about to head back out, "I'd really like to wear Drew's ring."

My hand instinctively clenched.

"But I know Drew won't ask for it back from you."

I was rubbing the ring with my free hand now.

"So, I was wondering . . . when do you plan on giving it back?"

"Soon," I said. This confused her.

"But why—"

"I don't know," I interrupted. I wasn't sure how to answer any of her questions, and this made no sense to her.

"I know Luke says it doesn't bother him, but it has to," she said.

I tried to move to the doorway, but she stood in my way. "Maybe it does. But when his ring comes in, I'll wear his."

"But why do you have to wear Drew's until then?"

"I want to," I said, sounding childish. I reached for the door again, but she blocked me. "Holly, I really don't want to have this discussion right now."

"But I do," Holly said. "And I know Luke rescued you from the conversation earlier today, but we're alone now and I want answers." The kindness in her voice was gone and she was back to standing firm with attitude. "Why won't you give it back to Drew? You're not together. He says you were *never* together. And it's his ring. It's not right, Sarah, and you know it."

My face reddened and my eyes began to sting. If Luke hadn't berated me earlier for almost taking it off at lunch hour, I would've caved and given it to her now. I hated wearing a ring that wasn't meant to be mine. A ring that symbolized commitment and love, but those things were obviously not meant for me.

"No!" I shouted, not realizing until after it was out that it made no sense.

Holly backed up a step, freeing the doorway. I pulled open the door and hastily walked back to the table. She didn't follow.

Luke stood up as soon as he saw me coming. "What happened?" he demanded, looking past me for Holly.

Drew stood up too when I took Luke's arms and steadied myself by holding my gaze with his.

"What the hell, Sarah?" Drew said.

"She wants your ring," I told Drew. "Do you have any idea how hard it is to give her a reason why I should keep it?"

Drew and Luke were quiet.

After what seemed like a minute, Maddy said quietly, "So . . . why *don't* you give it back?" She winced as if she were expecting me to lash out at her.

"No," Drew said, silencing Maddy with the raise of his hand. "She's keeping it."

Maddy propped her eyebrows and looked at Luke.

"And you're okay with that?"

"I don't care," Luke said, agitated.

My heart pounded against my chest and I wanted to scream. I hated lying to Maddy about this, too.

"Why do you want her to keep it?" Maddy asked Drew.

"Because . . . because she likes it and I don't care about it."

"Why would you *want* to keep it, Sarah?" she persisted, raising my level of impatience.

"I don't!" I yelled. "I don't want to keep it. I wish I didn't have to. I wish I could completely disconnect myself from Drew. I wish he didn't have this hold on me."

No one said a word for a long ten seconds, and the ring burned on my finger, begging me to take it off.

"I know I promised you, Drew," I said quietly, "but I don't want this. I can't do this anymore."

"Sarah," Drew began, "just a little while longer. I promise everything will—"

"Be fine?" I finished for him. "I shouldn't worry? Just relax? Everything will be fine?"

"Sarah, don't do this," Luke interjected.

"Am I the only one who is confused as hell right now?" Caleb wondered aloud.

Maddy was on her feet, hands pressed into the table in front of her as she watched the three of us intently. "No," she added, "I'm pretty lost, too."

"Sarah, listen to me," Drew said, drawing my eyes to his. They were cold, unfeeling, angry, even. "Just wear the stupid ring. It means nothing to me. I don't want to be with you. I only want you to have it so you don't die on my watch."

In that split second that his last word came from his mouth, everything around us went dark. I only saw him now. No one else in the world existed—just me and this monster of a guy who just hurt me so severely that I wanted to hurt him equally as bad. *He doesn't deserve you,* I thought to myself. *He is bitter, angry, hurtful. Get rid of him. Take off the ring. Break your ties from him. He doesn't love you, or even care about you. Take off the ring. The only reason he wants you to wear his ring is so that you don't die on his watch. Show him you'd rather die than be his slave. Take off the ring.*

Drew's voice repeated, painfully, in my mind over and over, in slow motion, as an incredible pain seared through my brain. The room was dark, but it was spinning. I groaned and held my head.

"She's coming around," I heard a muffled female voice say. Maddy?

"Try sitting her up," came another voice. Caleb?

An arm slipped under my back and pulled me upward. My head lulled back and I couldn't hold it up. Nausea gripped my body and I could do nothing about it—my head turned sideways and I vomited. Once. Twice.

272

Three times.

"It's okay. It's okay," someone else said. This time, I knew the comforting voice. It was Luke.

"Here's a towel," Maddy said.

"I said it's okay," Luke said more firmly. "Sarah, I'm right here."

"What happened?" I moaned. "Where am I?"

"You like totally passed out," Maddy said. "Right in the middle of the restaurant."

"Where am I?"

"We're at Drew's," Luke answered. "You've been out for a while."

"Where's Drew?"

"He's, uh . . . he's gone right now."

"I still can't believe he just took off with Holly and left us," Maddy grumbled. "What the hell does he see in her anyway?"

"Ease up on him," Luke defended, which told me that Drew had business to take care of. I just hoped it didn't have anything to do with my apparent blackout.

"I still think we should take her to the hospital," Maddy said.

"We can't," Luke said quietly.

"Why not? Why are you and Drew so insistent on keeping her here? You're not doctors, you know. This is the second time she's fainted this week. This could be serious."

Luke sighed. "Maddy? Could you please give us a minute?"

"Why?" Maddy snapped, but Caleb was at her side now and pulled her to the door. "I'll be back in a minute, Sarah," Maddy called before leaving the room.

As soon as she was gone, Luke rested my head on his lap and stroked my hair.

"I threw up," I realized.

"You did."

"On you?"

"A little."

"I'm sorry."

He chuckled. "It's okay. It's the stuff I gave you to drink. It doesn't settle well on an empty stomach."

"What was it?"

"Something to pull you out of your unconsciousness. The same stuff Drew gave you in the nurse's office the first time."

"What the hell happened?"

Luke sucked in a deep breath. "Drew made you angry. I think that, combined with how hungry you were, just made you collapse."

"What?"

"I think you meant to storm out in protest, but you only spun around and then fell flat on your face. . . . Well, not *flat* on your face—the table broke your fall a little."

"My head," I said, as a shock of pain pierced my skull.

I brought my fingers to the top of my forehead.

"Yeah, right there. Don't touch it. You've got a cut."

"Where's Drew now? Not with Holly?"

"No," Luke said, shaking his head. "He only said that for Maddy's sake. He's at the portal. Had something to take care of."

"What is he doing?"

"He's . . . putting more protection on the portal." I could tell this was an admission, but that he didn't want to tell me any more.

"Why? Did something else happen?

"Just you blacking out."

"But I have his ring on, so I was safe, right?"

Luke looked down and mumbled, "You didn't have it on when you blacked out."

"What? What do you mean?"

Luke sucked in a deep breath and clenched his jaw. "You threw it at Drew."

"Oh," I said, lowering my head.

He didn't answer.

"I'm sorry."

"It's Drew's fault. He shouldn't have provoked you like that."

I remembered Drew's words, and the sting of them made my head hurt even more. I was angry with him, I remembered. Hurt. It was hard to breathe as I recalled my last moment with him.

Luke squeezed my arm. "He didn't mean it."

I didn't argue. It hurt too much. "Where's Holly?" I asked, pushing the thought of Drew from my mind.

"Home now. She saw you pass out, but didn't see why. All she knew was that you fainted, and Drew was crawling around the floor looking for his ring that you threw. It took a few minutes to find it, which is probably why it took so long to pull you out of it. He put it back on your finger as soon as he found it. So naturally, Holly was confused as hell. She ended up storming out. Drew caught up with her, gave her a potion to make her forget what happened and then took her home while Maddy, Caleb and I brought you here."

"I am *so* sorry," I apologized again.

"Don't be hard on yourself. You didn't ask for any of this."

"What did Caleb and Maddy think?" I figured after this, we'd have to explain to them what was going on.

"Caleb didn't say much. He helped Drew find the ring. Maddy was quiet until we got into the car. She hasn't stopped yelling at me ever since."

"Yelling at you? Why?"

"Well, yelling at me about Drew, I should say. She blames him for getting you all worked up and caring more about finding the ring than about helping you."

"Oh man," I said. "She must think Drew's the biggest jerk right now."

"Pretty much," Maddy said from the doorway. "First he treats you like crap, then he cares more about finding his ring than he does about you fainting, then he chases after Holly and leaves you on the floor. I'll tell you this, if Luke hadn't hit him when he did, I sure as hell would have."

"Wait, what?" I turned quickly to Luke. "You hit him?"

He hung his head, as if it had been a moment of weakness that he wasn't proud of.

"You should've seen it—it was beautiful," Maddy said with a giggle. "As soon as you threw the ring at him, Luke just turned and smoked him right in the jaw."

"Luke!" I scolded, although I felt a surge of love for him at the same time.

"I know I shouldn't have," he said, then added in a whisper, "but it's not like he feels it anyway."

I smiled and rolled my eyes at him.

"He was out of line," he added.

"I totally agree. I deserved it." Drew was standing in the doorway behind Maddy now. His hair was messy, his clothes dirty and sweat-stained, his jeans ripped in the knee.

Maddy swung around, fists raised.

"Settle down, tiny terror," he laughed.

"Drew, I have to tell you—I lost a lot of respect for you tonight," Maddy said, lowering her fists, but raising her chin.

"I know. I'm sorry." It didn't seem to bother him that he couldn't explain to her what was going on. "Did she say anything about what happened during her black-out?" His question was directed at Luke.

"No, we didn't get there yet. She just woke up. Just getting her bearings."

"Sarah," Drew said as he came toward me, "what did—"

"Please don't come near me right now."

Luke started to stand, but he didn't need to. Drew had stopped the moment the words left my mouth. Lines of shock and hurt painted his face.

"Sarah, I'm sorry, but—"

"Drew," I said, interrupting him again, "I'm not ready to talk about it."

"I know, but I—"

"Why do you keep saying 'but?'" Maddy demanded. "Can't you just apologize? What possible excuse could you give that justifies how you treated her tonight?"

Drew looked over his shoulder at Maddy, then back to me. Luke sat down again next to me and held my hand.

"I'm sorry," Drew finally said. "I only wanted you to hate me."

Maddy scoffed. "Well, congratulations. I think it worked." She threw her arms up and paced back to the door, waiting for Caleb to return.

"Why?" I whispered. "Why would you want that?"

He hung his head. "Because I know you feel torn between Luke and me."

"I do not!"

"Just listen to me." Drew glanced at Luke. "You feel guilty for wearing my ring because you still have feelings for me. So I—"

"You have some nerve!" I was trying to stand, but Luke held me down.

"So I wanted to make the decision easy for you. I hate seeing you so torn. I figured if you hated me, you wouldn't have an issue wearing my ring."

"You realize that pushing me away like that makes me *not* want to wear it at all, right?"

"Yeah, I see that now. It would've worked with the old Sarah, but this Sarah is a little more assertive, and a little more defiant than she was a few weeks ago."

Luke grinned.

"So what? You thought you could push me away like that and I'd just feel powerless and do whatever you told me to?"

"Pretty much."

I shook my head.

"You don't need to reprimand me for it, Sarah," Drew said. "Luke already did." Drew rubbed his jaw, indicating the place where Luke had hit him.

"If only it had really hurt," I mumbled, reminding

him that I knew he was immune to most pain in his world.

"I said I was sorry." Drew approached again. Luke watched for my consent, and I nodded my approval. He sat down next to me on the bed. "Sarah, I need to know. What did you see when you were unconscious? Where did you go?"

Maddy sneered from the doorway. "Are you kidding me? Did you just ask her that?"

Drew paid no attention to her. Luke appeared not to be concerned by her presence, either. He pulled a vial of yellow liquid from his back pocket and held it in his hand. Drew saw this and nodded his approval, but nothing happened.

I watched Maddy, her perplexed expression telling me that nothing about this night made sense to her.

"I don't remember anything," I said, honestly.

"Damnit!" Drew threw his fist into the wall. The plaster crumbled onto the floor.

"What does this mean?" I asked.

"Someone's messing with us!" Drew growled, thrusting his hands into his hair. He pushed himself off the bed and paced the length of the room.

"What the hell is going on?" Maddy demanded, coming into the room, but keeping her distance from Drew who looked angrier than I had ever seen him.

Having had enough lies and secrets, I blurted, "Someone wants to kill me. Someone from a dream world. Another dimension. They're trying to lure me to their world so they can kill me. But why"—I was looking at Luke now—"why wouldn't they have just killed me then?"

"I don't know!" Drew yelled before Luke could answer. "That's what we can't figure out. Maybe they intended to, but we gave you something to pull you out. What are they doing to you when you're blacked out? What are they saying to you? Telling you? *Think*, Sarah! THINK!"

"I can't!" I yelled. "I can't think! It hurts. My head hurts. I don't want to do this anymore, Drew! I don't want this life. I am done!" I tried to get up, but the pain in my head pulled me back to the bed. Luke had his arms around my shoulders.

"Holy hell! Someone has *got* to explain this to me," Maddy yelled.

"Okay," Drew said, pulling Maddy further into the room. "Where's Caleb?"

"Outside. The vomit made him sick. Why?"

"He can't be here for this. Sit down."

"I will not sit," she said, folding her arms across her chest. "And whatever you tell me, I'll just tell Caleb later. It's his right to know, too. We're all friends here."

"Sure," Drew said, not really caring. "If you can remember." Drew took the yellow vial from Luke's hand.

"Drink this."

"Why?"

"Because it will help. Just . . . just do it." Drew was agitated, which made Maddy drink faster. The vial was gone in a few seconds. Drew hugged her.

"Get your hands—" Maddy tried to protest, but before she could finish her sentence, she fell limp in Drew's arms.

"What the hell was that?" I shouted as Drew carried Maddy to a chair and propped her up in it.

"She'll be fine. She'll wake up in a minute and won't remember a thing."

"But why?"

"You said too much, Sarah. You can't go around telling everyone about us," Drew scolded.

"Why not? Maybe she could help."

Luke and Drew both shook their heads. "Not likely," Luke said.

"She may be small, but she's clever. Maybe it isn't a problem we need to solve with brute force; maybe we just need to outsmart them."

Drew looked at me as if that were the stupidest thing he had ever heard. Luke just took my hand. "Not these type of people, Sarah."

Maddy made a groaning noise in the chair and started to move.

Drew squatted next to me and whispered, "So you really don't remember anything?"

"I'm sorry, Drew, I don't."

Maddy yawned. "Oh, man. I must have dozed off. How long have we been here?"

I couldn't answer her. I was done with the lies. I pushed myself up off the bed and fought through the burning pain in my forehead.

"I see you're feeling better," she said as she came to my side. "Ew. What is that? Did you throw up?"

Did she really not remember?

"She did," Luke answered. "When she came to. Must be the knock on the head."

"She should really go see a doctor."

"I'm fine," I assured her. "I'm just going to go home to bed. Did you want to walk with me?"

"I'll take you home," Drew said.

"I got her," Luke countered.

Maddy laughed. "If you're just going to call it a night, I might head out for dinner with Caleb. We haven't eaten yet." Caleb walked into the room, as if in answer to his name.

"I'm ready to go eat if you are," Caleb agreed.

I nodded and smiled. "That's fine. I can walk myself home anyway. You guys can stay here," I said to Drew and Luke.

"Not happening," Drew said at the same time Luke

said, "Nice try."

AT MY FRONT door, Luke leaned in to kiss me while Drew looked away.

"Will you be okay?" Luke whispered into my ear as he held onto me.

"I'm fine."

"I can stay if you want. Just say the word."

"I need to be alone," I said, feeling a lump quickly form in my throat.

Luke's embrace weakened and he let me go. Drew was watching me now, pity in his eyes.

"I'm sorry, Sarah," Drew said.

I nodded. I wasn't sure if he was still apologizing for what he said earlier, or if it was something more. He had enough reasons.

I unlocked my door and pushed it open. The two guys that my world revolved around stood at the bottom of the front steps, both wearing looks of anguish and helplessness. It didn't have to be that way. Drew could've told me about the dream worlds years ago.

"Good night." I turned and went inside, leaving them to their misery.

WITH DREW'S RING back in place on my hand, I knew I wouldn't dream, but as I drifted off to sleep, I couldn't help but think about what it would be like to have a key like Drew and Luke. To be able to travel to different dream worlds and discover new things. I wondered if I were at Drew's house and I found his key, what would happen if I said "Etak" or another world. Would I be able to go? Or would it just be the bearer of the key that could make it work? Maybe only he could touch it. Maybe if I tried, I would get a shock, or burned. All these thoughts carried me into a dreamless sleep that was filled with wants, desires and adventurous creations of my overactive imagination.

Where would Drew even keep such a key? It must be in his room. I am lying on his bed now, as I have done many times before, waiting for him to get home from being with his dad. If only I had known back then what he was really up to. Where does he put his key when he's in the shower? In his nightstand? I am checking in his nightstand drawer now. Nothing but a few trinkets, a Bible and a notebook and pen. Hidden on his bookshelf, maybe? I am rummaging through his books, checking each one for a hidden compartment inside. Nothing unusual. Under his pillow? His pillow is neat, fluffed and hard, suggesting he has been too busy for rest. In his closet? His clothes are neatly pressed and hung meticulously. In a shirt pocket? His clothes smell so good. I pull one from the hanger and hold it to my face. Suddenly, I hear a noise. Someone is coming. I panic, and begin to run, but then I realize, I am just dreaming. Well, not really dreaming, but thinking. Imagining. Daydreaming. So I don't need to run, but I want to. I slip out his bedroom window and make my way back home. I'll find his key another day, and then I will use it to travel the worlds and discover their hidden secrets.

I sat up straight in my bed and checked the time. It was three in the morning. I was alone, shivering from the coldness of the room. Lucia wasn't next to me keeping me warm, but instead, she was pawing at my bedroom door, on the outside trying to get in. I opened the door and she came scurrying in, sniffed me incessantly and then ran directly to my bed and hopped in. A cold breeze encircled me, and I realized that the window was open a few inches, causing the curtains to move in and out in response to the wind's whisper. Slowly, I made my way to the window. Lucia whimpered. I looked back at her and hesitated before pushing the curtains aside. Lucia growled, which startled me so I slammed the window closed and ran back to my bed, diving in next to her furry body. I pulled my blankets over us and stayed quietly in the darkness with Lucia keeping me warm.

CHAPTER 20

Midnight Kiss

~ SARAH ~

THE DOORBELL WOKE me the next morning, but I figured it had to be far too early to be for me. I rolled over and buried my face into Lucia's fur while she kept on breathing deeply as if she hadn't heard a thing.

A minute later, my bedroom door opened. "What are you still doing in bed?" Maddy said, too loud for this hour in the morning.

"What time is it?" I groaned as she plunked herself down next to me and tried to pull the covers from my face. "Leave me alone," I complained.

"It's almost eleven o'clock. You need to get your ass out of bed."

"Eleven?" I sat upright and reached for my phone.

"Holy crap, it is."

"Yeah, I've been texting and calling you all morning. You must have your phone on silent, do you?"

"Yeah, sorry." I checked my list of notifications—three missed calls from Maddy (the first one from five o'clock in the morning), two from Drew, one from Luke, and numerous texts from each of them.

"Darlene said Luke was here earlier looking for you, too. She wouldn't let him up."

"Crap." I texted Luke right away.

LUKE

Today at 10:53am
I'm awake. Was sleeping. No dreams. All okay.

Then I copied and pasted the same message to Drew.

"Why were you calling me at five this morning?" I laughed as I scanned her texts.

"Couldn't sleep," she said quickly.

Her eyes were sunken and encased in dark circles, then my eyes darted to her necklace. "Were you with Caleb all night?"

Maddy laughed. "No!" She stood and walked to my mirror where she assessed her face. "Just have stuff on my mind, I guess." She widened her eyes and puckered her lips before applying another layer of lipstick. "I see you're still wearing Drew's ring."

"Yes," I answered, hoping this wasn't going to become a full-fledged discussion, or worse, lecture.

"Why even bother, Sarah? I mean Luke clearly likes you. And you clearly like him. Why can't you just let Drew go?"

"I don't know," I lied.

"To each his own, I guess." She tucked her lipstick back in her bag and sighed heavily. "Anyway, Holly is planning on meeting us at the mall in an hour."

I fell back on my pillow and groaned. "I forgot about that. Do we have to go?"

"I hear ya. She's already called me twice this morning to confirm, though."

"Okay, okay. I'll go get ready."

Luke texted back first.

LUKE

Today at 10:53am
I'm awake. Was sleeping. No dreams. All okay.

Today at 10:54am
Okay, babe. Hope you had a good sleep.

Then Drew . . .

DREW

Today at 10:53am
I'm awake. Was sleeping. No dreams. All okay.

Today at 10:54am
NP

No problem. That was typical Drew. Short. To the point. He couldn't care less.

I ignored Drew and replied to Luke.

LUKE

Today at 10:54am
Okay, babe. Hope you had a good sleep.

Today at 10:54am
*Going shopping with Holly and Maddy. *groan* Wish me luck.*

Today at 10:55am
Ha. I almost forgot about. Call me when you're done. We can meet you guys for dinner.

Today at 10:55am
Hoping not to be out that long,
but a late lunch sounds good.

Today at 10:56am
You'll have fun. Can't wait to
see you.

I read the words over and over again as my heart sang a tune of happiness and contentment.

LUKE

Today at 10:56am
You'll have fun. Can't wait to
see you.

Today at 10:56am
Me too.

I got out of the shower and rummaged through my closet for a decent outfit to wear shopping.

"Why is your room such a mess?" Maddy asked as she fixed her hair in my closet door mirror.

"Couldn't decide what to wear for dinner last night," I told her. "And was too *cranky* to be clean about it." I knew she would catch my sarcasm.

"That was pretty funny, though." Maddy snorted. "I love that Drew carries a granola bar around for you, too."

I picked up a few shirts from the floor and found a red shirt that didn't belong to me. Being a redhead with hair the colour of a pumpkin, red was not a colour I could pull off very well, so I just did not own a single red piece of clothing. But Drew did. And this was his shirt. Why was it on my floor?

I held it up in the mirror, studying it, trying to recall when Drew wore it last and why he would've left it at my house.

"You cannot wear that colour, Sarah," Maddy said, definitively.

"I know," I laughed. "It's Drew's. Just trying to re-member why it's here."

"Has he ever slept over?"

"No!" I laughed.

"Did you ever borrow it?"

"Why would I? It'd look hideous on me."

"Must have fallen out of his bookbag at some point. Anyway, hurry up and get ready, would ya?"

"Yeah, right." I threw the shirt into my hamper and continued to sift through my closet.

MADDY FOUND A dress fairly quickly. Teal was easily the best colour on her as it went so well with her blue eyes and blonde hair. It was a shorter dress, cut above her knees, which we decided made her legs look longer. She picked out a tiara to go with it, and we found a pair of white pumps that looked as though they were made for the dress. I had to admit that I was a bit envious of how beautiful she looked.

Four stores later, Holly decided on a pink dress, three inches shorter than Maddy's. It felt wrong even looking at the dress on the hanger, it was so small. Maddy tried to talk her out of it, suggesting it was too inappropriate, but Holly had her mind set on it. I was pretty sure she didn't care what colour it was, as long as it was the smallest dress in the mall.

"*Please* come to the prom," Maddy whined as Holly went back into the changing room after parading around the store in her dress for nearly half an hour. "I can't be stuck hanging out with her and Drew all night."

I grinned. "I just don't really want to."

"Why not? You've always secretly wanted to go to prom."

"I don't know," I said, picking at a thread hanging from my shirt. "It's hard being around Drew and Holly, you know?"

Maddy nodded and looked down at the floor.

"I mean, I'm glad he's happy, and I really like Luke, but I still feel jealous. I don't know why. I shouldn't."

"Jealousy is a part of everyone," Maddy said.

"But it's not a good quality, and I don't like the feeling."

Maddy hesitated before touching Drew's ring on my

finger. "Why?" she asked. "Why haven't you given it back?"

I shrugged. "It's a piece of Drew, you know?"

She nodded, sympathetically. "I'm sorry that you have to watch him and Holly do this stupid couple thing. I say wear it as long as you want. Keep it forever if you have to. So long as *she* doesn't get it."

I smiled. Did I need to tell her that once Luke's ring arrived, I would give Drew's back? Or would that just confuse her even more?

"Do you think Caleb will love my dress?" she asked after a minute.

"Oh, he's going to love it alright."

"I really like him. I think . . . I think I really love him."

"He seems like a good match for you." I was referring to the fact that he was quiet, and supported every crazy idea and outburst that she had.

As Maddy talked about all the things she loved about Caleb, my eyes wandered the store, then carried me out the door and into the window display across the hall at the most beautiful yellow dress I had seen all day. I gasped.

"What is it?" Maddy asked.

"That dress," I said, making my way out of the store and across the hall.

Maddy followed. "Sarah, this is an old lady's store," she said, disapprovingly. "Actually, correction—this is an old lady's second hand store."

The dress was a floor-length, sleeveless design in a vintage, pale yellow material that flowed from the waist to the floor in one elegant movement. The bodice was pulled together with an embroidered lace that held the mid-section with class and valour. The neckline dipped discreetly, leaving everything to the imagination. And it was the most beautiful, classic dress I had ever seen.

"It's ugly," Maddy said, holding nothing back.

I sighed, realizing that it didn't matter how beautiful the dress was in my eyes, it wasn't a prom-worthy dress. Not in this era, anyway.

"Yeah, guess it looks different up close," I said, turning around.

"I'm starving," Maddy complained. "I'm going to text Caleb and have them meet us now. I think Holly's finally done."

THE GUYS WERE waiting at Boston Pizza when we arrived a half hour later. Luke stood up and greeted me with a hug and kiss.

"How'd it go?" he asked, a sly grin on his face.

"I survived."

"So my dress is pink," Holly chirped as she slid into the booth next to Drew, "which means *you'll* be wearing a pink tie." She touched Drew's lips with her index finger.

"Pink," Drew repeated, and it took everything in me not to laugh.

"You'll look so hot."

"Pink," he repeated.

"Is that a problem?" Holly pouted.

"No, not a problem at all," Drew assured her. "Did Sarah help you pick it out?" he glanced at me, but I avoided his eyes.

"I did," I said proudly. "I know how much you like *pink*."

Luke squeezed my leg. "Did you find a dress?"

"I did not," I said. "I was thinking dinner and a movie for us." I puckered my lips and he brought his to mine.

Drew cleared his throat and I realized that we had an audience. Well not a full audience—Holly was busy watching how her fingers looked as they mingled with Drew's.

"Oh, Drew," I said, suddenly remembering I had something of his. "I have your red shirt at my house."

"My red shirt," he thought aloud.

"It's a faded red v-neck . . . a small hole near the bottom." *Ringing a bell?*

"Yeah, I know what shirt it is, just trying to figure out why it's at your house."

"I know. I was confused, too. It was on my floor this morning but I have no idea why."

Drew and Luke exchanged a strange but meaningful

look that they didn't care to elaborate on.

"Let's order," Luke said.

AS I FELL asleep that night, Luke was on my mind. Luke, my sensitive, strong, loving, caring, supportive boy-friend. The guy who still loved me regardless of how I continued to prove my affections for Drew. And what did that exchange between the two of them mean at Boston Pizza? When I told Drew that I had his shirt at my house, why did that mean something to both of them? My eyes were heavy and my thoughts were all mine now. The voice in my head spoke to me, as if lulling me to sleep.

I'm in Drew's closet now, returning his red shirt. Hanging it up where it belongs. I do not want a piece of him in my house. No, I am Luke's. Luke is mine. Drew does not belong here with us. I smooth the fabric of his shirt on the hanger and turn to go, but I want so badly to see Luke. Luke, who has to go back to Etak every night, feels so far away from me. Because he is. I search Drew's room for his key again, dangling from the black cord that I know he is wearing around his neck, but for some reason, I still need to search. For a chance to see Luke. Kiss him with no one else watching. Hold him. Be with him. But now the door opens and Drew walks in. He is standing in front of me now, breathless and aware. He is handsome and tall. He's not Luke, but he is familiar and comfortable. He is not surprised to see me here. I have to stop to catch my breath, as this is what he always does to me. He comes to me, asks what I'm looking for, but I only see his lips moving. His words aren't registering and I can't resist the temptation. I reach up and press my mouth to his and feel his lips react. He wants me, too. I know I'm imagining this, but I still feel guilty. I am enjoying it. He asks me again why I'm there. I tell him I miss him, although it's Luke I really miss. It's Luke's lips I want on mine. I convince myself of this as we walk.

Suddenly I was no longer dreaming—imagining. I was outside and the bitterness in the air was making me shiver. I was being carried over someone's shoulder, my head hitting his broad back with every step he took. I stifled a cry when I heard him start talking, but then I recognized his voice.

"It's the third time this week," Drew said. He paused and then added, "Yeah, I think it could've been her the first time, too."

"Drew?" I said, squirming in his arms. He let me down, but held onto my arm with one hand, the phone to his ear with the other. "What's going on?"

Drew slid his phone back in his pocket and smiled. "You were sleepwalking."

"What?" *Sleepwalking? I've never done that before!*

"Yeah, it's no big deal," he said. "You just came to my house, knocked on my door, and I walked you back."

"I walked to your house?" I look down and saw, with mild embarrassment, that I was wearing my green flannel pyjamas with white stripes. "Why would I do that?"

"Sleepwalk? It happens sometimes."

"But . . . but what if I went somewhere else? This is scary, Drew!" I wrapped my arms around myself to still the shudders.

"Relax, Sarah. You wouldn't have gone anywhere else."

"How can you be so sure?"

He looked at me tentatively. "Sarah, I'm the keeper. Nothing happens in sleep that I don't know about."

"So, what? Did you *want* me to go there?"

He slid off his coat and put it over my shoulders, then shrugged.

My body was heating up, but not from Drew's jacket. Had this been his idea of a joke? Luring me to his house so he could see what I would say to him in my sleep? "Did you *lure* me there?"

"What? No!" he said, appalled that I would make such an accusation.

"Then what?"

"You lured yourself there," he said in an exhale, a tiny smile forming at the corner of his mouth.

"What do you mean?" I didn't like what he was suggesting.

"Well, I think," he began, watching me wryly, "that you miss . . . *us* . . . and that's why you're sleepwalking."

I scoffed at this theory, but didn't dare look at him for

fear I'd blush. "But I'm wearing your ring. I'm not dreaming."

"You don't have to dream to sleepwalk. It's your body's needs and desires that make you sleepwalk."

At that, I donned a crimson red and turned away. How could he suggest that my body wanted him? What did I say or do when I got to his door? Maybe I gave him good reason to believe this.

"Did I . . . uh . . . say anything?"

"What?" he said, continuing his slow steps toward my house.

"When I was at your house. Did I talk to you at all?" I almost didn't want to know the answer, and I pretended to be more interested in the stars in the sky than what he had to say next.

"Not much," he said, much to my relief. "A few things, but mostly mumbles."

I nodded as if I suspected as much. "What if . . . what if it happens again?"

"Then I'll take you back to your house . . . again. You'll be fine," Drew promised. "It's all good. Luke and I will take care of you."

"Thank you, Drew. You're a good friend."

He took my hand in his and squeezed. By the time we reached my front door, Luke was there. Drew let my hand slip from his as I ran to Luke.

He lifted me into his arms. "Are you okay?"

A flood of tears poured out of me at the sound of his voice.

"It's okay," he soothed.

"She's fine," Drew said.

"What is happening to me? What is going on?"

Luke's eyes flashed to Drew, and then he took in a deep breath. "You have a shadow in you."

"A what?"

"Luke," Drew warned, "she doesn't need to know this."

I silenced him with my hand. "Stop babying me, Drew." I turned back to Luke. "Go on."

"A shadow," Luke continued. "It's like a demonic presence." He watched me closely for my reaction. "They're rare, but dangerous. They usually attack your mind, causing mental illness, but we didn't notice any of that in you, so we didn't pick up on it right away."

"So, it's in me like right now?"

Luke nodded.

"Well, how do we get it out?" There was a slight panic to my voice, but I tried to keep calm for Drew's sake. I didn't want him to think that he was right to have kept it from me.

"We don't yet," Drew said before Luke could offer an answer.

"What do you mean *yet*?" I pressed.

"It's too dangerous to extract," Drew said. "You could

die. We wait it out. We find out who's controlling it, then we . . ." His voice trailed off.

"Then we *what*?"

"Once we know what world the shadow came from, we have to go there and extract it. It's the safest way for you."

My surroundings began to sway, but I held firm to my composure. "So, there's a demon inside of me and I can't do anything about it."

"It's not a demon," Drew said, frustration on his tongue. "It's a shadow."

"Oh, sorry, a *shadow*," I said sarcastically.

"It's worse than a demon," Drew muttered.

"Okay, so why is it in me? What's it doing if it's not making me mentally ill?"

"It's controlling you in a subconscious state." Luke glanced at Drew. "That's why you've been sleepwalking."

"What do you mean *been* sleepwalking?"

"This is the third time. The first time was when Drew's house was ransacked. The second time was when you took his red shirt, and then . . . tonight."

I shook my head. "But why? Why would I do that?"

"Whoever implanted the shadow has you searching for something at Drew's."

"So I'm not sleepwalking from my own . . . ambitions?" I asked, my eyes not meeting Drew's. He had said my needs and desires led me to him. Was he lying? Was it the shadow that brought me to him?

Luke shook his head. "No. The shadow is controlling you."

"For what?" My heart pounded. What had I been doing?

"That part I don't know," Luke said, but I could tell there was more he wanted to say, and if it weren't for Drew's glaring, perhaps he would have. "What do you remember?" he asked.

"She doesn't remember anything," Drew answered.

Luke shot him a warning look. "*Sarah*, what do you remember?"

Why would Drew say I didn't remember anything? He hadn't even asked me himself if I remembered anything. And then I realized—I hadn't just gone to his door and knocked. I had been in his room. I went in his closet. I returned the red shirt . . . and I was looking for his necklace . . . and . . . I kissed him! I gasped.

"What is it? What do you remember?" Luke pressed. Drew groaned and looked down, shoving his hands deep in his pockets.

He *let* me kiss him. He didn't try to stop me. He kissed me back. How could he do that to me? Was his sole purpose in life to mess with me?

"Sarah?" Luke urged.

"I was in Drew's room," I said. Drew flinched. "I was

looking for something."

"What were you looking for?" Luke asked.

I lowered my gaze, embarrassed that I was actually admitting all of this. "His key," I said.

"Do you know why?" he asked carefully.

"Because I wanted to see you. I wanted to go to Etak."

Luke sighed and sat down, pulling me with him. "So you were looking for his necklace."

"Yes."

"And then?"

Drew rocked back and forth on his feet, humming softly to himself.

"And then I . . . I . . ." How could I tell him? How could I admit that I kissed Drew? How could I crush Luke like that? Maybe I didn't have to. Maybe I could pretend that was all I remembered.

"I kissed her," Drew said before I could decide how to answer.

"What?" Luke stood up faster than I could hold him down. "You kissed her while she was *sleeping*? You son of a—"

"Wait!" I shouted before Luke's fist reached Drew's face. Luke kept his fist raised, but paused long enough to hear my explanation. "Drew," I whispered, "why would you say that?" Why would he want to hurt Luke? Did he want us to break up? How could he be so cruel?

"Because it's true," Drew said, and then Luke's fist

connected with his face. Hard. Drew fell back. He knew it was coming and he made no attempt to stop it. "I deserved that." He stood up and cracked his jaw back into place. "But," he said, holding out his hand, "I only deserved the one. If you hit me again, Luke, I'll be hitting back."

"I'll take my chances." Luke hit him again, square in the nose.

"Luke, no!" I screamed as Drew came back at him, tackling him to the ground.

"Drew, stop this!" I shouted again. Luke got on top of Drew and pushed him down before backing off.

"Lay one finger on her again without her permission and I'll—"

"I got it," Drew said, his breath heavy.

I stared at both of them, angry at Drew for upsetting Luke to the point of combat, and for fighting him back. Drew, although sporting a bloody nose and swollen eye, at least couldn't feel the pain from each fist, but Luke wasn't immune to pain here.

Drew wiped the blood from his face and the swelling in his eye was already going down. Blood still trickled from Luke's mouth. I touched his lip, wiping the blood away. "I'm sorry," I said.

"It's not your fault," he said.

"But it was, I—"

"It wasn't," Drew interrupted. "It was my fault. I

shouldn't have kissed you."

I saw the hurt in Luke's eyes and couldn't stand it. I was so angry with Drew for telling him that we kissed. "Drew, go home," I said.

Drew looked down, but didn't argue.

"Luke?" I took his hand in mine.

He softened when he saw my face, wet with tears. "Yes?"

"Will you stay with me tonight?"

"I will." He turned to Drew. "You heard her—go home."

"Sarah," Drew started, but he didn't finish. His gaze fell to my necklace. There was a deep agony in his eyes that I tried to ignore, and then he stalked away, frustration evident with every step he took.

CHAPTER 21

The Ring

~ SARAH ~

LUKE WAS GONE when I woke the next morning, though his place next to me was still warm. I ran my hand across the crinkled sheet and smiled. He had held me all night. At first I thought it would be impossible to fall asleep with my heart thudding and my mind racing, but only seconds later it was morning and Luke was gone. I tried not to begrudge the fact that he had business to take care of back in his own world. I knew he'd be back, and I wasn't wrong—before lunch, the doorbell rang and George announced that Luke was there to see me. We spent the day together watching movies and cuddling on the couch. He had dinner with our family, and George even said that he liked "the young chap." Drew called twice, but I ignored it. He needed to know when to keep his mouth shut and when to mind his own business. I never ignored Drew for very long, so shutting him out for the whole day would send a clear message.

When my parents were fast asleep, I crept downstairs and let Luke in so he could stay with me while I slept again. I felt better knowing that he was with me—knowing I wouldn't sleepwalk to Drew's again.

When I woke in the morning, the sheets next to me were warm again. The plan was for him to meet me at school in just over an hour, so that kept me going. I wasn't looking forward to first class—Math with Drew. Why did he have to keep throwing me under the bus? Why had he told Luke about our kiss? Why would he say hurtful things to me? Why did he feel the need to flirt with Holly right in front of me?

"Hey," Drew said when I walked into the classroom and took my seat next to him. "You still mad at me?"

I shrugged. Of course I was.

"I'm sorry. I thought I was doing you a favour."

"A favour? How do you figure telling my boyfriend that I kissed you was a *favour*? Do explain this one, Drew." I flipped open my math book a little too hard.

"I didn't tell him that you kissed me. I told him that I kissed you."

"Oh, sorry. Details." The sarcasm was thick.

"Sarah, I knew you were going to tell him about the

kiss, so I took the blame. That way, he would be mad at me instead of you."

My hasty movements softened as I considered what he had just said.

"I know you think I ousted you, but really, I was trying to help you."

"I wasn't going to tell him," I said, picking up my movements again.

"Yeah, right. Sarah Marley, you do not know how to lie."

I clenched my jaw. Did I know how to lie? Would I have lied to him? Would I have been able to keep that from him?

"Look, I'm sorry," Drew said, interrupting my thoughts. "But I wouldn't change how it played out. Well, maybe I would've changed the fact that you asked him to stay the night with you."

I grinned. "Nothing happened."

He grunted his disbelief. "Where's your necklace?"

I pulled my necklace from inside my shirt. "Happy now? I didn't give it to him."

His features settled slightly, but he wasn't done being sour. "Did he stay again last night?"

"He did," I confirmed. "I don't want to be alone while I'm sleepwalking. I'm scared."

Drew chuckled. "Scared you'll kiss me again?"

"Shush!" I said. "That didn't happen!"

"Sorry." He hid his cheeky grin.

"Well, thank you, I guess. For *helping* me, as you say."

"No problem."

"And I'm sorry that I kissed you," I added in a whisper. "I don't know where that came from."

"It's okay. It was nice."

I blushed and played with my hair until it covered the side of my face from his view. "It was meant for Luke."

"Ouch," he said. And then, "He's a lucky guy."

I HAD EXPECTED Luke to catch up with me in the hallway before I reached Biology, but he hadn't. I even walked extra slow, anticipating his hand sliding into mine and his warm kiss on my cheek. Butterflies swarmed with expectation, but soon died off when I entered the classroom alone. He wasn't in his seat, either. Just Holly, watching me idly.

"Hey, Holly," I said as I took my seat.

"Where's Luke?" she asked, suddenly aware that I was alone. "Is there trouble with you two?"

"No," I said quickly.

She let out a small sigh of relief. "Oh good." Her eyes traced a line from my face down my arm and stopped at my finger adorning Drew's ring.

Ahhh . . . makes sense now.

My knee bobbed restlessly as I watched the door for Luke, but he didn't come before Mr. Chase closed the

310

door and took attendance. When he reached Luke's name and there was silence, Holly poked me with her pencil.

"Where's Lover Boy?"

I shrugged, trying to keep the worry from my face. Maybe it was nothing. Maybe Drew had just met up with him in the hall and they discussed my sleepwalking. Maybe that was it.

DREW

Today at 10:35am
Have you seen Luke?

Today at 10:35am
No. All ok?

Today at 10:36am
He isn't in bio yet.

Today at 10:36am
It's fine. Don't worry.

Don't worry. The story of my life. *Don't worry. Just relax. Everything's fine.* Everything is *not* fine. I *do* worry. I *can't* relax!

A tiny knock sounded at the door and I nearly jumped out of my seat. The doorknob turned and Luke slowly came into the room.

"Sorry I'm late, Mr. Chase," he said as I processed his return. His arrival. His presence.

311

"Luke!" I jumped out of my chair and nearly ran to him, relieved that he was okay. As soon as I realized what I had done, though, I sat back down as my face reddened.

Luke smiled from ear to ear, not taking his eyes off me as he walked straight to my desk and knelt down on one knee. "Sarah Marley, will you be my girlfriend?" Between his finger and thumb, his brand new school ring shined.

My eyes flooded with tears as I threw my arms around his neck.

"I'm sorry," he whispered into my hair. "I didn't mean to worry you."

The class erupted in applause around us while I slid off Drew's ring, buried it into my pocket, and Luke slid his ring onto my finger.

"Of course I'll be your girlfriend." I kissed him softly. "I already am."

Mr. Chase cleared his throat. "Very cute. Very cute. Well done, Luke, but if you could take your seat, I'd like to get this class started."

Luke stood up, nodded to Mr. Chase, winked at me, and then took his seat.

My smile was permanent. No matter how hard I tried to return my face to normal, it just wouldn't go. Even though his ring was an exact replica of Drew's ring . . . and Caleb's . . . and every other guy's ring at Xavier High, I couldn't take my eyes off of it. It was perfect. It was new.

It was Luke's. It was . . . mine.

"YOU MIGHT AS well just hand it over now," Holly said only seconds after the bell rang.

"What are you talking about?" I tried to ignore her burning stares on my back as she waited for me to load my books back into my backpack.

"Drew's ring," she said matter-of-factly.

I turned and looked up at her smug face, wide eyes, and expecting smile. Luke stood behind her, watching me carefully and analyzing my hesitation.

I pulled Drew's ring from my pocket and held it out, but then changed my mind. I couldn't. It was like a magnetic force that would not allow me to give his ring to her. To give *him* to her. I looked to Luke for assistance, but his face was sorrowful. Disappointment? Hurt?

"It's not my decision to make," I said, stuffing the ring back into my pocket. "If Drew wants you to have it, he should be the one to give it to you."

"He already said he wants me to wear it and you know that."

I shrugged. "Maybe he does. Maybe he just said that to stop your incessant whining."

Holly gasped. And if I couldn't be sure, so did Luke.

"Sorry," I said, hanging my head a little and feeling more than ashamed for stooping to her level. "I'm okay with you having it, Holly. But I really think Drew would want to be the one to give it to you. Maybe he has a special way he wants to . . . present it." I tried to sound sweet, referring to Luke's presentation of his ring, but the words sounded a bit sour. To my ears, anyway.

"Yes, I'm sure he does, actually." Holly didn't seem to notice. "Thanks, Sarah. Yes, give it back to him right away so he can give it to me over lunch."

I raised my eyebrows for a second and smiled, giving her the message that I understood. After she left, I let myself fall into Luke. He held me in his firm arms for a minute and we didn't move.

"You sure you're okay with Holly having Drew's ring?" His voice was tender and careful.

"Of course I am." But my lie did not reach my eyes; I could tell by his smile that did not reach his. "I mean, I don't like her, but if that's what Drew really wants, then that's up to him."

He nodded. "It is."

"It just kind of hurts," I said, without regard for how this would sound. I trusted Luke. I knew he would understand. He would forgive me. "It just hurts that he never wanted me like that. I loved Drew. I would've done anything for him at one point, and he never paid me any mind. But now . . . *she* gets everything."

My heart sank. Had I really just admitted that to him? Luke tightened his hold around me and his soft lips rested on my head, letting me know he wasn't angry.

"Drew loves you," he said, and I could tell it pained him to admit this. "He would still choose you, if he could."

"What do you mean?"

"I can't figure out for the life of me why, but Drew always chose to keep you at arm's length. Maybe he knew he couldn't protect you fully if you were his girlfriend. I don't know. I think now that he sees you and me together, he's just bitter that he never jumped first. He's jealous. That's all, Sarah. Trust me—he cares about you ten times more than he could even pretend to care about Holly."

It had to have taken a lot for Luke to admit this . . . and to *me* of all people. It made me love him all the more for it. I pulled away from him and stood on my tiptoes to reach his lips with mine.

I wanted to tell him that I loved him. I wanted to hear how it would sound and see his expression as he heard me say it, but I didn't want to get hurt. He still wasn't a hundred percent real to me and I was so afraid that at any moment I would wake up from this perfect dream and once again be alone.

THE LUNCH BELL rang and as we were heading toward the arboretum, I caught sight of Drew's blonde hair ahead in the foyer.

"I'll meet you at the lunch table," I said to Luke as I

reached for Drew's ring inside my pocket.

Luke squeezed my hand. "Good luck."

I watched Luke leave and the further he got away from me, the weaker and unsure I felt. But I had to do this. I had to return Drew's ring. It wasn't mine to keep. I had Luke's now.

"Drew?" I said as I touched his back. He had been talking to two guys that I recognized from the football team.

Drew spun around. "Hey, you." He turned back to the guys. "I'll catch you boys later." We started walking together. "What's up?"

"Wanna go outside?" I asked, leading the way to the front doors.

"Sure, yeah. Is everything alright?" He stopped by the front garden and pulled me down to sit next to him. The sun was warm and comforting.

"It's totally fine," I said, feeling the weight of Luke's ring on my finger. "In fact, everything's great. Luke's ring came in today, so I wanted to give yours back to you." I held up his ring between us. He just looked at it.

"It's okay," I said. "I'm already wearing Luke's."

He nodded, still hesitating to take it.

"I mean, you don't have to give it to Holly if you don't want to, but I can't keep it. I don't have a reason to." My eyes stayed fixed on the ring.

"How did it feel to take it off?" His voice was deep,

carving the words into my soul as he spoke.

How did it feel? Like I was ripping him from me. Like I was saying goodbye to the last piece of Drew that I held. It was like closing the door on a chapter in my life and knowing that I made a choice.

"I have no reason to keep it," I reiterated, refusing to tell him how much it hurt to give it back.

"That's not what I meant," he said, smiling slightly. "I meant when you took off my ring, did you feel anything before you put Luke's on? And do you feel different now? Is his ring working the same as mine?"

Oh . . . how did I *feel*? Physically. Embarrassment only lasted for a few seconds over the misunderstanding—I thought he wanted to know how I felt about letting him go; he actually just wanted to know about my physical symptoms in response to removing the ring of protection—but relief quickly washed over me, and I was happy to finally share my symptoms with someone. It had been bothering me since it happened. In the five seconds that spanned from when I took Drew's ring off and when Luke slid his ring on, the room had spun viciously, my head was light and hazy, and my stomach filled with nausea. But then Luke slid his ring on and the symptoms completely evaporated. I hadn't wanted to ruin the moment by telling Luke how I felt, and really, was it important anyway? Luke had enough to worry about—he didn't need to hear about my physical reaction when I wasn't wearing Drew's ring. But now that Drew was asking, I had no reason to keep it to myself. I could share it now. Share my fear and uncertainty of what was happening to me without the intervention of this piece of metal around my finger. This confirmed that when I took Drew's ring off at the restaurant (and threw it at him, apparently), it wasn't frustration, fatigue and famine that made me faint, it was the absence of the ring of protection.

"It was weird," I started, monitoring the words carefully as they threatened to rush out of my mouth. "It was only a few seconds, but I swear I thought I was going to pass out. I was completely weak and nauseous and dizzy all at the same time."

Drew's jaw clenched as I spoke. "I was afraid of that," he said. "The shadow is trying to pull you into a blackout. Whoever is behind all of this can only get updates from the shadow when you're unconscious. That ring is the only thing keeping you safe. That's why you blacked out on Friday night at the restaurant when you took the ring off."

"So when I blackout, the shadow is giving these people updates on . . . what?"

Drew shrugged. "Anything that could help them get what they want. They have you searching for something at my place. My concern is, I don't know how long they'll keep looking before they give up."

"That'd be a good thing, right?"

Our eyes met and a chill went up my spine. It wouldn't be a good thing. If they decided I was useless, then they would kill me.

"You have to make damn sure that ring doesn't come off until I solve this thing, okay?"

"Okay," I promised. "Do you know anything yet?"

He shook his head. "Nothing yet. But I won't give up, Sarah. I promise you that."

"And do you know *why* yet? Like, why me?"

"I assume someone is trying to offset the balance of Earth, knowing that if anything were to happen to you, both Luke and I would be angry and vengeful and careless. And that would help ensure Earth continues on a path to darkness." He narrowed his eyes into the distance, deep in thought.

"So someone actually thinks that they can do that much damage to Earth by hurting me? That's insane. Don't they know you don't love me? Why aren't they after Holly?"

He looked at me again, his eyes tunnelling into mine. "Do you honestly think that I don't love you?"

And my breath ceased.

"Sarah, if I could *stop* loving you, maybe things would be different, but I can't, so—"

"But Holly."

"Yeah, Holly."

"And Luke."

"Yeah, him."

"I love Luke."

"I know you do."

We were only inches from each other now. How we got closer during this completely awkward exchange was beyond me. I pulled away. "I have to go. Luke's waiting."

"Yeah." He held up his ring. "Thanks for this."

"Yeah. Thank you for . . . lending it to me."

"Anytime."

I hurried off to the arboretum, leaving Drew behind with a piece of my heart in his hands.

I FLUNG OPEN the door to the lunch room and my eyes rested on Luke. He stood the second he saw me and came right to me. I didn't need to say anything, he just folded me in his arms and held me there. He knew it would be hard for me to give Drew's ring back. He knew I would need him to understand and forgive me for the feelings that still lingered for Drew. And he did.

"Come get something to eat," he said, moving me to the table. "I got pizza for you. Is that cool?"

I nodded. "Thank you."

I sat down across from Maddy who was hunched over eating her sandwich.

"You okay?" I asked as I took a bite of my own lunch. The pizza was still hot and my stomach was immediately grateful.

Maddy nodded as she watched me bring my pizza to my mouth.

"You want some?"

She shook her head. I looked to Caleb, who had an expression of impatience about him. Had they been fighting before we arrived?

"So," I said, trying to brighten the mood, "Luke's ring came in today." I displayed my hand so they could get a good look at my new Xavier High ring, which looked exactly the same as Drew's without the minor wear and tear.

Maddy dropped her sandwich and snatched my hand. "This is . . . Luke's ring?" she asked, a new interest in her voice. "Where's Drew's ring? Did you give it back?"

I pulled my hand from hers, unnerved by her peculiar interest. "I did," I confirmed. But as I studied her, I noticed, for the first time today, her face. Dark, puffy circles cradled her tiny, tired eyes. Her skin was paler than normal, and she sat with a hunch that told me she was hardly awake or aware. "What the hell is wrong with you? You look exhausted."

"You know that's just a polite way of telling someone they look like shit, right?" Maddy mumbled.

I nodded. She wasn't wrong.

"She hasn't slept in three days," Caleb said before attacking his sandwich with an angry bite. Luke and I watched him for a moment, his eyebrows pressed down in an irritated fashion.

"Why?" I finally asked.

"Why don't you tell them, Maddy?" Caleb said, his annoyance prevalent.

"Give it up, Caleb," Maddy scolded, and Caleb apologized with a nod and continued on his sandwich. "It's not a big deal. I haven't been able to sleep well, is all."

"Any reason?" Luke asked and I could tell he was processing his own list of possible reasons.

Maddy shrugged.

"Nightmares," Caleb said. Maddy glared at him, but he continued anyway. "I've been telling her she needs to go see someone about it or get some sleeping pills or something. It's clearly affecting her in a bad way."

"Nightmares about what?" Luke and I both asked.

"I'm fine!" Maddy shouted as she stood up and threw her lunch back into her bag. "It's nothing. Forget it." She turned quickly and left before I could convince her otherwise. Caleb quickly followed, passing Drew on his way out.

"What's going on there?" Drew asked as he took Maddy's place across from us.

"Maddy's been having some nightmares, apparently," Luke said nonchalantly, but I caught his wordless exchange with Drew.

"About?" Drew asked, also pretending not to care.

"Dunno. She didn't want to talk about it."

"I'll look into it tonight," Drew finished before Holly left her table of friends and headed our way. She slid in next to Drew and ran her fingers through the back of his hair. I focused on my pizza slice and Luke's hand on my thigh.

"Oh yeah, so I've got something for you," Drew said as he pulled his school ring off his finger. Holly gasped and threw her hands over her mouth.

"Really?" she said, as if he were actually asking her to marry him. "Are you like *officially* asking me out, Drew?"

Drew swallowed and smiled at the same time. "Yes."

She took his face in her hands and kissed him on the lips. He was caught by surprise, but after a few seconds, his eyes closed and he kissed her back. Drew was kissing Holly. Drew. My Drew.

Snap out of it, Sarah!

I looked to Luke who was holding back a grin. "Walk?" he asked.

"I'd love one." I took his hand and we left just as Drew and Holly were coming up for air.

"Where are you going?" Drew asked.

"For a walk. We'll see you guys later," I answered through the lump gathering in my throat.

When we were in the hall, Luke said, "You did well.

That must have been hard for you."

"Just a little."

He led us outside.

"I'm sorry," I said. "I shouldn't be admitting this stuff to you."

"What? You should lie to me about it? Sarah, if we can't tell each other this stuff, what do we have?"

"True."

"I'd rather hear the painful truth than pretty lies."

"I'm so glad." I breathed a sigh of relief. "Because I'm a terrible liar."

"Yes. Yes, you are."

IT HAD BEEN a long day. My exhaustion was, no doubt, in part due to sleepwalking and spending the rest of my sleeping hours in Luke's arms, trying not to fall asleep. But the emotional turmoil of giving Drew's ring back and watching him move on without me could also have had something to do with my exhaustion. Regardless, the last class of the day was long, and I could not wait for it to be over. Maddy obviously felt the same as she had her head down on her desk on the other side of the room. Her book was propped open beside her, but she was fooling no one—her eyes were already closed. How could they think assigning *reading* was a good idea for the last class on a Monday? My eyes were struggling to stay focused on the pages in front of me, and each word blurred in and out, burning my eyes. Luke sat behind me, nudging me every few minutes to make sure I didn't fall asleep like Maddy.

Suddenly, an ear-piercing scream woke me from my stupor. Maddy's head was pressed to her desk and both of her hands were gripping the sides. Her eyes were tightly closed, and her face was blood red as she screeched at the top of her lungs.

"NO! PLEASE NOOOO!" She inhaled sharply. "WATCH OUT, SARAH!!"

CHAPTER 22

Maddy's Nightmare

~ SARAH ~

BEFORE I COULD react, Luke was there beside her, waking her. He shook her and she immediately bolted upright, her face white with panic and eyes wide with terror. She gripped Luke's shoulders and searched the room fearfully.

"Sarah!" she cried. "Where's Sarah?!"

I jumped from my seat, thawed by the sound of my name, and ran to Maddy. I crouched beside her. "I'm here, Maddy. I'm here. I'm okay."

Maddy clung to me, sobbing into my shoulder, her wails being carried out of the classroom into the halls.

Mrs. Watson was at our side now. She placed a hand on Maddy's shoulder. "Are you okay, Maddy?"

"She's fine," Luke assured her. "She fell asleep. Had a nightmare."

"It was *real!*" Maddy sobbed uncontrollably. "Sarah, you're going to die!"

A few gasps were heard around the room. Luke stood up quickly and I looked to him for reassurance. His eyes were wide with fear, like Maddy's. It wasn't reassuring.

"Maddy, I'm alive. I'm right here, sweetie," I said, a small quake to my voice.

"Let's get her out of here," Luke said, pulling me to my feet. He helped Maddy up and we both carried her to the hallway.

"We'll take her to the nurse," I said to Mrs. Watson over my shoulder. "She's really hot. Probably a fever." She nodded and dismissed us.

Once in the hallway, Luke closed the door to the classroom and set Maddy on the floor. "Maddy, look at me. You need to tell me exactly what happened."

Maddy was breathing normally again, but still clinging to me.

"It's okay, Mad," I soothed. "Nothing is going to happen to me."

Maddy shook her head, eyes wide as they held mine. "Sarah, this isn't the first time I've had this dream. I can't sleep anymore. It wakes me every night and I'm too afraid to go back to sleep."

"But it's just a dream," I said again, trying to keep the

shake from my voice.

"But it's not," she said again, her voice lighter and more calm, but accurate. "It's so vivid. It's so *real*."

Luke stiffened at this comment. If Maddy remembered her dream so vividly, then was it possible she was supposed to? The keeper didn't put a memory fog on her because he wanted her to remember it? Luke's eyebrows came down and he watched Maddy carefully. "What was your dream, Maddy?"

"It's the exact same dream every time. I'm lost in the woods and there's all these things after me, but I can't find my way out. I'm just going around and around in circles. Then this . . . guy dressed all in black with a black hood finds me and he . . . he wants me to do something for him, but I won't . . . I can't . . . and he said he'll kill me unless I do—"

"What does he ask you to do?" I pressed.

Her eyes slowly found mine. "He . . . wants me to steal Drew's ring."

Luke's head snapped up. "His school ring?" he asked, though we both knew that it was.

Maddy nodded while goosebumps covered my arms. "I know it doesn't make any sense, but he's adamant that I'll keep having nightmares until I somehow take the ring from Sarah. And every time I have the nightmare he's angrier because she's still wearing the ring. Each time I wake up, I'm determined that I need to take it from her.

I'm obsessed with it. I'm almost entranced by the thought. But the longer I'm awake, I'm able to convince myself that it was just a dream and it's stupid." Maddy sniffled and hugged herself tighter. "Then this last nightmare, he decides he's done waiting. And I see him go to Sarah's house and . . ." — she began to sob again — "he has a sword . . . and she's sleeping . . . and he doesn't even hesitate, he just — "

"Okay, that's enough," Luke said, and I noticed his hands were trembling. He took Maddy's shoulders and knelt down in front of her, forcing her to look at him. "What does he look like?"

Maddy squeezed her eyes closed as if trying to forget. "It doesn't matter," she said, shaking her head. "It's not real. It's not real." She rocked back and forth, repeating this to herself.

"Maddy," Luke repeated, "what does he look like?"

"He . . ." her voice trailed off.

"What, Maddy?" I pressed. "He what?"

Her eyes found mine and she took in a breath, giving herself strength. "I'm sure it's just because we had that talk the other day about how Luke must be jealous that you're wearing Drew's ring."

"What do you mean?" Luke said.

"I asked Sarah why she was still wearing Drew's ring now that she's with you, and she said she just wanted to. And I wondered if that bothered you. Because I think it would bother me."

We both stared at her. "What does this have to do with your dream?" I asked.

"Because the guy in the black hood . . . was Luke." She flinched as if she had personally hurt his feelings. Though her nightmares had felt intensely real, the longer she spent in Earth's reality, the less afraid she felt. Her eyes softened, and confusion replaced her fear. "I . . . I'm sorry," she apologized. "I haven't slept in days. I'm just so tired." She whimpered and I took her in my arms. "I just want to sleep without being scared to death."

"We'll take you to the office," Luke said. "You should go home. I know you're tired, but try not to go back to sleep."

"Isn't there something you can give her so she doesn't fall asleep?" I asked under my breath, as we helped her to her feet and began walking down the corridor.

"She'll be okay. I'm putting an end to this right now."

As we walked, his face hardened with a profound anger, and his eyes darkened to the deepest blue I had ever seen. When we reached the office, Luke helped Maddy into a chair. "Stay with her. I have to go."

Caleb burst into the office at the same time that Luke was leaving. "What happened?" he demanded as he struggled to catch his breath. "My phone blew up with texts that she freaked out in class. What happened?"

"She had a nightmare," I said. "Stay with her." I ran

out into the hallway. "Luke, wait!" I called after him, catching him before he got to the main doors. "What does all this mean?"

"I think I just figured out who's after you." There was an urgency to his voice that was unnerving. "I have to go, Sarah. I'm so sorry." He kissed my forehead and tried to leave again, but I held onto his arm.

"No," I said firmly, but with an audible shake to my voice. "Shouldn't you stay with me then? Why do you have to leave me now?"

"I have to put an end to this."

"Who is it? Who wants me dead?"

He narrowed his eyes. "Nitsua's keeper is a shapebender, which would explain why Maddy thought she saw me. I need to go now."

I felt my eyes fill with water and then overflow.

He pulled me in and squeezed me harder than normal. "I need to do this and I need to do it now. Call Drew. Tell him what's happened. He'll protect you."

"I don't want Drew to protect me. I want you."

"Sarah, if I don't stop this now, you'll need more than just me and Drew protecting you. I know Nitsua's keeper and I may know a way to stop this." He pulled away and was gone before I could swallow my grief. I fell back into the wall and stared at the doors, willing him to come back. *Don't leave me. I need you.*

My head was reeling with thoughts, questions and

confusion. Maddy's nightmare. Someone was after me. Was this a premonition? Was this meant to come true? Was I to die? And why? Why me?

"Sarah?" the nurse interrupted my gyrating thoughts. "Maddy should go home. Caleb has offered to take her. Are you okay with that?"

I shook my head, ridding it of the swirling mess inside. "Yeah, sure. Yes, that's okay." I took my phone from my pocket and stared at the screen, imploring my fingers to stop trembling long enough to dial Drew's number.

"Are you okay?" he answered in a whisper, reminding me that I was interrupting him in the middle of class.

"No," I said, and the floodgates holding back my tears broke open. I fell to the floor gasping for breath.

"Where are you?" he demanded, his voice no longer a whisper.

"Nurse," was all I could say as I continued to grasp at reality.

"I'm on my way. What happened?" I could tell he was running now.

"Maddy. Luke." I gasped.

"Luke!" Drew said, accusation, anger and a deep concern all mingled together in that one word.

Rapid footsteps were coming from the south corridor. I stood up and stumbled in that direction. Drew flew around the corner and had me in his arms before I could fully stand up. His embrace brought breath back to my lungs.

"I got you. I got you. I'm here," he said over and over as he stroked my hair. "Sarah, you need to tell me what happened."

I steadied my breathing and focused on his bright green eyes for strength. "Maddy's been having nightmares. Someone's been trying to get her to take your ring from me." I paused, and he waited, knowing that wasn't the worst of it. I shook my head as my eyes filled with tears. "Time's up. They're coming for me."

"Where's Luke?" Drew looked around indignantly.

"He's gone." The anxiety came back and my breath was hitching in my throat again.

"It's okay, Sarah. Just breathe," Drew commanded as his eyes shot back and forth as if in quick thought. "Where did he go?"

"To find Nitsua's keeper, I think. To try to stop it before it happens." Could I tell him what Maddy said? About Maddy's accusation? Could I *not* tell him? "Maddy said the guy from her dream was Luke. But Luke said Nitsua's keeper is a shapebender and he thinks it's him."

Drew let go of me and pushed his hands through his hair as he paced the hallway. "Nitsua's keeper is a *she*. Ella Ingram. And last I heard, she and Luke were . . . good friends."

"But that wouldn't make sense. Why would she want

to kill me if she and Luke are friends?"

"You don't get it, do you, Sarah? Luke was never on our side. This was all a game to him."

"No." I shook my head.

"How could I have been so stupid?"

"Luke is not behind this," I said confidently. "He's on our side, Drew."

"Sarah." Drew took my shoulders and held them firmly. "Luke is a dark prince of a very dark world. No matter how much he cares about you, and I believe that he does, in the end, he can't beat the darkness. It's who he is. It's in his blood."

"You're wrong!" I cried, pushing his hands away from me. "You're just . . . you're just jealous." I spat the last word at him.

"Jealous! Is that what you think??" He was angry now, too. "You really need to wake up, Sarah. You live in this fantasy world where you actually think your dreams are just that—a figment of your imagination. This shit is real. You are in serious danger here and all you can think about is protecting a dark lord and blaming me for being jealous?"

My mouth fell open, but I quickly closed it. I wanted to tell him he was wrong, but none of this made sense enough to me to know what was right and what was wrong. Maybe he was right. Maybe my common sense was clouded by how Luke made me feel. But what if he was right? What if Luke didn't care about me? What if he played me so that he could catch Earth keeper's off guard? These thoughts made my heart squeeze with pain and my eyes sting with fear.

Suddenly Drew's eyes widened. He took his key and studied it. I had never seen it glow before, but it was definitely glowing now.

"What's wrong?" I pressed.

"Someone's here."

"What do you mean?"

Drew took my hand and dragged me down the hall and into an empty classroom. "I'm taking you to my house and you'll stay with my dad." We vanished and reappeared seconds later in Drew's living room.

My head spun for a few seconds while I readjusted to my surroundings. "Wait—where are you going? And what do you mean someone's here?"

Drew hurried to the dining room and opened the china cabinet. Then he pushed back the shelves adorned with dishes, revealing a stash of swords, knives, and bows. "A dark lord is here."

Drew's dad was behind us now. "What is it, Drew?" he demanded.

"Someone's at the portal."

Mr. Spencer's eyes fell to Drew's key as Drew belted a sword around his waist.

"Keep Sarah with you. Protect her with your life."

"Of course," his father said.

"How do you know it's a dark lord?" I pressed.

"I can feel it," Drew said. "And it's not just a small shift in energy. Someone's here for a fight." Drew finished stashing knives into his boots, then collected me into his arms and kissed the top of my head.

"Please don't go," I begged him.

"I have to do this, Sarah. We have to end this thing." He backed away.

"Can you tell what keeper is here?" Mr. Spencer asked as Drew took his key, and readied himself for his departure.

Drew looked at me for a few seconds before answering. "Etak's," he said, making my heart stop. And then he was gone.

Mr. Spencer was holding me upright. I hadn't realized I had stumbled. Drew was gone to fight—but worse, he was gone to fight Luke. Why had Luke come for a fight?

"Where did he go?" I demanded, my breath getting caught in my throat.

"The portal." Mr. Spencer tried to help me into a chair. Once his hands were off me, I stood up and began pacing the room.

"But this doesn't make sense. Luke is Etak's keeper. Why would he call Drew to the portal? Why not just show up *here* if he really wanted to fight him?"

Mr. Spencer began arming himself with the weapons from the china cabinet. "The portal is the only place shielded from mortal eyes. Perhaps he doesn't want a war of the worlds, but just a battle for something much smaller." His eyes fell on me. "Or someone much smaller."

"Luke wouldn't fight Drew. He has no reason to."

"Sarah, my dear, Luke is a dark lord. A master of deception and deceit. If Drew was able to feel the dark energy with his key, then Luke brought backup and he's not here for a tea party."

Could this really be happening? Maybe Drew was wrong. Maybe it wasn't Luke. Maybe Mr. Spencer was wrong. Maybe there weren't reinforcements. What if Drew didn't come back? What if this was the end?

"Sarah, where are you going?" Mr. Spencer called. I was at the front door with my hand on the doorknob.

"I can't just sit here and wait for him to come back, Mr. Spencer. I'm sorry, but I have to go help Drew." I pulled the door open.

"Sarah, you won't be able to—" but before he could finish, I took a step outside and was immediately propelled back into the house.

I landed hard on the floor and it took me a few seconds to realize what had just happened. "What the—?"

"You won't be able to leave the house, my dear," he said calmly.

"Why?"

"Drew wanted to ensure your safety."

"No," I corrected. "Drew didn't trust me."

Mr. Spencer smiled and turned back to the weapons cabinet. "There's more to it than that."

I slowly sat up, trying to decode his last sentence. "What do you mean there's more to it than that?"

"Has Drew ever told you about how his mother died?"

I shook my head. Drew never elaborated on the details of his mother's death, just that she had died when he was old enough to remember her, but young enough to forget.

Mr. Spencer picked at the end of a blade with his fingernail. Then he cleared his throat. "She died at the hands of a dark lord."

"I . . . I didn't know."

"Drew probably never wanted to tell you for fear it'd upset you. The dark lords . . . they can't be trusted. They don't know mercy or kindness. They'll kill you just to see you bleed. Just to hurt Drew. And this is why he is so fiercely protective of you, Sarah."

There was a moistness to his eyes that I had never seen before and that contrasted his otherwise rugged features. I spoke softly, "If and when I die, Drew needs to know that he isn't responsible. . . . But not letting me live . . . that's worse than dying."

Mr. Spencer nodded as if he understood. "She said the same thing to me." He smiled and flicked away a tear that was sliding down his cheek. "So I never stopped her. I let her live the way she wanted to. You remind me of her, actually."

"I'm sure she died happy," I tried.

"She did," he said, without hesitation. "She died doing what she loved, and as much as it tore me apart, I probably wouldn't have done things any differently." He turned away from me. "Drew, on the other hand, doesn't want the same fate for you."

"Mr. Spencer," I began, "I know you don't agree with him on this. I know you don't want to keep me prisoner here."

"It's not my call," he said, returning to the table of weapons before him. "Drew is your keeper now."

I slumped down in a chair, frustrated at my imprisonment. Drew didn't trust me to be able to help him. He was off fighting Luke, and for what? Me? Drew obviously blamed Luke for everything that was happening to me. So did that mean Luke blamed Drew? I had a hard time believing that Luke was as bad as everyone made him out to be.

"Can we go there together?" I asked, still hoping I could sway him.

Mr. Spencer shook his head.

"Don't you want to help your son? How can you let

him go into this all alone?" I knew he wanted to be there for Drew, especially after losing his wife to these dark lords. Mr. Spencer might have been in his fifties, but he was fit and strong and had an edge to him that told me he was having a hard time sitting this one out. Besides, he was dressed for it. He was armoured and ready to go. Maybe it wouldn't take much more convincing.

"It doesn't matter if I want to help him or not. He gave me a direct order—to keep you safe—and I won't disobey that order."

"Okay," I said, nodding, as an idea suddenly came to me. "Your order was to keep me safe, right? . . . What if keeping me here is unsafe?"

He studied me, his eyebrows pulled together in thought. "What are you talking about?"

I took a quick inventory of the sharp objects laying on the table next to Mr. Spencer. I went to him, but avoided looking at the small knife closest to the edge. "Mr. Spencer, please," I said. "Drew needs us. We have to help him. I'll never forgive myself if something happens to him out there."

When his face softened I quickly snatched the knife and jumped back. First, I held it to my wrist, but then I realized that wasn't dramatic enough. I pressed it into my stomach. The blade was sharp, but it wasn't piercing my skin yet.

"Sarah, what are you doing?" he said, as if calling my

bluff.

"Your job is to keep me safe. If you don't take down that . . . barrier, or whatever it is, then I will cut myself."

He eyed the knife suspiciously, then grinned. "You're still safer in here."

I took a deep breath, and realizing that time was sensitive, I pushed the end of the knife into my side. I winced at the cruel pain of it.

"Geez, Sarah, what the hell are you doing?" Mr. Spencer came to me, but I stepped back and held the knife to my throat now. "You do know I can't heal you, right?" he pressed more urgently.

"I know," I said. "But Drew can."

"Don't be selfish, Sarah."

"That's exactly what I'm trying not to do, Mr. Spencer. I want to help Drew." The tip of the knife was sharp and I already felt it piercing my skin just under my chin. "If Luke is at the portal, then I know I can stop this."

"Okay, okay!" he said, raising his hands. "Get suited up. We'll go together."

CHAPTER 23

The Battle at the Portal

~ DREW ~

HE STOOD IN the center of the portal, the large apple tree wading in his shadow. The black hoodie shielded his eyes, but his stance and the contour of his mouth gave him away.

"Luke, what the hell are you doing?" I demanded as his guards slowly surrounded me. There were at least a dozen of them, all dressed in black, and all bearing weapons, but I wasn't afraid.

"You have something I want," he said. His voice was deep and dark, and although it was familiar, it wasn't Luke's.

"Riley," I said, suddenly realizing my mistake. The same one who tricked me into thinking he was Luke the first time.

Riley slid his hood back. "Can't fool you this time, can I, Drew?"

"What do you want?"

"I've come for the girl."

"I don't know what you're talking about."

He chuckled to himself. "Alright then, plead ignorance. You won't mind then if I take a quick look around?"

"Riley, I'm warning you."

"And I'm warning you, Drew. You can either hand her over and no one gets hurt, or I can take her myself and kill anyone who gets in my way. You included."

"Get the hell out of my world," I hissed. "You have no authority to be here, Riley."

"But I do," he continued, arrogantly. "You see, my brother left me in charge when he went on his little adventure to Earth." Riley held up his key as if this was the proof he needed. "And now he's nowhere to be found, and the last place he went was . . . here. So in fact, I have every right to be here."

"Why do you have Luke's key?" I demanded.

"What'd you expect? He had to leave someone in charge while he took on the task of luring the girl."

Luring the girl? My insides twisted. I should never have trusted Luke. I should never have let Sarah convince me. Riley moved forward.

"If you take one more step, I'll have no choice but to kill you, Riley. Go back where you came from and I'll pretend you didn't just try to break the rules."

Riley grinned and pulled a knife from his boot.

"Honestly, Riley," I said. "You haven't a hope in hell of beating me. This is *my* world. Have you forgotten?"

"It's not you I want, Drew." He played with the knife in his hand for a second, then said, "It's her." He turned a quarter turn and hurled the knife into the woods.

Sarah's cry filled the air. "No," I gasped. Then came my father's panicked voice: "Drew! . . . Sarah, hang on!"

I ran toward Sarah's scream, but the air grabbed me and threw me back into the ground. "RILEY, NO!" I boomed as I fought against the wind.

Riley wore a disturbing grin as he turned his hands in the air, pulling the breath from my lungs. I gasped, still struggling to get to Sarah.

"Kind of cool, isn't it?" Riley mused. "It's amazing what Etak's craft can do if you add just a little more darkness to it." Riley threw his hands toward the ground, letting go of his grip on me, then he stretched his hand out toward Sarah, and in one calculated movement, he grasped the air between his fingers and pulled it into his chest. Sarah flew through the air toward him, and I leaped into the air, over the heads of several guards advancing on me. I intercepted Sarah's flight and we both fell to the ground, too close to Riley. I fumbled for my key, but Riley gripped me again and hurled me across the field, away from Sarah. I jumped into the air again, bringing myself back to the dozen fighters ready to tear me apart.

I drove my sword into the chest of a guard, pulled it out and turned to behead another. I heard nothing but the sound of Sarah pleading for her life. *Drew, help me. Please. I can't breathe.* With each plea, I beheaded another and another. Their strength was no match for me. Not in my world. Maybe in Etak, or even a more neutral world, but not here. There were only three guards left to go through to get to Riley who was deep in combat with my father. Dad was more seasoned with his craft than I was, and he evaded Riley much better than I had. Sarah was lying on the other side of them, her shirt soaked in blood below her chest and down one arm. She clung to the knife stuck deep in her shoulder. She spotted an abandoned bow on the ground near her and she scrambled to retrieve it. I had taught her how to aim and shoot. She could do this. *Come on, Sarah.*

"I've always wanted to kill you, Spencer," Riley said as his sword slashed against my father's. "As vengeance for killing my father."

"You know I didn't want to do that," Dad said as he pushed Riley off of him with his sword, "but he left me no choice. After what he did to my wife . . ."

Riley's eyes moved to Sarah's, and I saw the grin on

his face as she released the arrow. He dropped his sword, thrust his hands toward the arrow and then pushed the air toward my father. The arrow curved before reaching him and spun in an arc, piercing my father right in the chest.

"Nice shot, Sarah," Riley mused as my father fell to his knees.

"No!" Sarah cried out.

At my hesitation, a cold blade went through my back, and I collapsed on the ground just as Riley reached Sarah, and they disappeared before I could stop them. I finished off the last guard, then I pulled his sword from my back and tried to regulate my breathing long enough to heal myself. A storm of emotions raged inside. If anyone could save my father, it was me. But every fibre inside of me wanted to follow Sarah and Riley to Etak.

"Drew," my father gasped. I hurried to my feet, ignoring the pulling and twisting of my back's healing. When I reached him, he took my free hand while I pulled the arrow out of his chest and began healing.

"It's no use, son." His voice was a hoarse whisper. "Leave me and go save your girl."

I let my tears fall on him. "No, Dad. I won't let you die."

He tried to chuckle, but his face contorted in pain instead. "Your job is to protect that girl. Nothing else matters, Drew."

Then he gripped his key, muttered something, and disappeared.

CHAPTER 24

Keeper of Darkness

~ SARAH~

HE WOULDN'T LET me see his face, which frustrated me since I hadn't gotten a good look at him while I lied bleeding at the apple tree. I closed my eyes, willing myself not to cry. His grip on my arm was tightening and there was no mercy to how he shoved me through the thick, humid jungle, my face and body taking the brunt of the abuse from the trees and bushes we pushed through.

An image of Mr. Spencer falling to his knees with an arrow protruding from his chest pierced my mind. What if I had killed him? A sob built up in my chest and I released a few quick breaths in order to override it. If I had to stay positive, at least I could breathe now. I hadn't expected him to heal me. I expected to die with cold, hard eyes staring down at me and grinning heartlessly while I took my last breath. My fingers found the rip in my shirt where the knife had gone through. My arm was still tender, but there was no open wound.

Finally we stopped. He pushed me to the ground and I scrambled to my feet, putting distance between us. But then I was back in his arms, wondering how I got there. How did he do that? And how had he made me fly through the air toward him at the apple tree?

This time we were chest to chest and I took in his features with alarm. His sculpted jaw and deep, dark eyes, were so much like Luke's that it took me a few more seconds to ensure that he wasn't.

"Riley," I guessed. "You're Luke's brother."

"Aah," he said. "Clever one, you are."

"Why are you doing this?" I asked, watching his eyes now and trying to feel him; see through the window to his soul. His eyes flickered with something reminiscent of a curious recognition that was deep and misunderstood even by him. He frowned and pushed me away and I wondered if he saw something in me that made him hate me less.

"You were the one who came to me in my nightmare, weren't you? You were the one who saved me from drowning."

"I didn't *save* you," he spat. "I preserved your death because I wasn't done ruining your life."

"But why?" I said. "What do you want from me?"

"Haven't figured it out yet, I see." He watched me curiously, a profound hatred lingering in the depths of his eyes.

"Drew's key," I said, remembering how he had bewitched me to sleepwalk and search Drew's house for his key. "Why did you want me to find Drew's key?"

He considered me for a minute. "This is interesting," he said softly as if to himself. "It doesn't change anything, but it's interesting to me how little you know."

"You wanted me to find Drew's key and take myself to Etak where you planned to kill me, then take Earth's key for yourself. I'm not stupid." I swallowed hard. "But when that didn't work, you came looking for me. You think by killing me, you'll have an advantage over Drew."

He grinned. "It is true that I want you dead, Sarah. If only for the simple reason that you are far too much of a distraction for my brother."

I meant to hit him, but he was too quick and blocked my swing with his left hand and backhanded me across the face with his right.

I stayed on the ground where I fell, breathing heavy and tasting the salt from my blood. "Why? Why would you want to hurt your brother like this?"

"What do you think dark worlds are, Sarah? Full of tea parties and happy family reunions? These worlds were created for misery. There is no such thing as happy endings here. There are no happily ever afters in Etak."

"But *why*?"

"It's in our blood."

This reminded me of when Drew told me that Luke wasn't capable of being good. That being evil was in his blood.

"Luke doesn't love you, Sarah. He's not capable of loving anyone and it's about time you come to terms with that."

The accusation hurt, but I tried to ignore him. I picked myself up off the ground and wiped the blood from my chin, ignoring his claim. "Why are you doing this?"

"Because I want to watch Earth burn," he said, a hiss of venom in his words. "I want to help turn it into the masterpiece of darkness that it was meant to be."

"And you think getting rid of me will somehow make that happen," I said, still unsure of how his plan fit together.

"Drew is a good keeper, I'll give him that," Riley began. "He's always been on top of his game. But he has an achilles heel—you. I have to applaud him really. He was smart to keep you at a distance, knowing that you would be too much of a distraction and burden for him. But then Luke took on the job as your new love interest and old lover boy Drew wasn't able to stand back and watch you be happy. Which, if you ask me, is just awesome. I'm so glad we finally found a way to bring him to his knees."

"You'll pay for this. When Luke finds out what you've been doing—"

"Sarah, don't kid yourself. Luke knows as well as I do that Earth deserves to be destroyed. It was always only a matter of time. Earth is already covered in darkness—suicide bombings, hate crimes, murders, violence against children. Humans are the most selfish, hateful creatures in all of the dimensions combined. It's beautiful, really."

My mouth was slack and my eyes were fixated on his lips as they moved. As he said those words. The same words that Luke had said while we sat at Peggy's Cove. They both shared the belief that Earth was on a path of destruction. And if they were in agreement over that, then it was possible Luke was more like his brother and less like the person I fell in love with.

Riley was standing directly in front of me now, his body touching mine. He slid one hand around my waist and before I could pull away, his other hand was in my hair, pulling my head back. He whispered in my ear, "I wish I could keep you alive just a little while longer."

I tried to pull away, but his grip was strong and only tightened at my resistance.

"But," he went on, "as long as you're alive, Drew has reason to fight." His lips brushed my ear, causing my stomach to tighten.

"So you're going to kill me now?" There was a shake

in my voice that I didn't like.

He grinned, and watched my lips for a few seconds before moistening his and saying, "I don't want your blood on my hands." He bit his lip but then looked away. "Obviously, you've seduced my brother, so killing you myself would only cause more problems for me. But that shadow inside you has been itching to have some fun. I'm going to let him have full reign and see how long it takes for him to kill you."

I felt a stirring of excitement inside my chest, but knew it was not my own.

"Drew will come for me. And then you'll be sorry," I stammered.

"Might be hard to find you given that I have Etak's master key and there's literally no way I'm letting him get near you . . . until you're dead, of course."

"Why do you have Luke's key?" I realized I was stalling for time now.

"Luke put me in charge while he was off falling for you." He said it with distaste, but it still made my heart light to think for a second that perhaps Luke did love me, and even Riley knew it.

"That key doesn't belong to you. Luke is Etak's rightful keeper, not you."

There was a sharp sting across my face and I fell to the ground, tasting more of my blood than before. I held my jaw and moved it slowly to check for brokenness.

"Drew will find me, and—"

"Yes, yes, I know. *I'll be sorry.*" He crouched down next to me and grabbed a fistful of my hair. "It'll be hard to do . . . when he's dead." He dropped my head and stood up. "Face it, Sarah—it's over."

I shook my head. *No. No, it isn't!*

Riley's hand went to the key around his neck and he paused, as if reading something from it. Then an unnerving grin crept across his face. "Too predictable," he laughed. "I wonder if your little boyfriend knows what's about to happen to him." He chuckled darkly. "I hope he came prepared. There's a whole army of my strongest men waiting for his arrival."

I charted the ground quickly and erratically, looking for something to use to defend myself. A stick, a rock— anything! But found nothing. Drew was here, walking right into a trap. I needed to find him. I needed to help him.

"I guess now is as good a time as any to unleash the shadow and see how you make out in a world full of nightmares without your little boyfriend to keep you safe." He grabbed me by the face and looked into my eyes, but he wasn't looking at me—I felt the shadow answering to his stare. "Destroy her." He snapped his fingers and everything went dark, sheathing me in a thick blackness that took my breath away. "Let the nightmares begin."

CHAPTER 25

Rescue

~ DREW~

LUKE'S CASTLE WAS in front of me now, but the gates were closed. My sword was already drawn, and I was half expecting an ambush when I arrived. But no one was around. All was quiet and still. Too still.

I pounded on the large wooden doors. "Riley!" I yelled. "Luke, let me in!"

Devon appeared seconds later. He sighed when he saw me pounding on the invisible barrier. "Seriously, man, do you not have anything better to do with your time than to chase after rebel dreamers?"

I grabbed Devon's shirt with my free hand. "Where is she?!"

"Who? The little redhead?" He pushed my hands off

of him, but kept his weapons at bay, for now. "Everyone seems so interested in her. I'm beginning to wonder why."

"Don't toy with me, Devon. You know she's here. Riley took her!"

Devon stared at me for a few seconds, then let his head fall back at a realization, but before he could say anything, Luke appeared next to us.

"Drew," he said, a look of confusion on his face. "Why are you here?"

"You know damn well why I'm here, Luke!" I jabbed him in the chest. "Where the hell is she? What have you done with her?"

"Whoa, man, what are you talking about?"

My fist connected with his face. He shook it off and cracked his jaw back into place.

"Nice work trying to make her believe this was all Nitsua's doing!" I shouted. "Put the blame on someone else because she was getting too close to discovering the truth about you?"

"I did think it was Ella, Drew! I went to Nitsua, but I couldn't find her. Why are you looking for Sarah here? What happened?"

He was lying to me and stalling for time and I knew I'd have to kill him or die trying. I punched him again and then wrestled him to the ground.

A shrill metal sound rang through the air—the sound

of a sword being drawn—and then a sharp stabbing in my back stopped my fists from hammering into Luke's face.

"Drew!" Luke said as Devon pulled me to my feet, the severe edge of his blade digging into my spine. "Tell me now what you're talking about." He wiped the blood from his chin.

"Riley took Sarah."

"Riley!" His eyes pinballed mine as a look of fear masked his.

"You didn't know?" The pressure in my back subsided and Devon lowered his sword.

A blackness covered Luke's eyes. "It wasn't Ella in Maddy's dream," he said as if this just occurred to him. "It was Riley. He wore a hood and covered his eyes so she'd think he was me."

"He came to Earth with a dozen fighters," I continued. "He threw an effing knife at her!"

Luke gripped his key and muttered Riley's name. I expected him to disappear, but he didn't. "Damnit," he hissed. "He's blocked me. I can't go anywhere."

"There's another problem," Devon said. "The beast in the vault. It wants out. Riley's been taking down the protections surrounding it. It'll be out soon if we don't do something about it."

"The beast," I said slowly, realizing the impact of this statement. The beast designed and created for human blood. The very beast that caused irreparable damage to the fate of the worlds, and had been imprisoned and dormant for more than fifteen years.

Luke took to running. "We'll go to the vault first. We can't risk it getting out. It'll find Sarah before any of us and she doesn't stand a chance against it. And if I know my brother, it won't be long before he meets us at the vault. We'll need to get my key back from him before we can find Sarah."

"Then we'll find Sarah," I added, frustrated that it was the third item on our list. Obviously we couldn't find her without Luke's key, and understandably this beast would need to be contained next. It all made sense, but each passing second felt like a punch in the stomach.

"Follow me," Luke said. "The vault isn't far."

CHAPTER 26

Abandoned

~ SARAH ~

THERE WERE NO sounds. No light. I could only feel my own heartbeat as I blindly wandered through the thick forest. It seemed endless. Was I walking in circles? Had I already passed that tree? I called for Luke, and then called for Drew, but no one came. But what was so scary about this anyway?

The forest was huge, and likely stretched for eternity. It was probably filled with every terrifying creature imaginable and my chances of survival would be slim to none. What was I doing even trying? It was hopeless. I sat down on the ground and felt an enormity of sadness and defeat wash over me. This was it for me. I was powerless here. My chest felt heavy with the realization that I was a failure. That I caused this. That if it weren't for me, Mr. Spencer would still be alive and Drew wouldn't have had to go to the portal to fight Riley and his thugs. This was all my fault. Drew loved me and was taking good care of me and I went and screwed it all up.

I closed my eyes tight, hoping that when I opened them, I would somehow be home. Nothing happened. I began to cry. My sadness was overwhelming, but there was a satisfaction that came with my misery. I was such a failure. Everyone would be better off without me. The only thing I was good at was hurting the people I loved and making a mess of my life. My tears turned to sobs and soon I was curled up on the ground wishing I were dead so I didn't have to fight anymore. So I didn't have to ruin anyone else's life.

Kill me, I thought desperately. *Please, just let me die.*

I cried like this for what seemed like an hour, constant nagging thoughts on the edges of my reality begging me to just die and escape the suffering. I had never cried like this before. I had never felt this desperate and alone before. Was I delusional all those years? This seemed like reality. This seemed more real than all those times I was happy. This misery was reality.

At these desperate, wretched thoughts, a darkness stirred inside, reminding me that a shadow lived in me.

I sat up, energized by this realization. There was a

shadow in me! A shadow that, according to Luke, at-
tacked the mind, causing illness of the mind. Was that
what was happening? Was the shadow attacking my
mind now? Was it making me sick? I was standing now,
a small ray of light and hope surrounding my thoughts.
What if Drew was still alive? What if Riley's guard didn't
kill him? What if he was here looking for me? What if
there was still hope? What if we could get out of here?
What if I could be happy again?

There was a frustrated churning inside that wasn't
my own. The shadow didn't like my newfound courage,
and he fought harder at darkening my mind. I wouldn't
let him take me, though. . . . But my despair had been
genuine. My reasons had been real. Maybe it wasn't the
shadow. Maybe it was reality. My life sucked right now
and I didn't deserve to be alive.

I began to sink back into hopelessness, which felt even
more tragic now that I had climbed up to a position
where I could see such a small glimmer of hope. And as I
cradled my legs against my chest, that deep, dark feeling
of depression blanketed me once again.

Now it was clear what was happening. The shadow,
quietly and furtively, was following his orders from Riley. He was destroying me—from the inside out. He was
manipulating my thoughts and burying my happiness
underneath heavy mounds of guilt and sadness.

It's not real, I told myself. *I am not a failure. My life is not a mess. This is not the end.*

My head pounded with an intense pressure, and I knew that the shadow was agitated. I pressed my fingers against my temples and massaged the pain as I continued talking to myself, ignoring the inner workings of the shadow. *You are beautiful. You are talented. You are smart and you are loved. You are stronger than the shadow and you don't have to go out like this.*

The shadow withered inside, slamming its presence against the sides of my brain until I thought that it would split open. But instead of bringing me to my knees, this empowered me. I knew I was stronger than the shadow, and the pounding in my head told me that the shadow knew it, too. The harder it pounded, the more sure I was that I could beat this.

I am a fighter, I thought. *And I am too strong for you. You won't win.*

The throbbing made me nauseous and I was soon on my hands and knees throwing up.

"Is that all you got?!" I cried. "I'm still stronger!" I threw up again. "Your best hope of killing me is to come out and fight like a real warrior!"

I felt the surge going through my veins and the next thing I knew my body had slammed against a tree. I vomited again, but this time a black tar came out with it. The tar spread across the ground, shifting and expanding into a long blob, and then transformed into a massive, grotesque snake!

Perhaps it was stupid to have provoked the shadow. I fumbled for my dagger with one hand while I instinctively threw my other hand in the direction of the snake. It hissed violently, but my eyes were stuck to my pant leg where I pulled desperately to release the hidden dagger that Riley had failed to confiscate.

I finally got the knife free and turned back to the snake who was swaying back and forth, seemingly unsure of what to make of me. Was he taunting me now? I lurched toward him, my dagger out front. The snake kept his eyes on my free hand; not the dagger, as if I had power in my hand that he saw but I couldn't. I waved the dagger, but he only watched my other hand. I slowly lifted my hand and the snake recoiled. Peculiar.

I stepped forward, causing the snake to hiss and spit. Then, distracting him with my hand, I threw myself onto him, driving my dagger into his leathery skin. I clutched his neck with one hand and then beheaded the beast with the other.

There was silence in the jungle again. All that lingered was a faint smell that resembled burnt flesh. I stood, cautiously, leaning on a tree for stability as my vision played with my surroundings. Soon I felt normal again. Normal and sane. The snake was gone, and more importantly, the dark place I had been only minutes before now seemed like an unreasonable state of mind. I marvelled at the power of the shadow and took a minute to gain momentum with my own positive, encouraging thoughts. *The shadow is gone. Drew is alive and looking for me. Luke isn't one of the bad guys.* All I had to do now was ensure I survived and Drew would find me.

Suddenly, the trees trembled with a stampede of heavy footfalls. My body shook with fear, but I tried to ignore it. If it was a world of darkness fueled by fear, anger and hate, then wouldn't courage, kindness and love be the perfect antidote?

The spaces between the trees filled with darkness as the rumblings became louder and heavier. The ground shook and I nearly fell. I tried to stand with courage, but a thick cold mist of fear swept over me, rendering me useless. Then the trees parted and the thundering stopped at the arrival of the creatures. All around me, in a terrifying circle, stood enormous, black horses. Their ears lay flat on the tops of their heads, they pawed restlessly at the ground, and then one reared up on its back legs and let out an enormous neigh that shattered the silence. At his war cry, the others reared up too and then raged toward me.

Any second, the herd would reach me and my worst fear—to be trampled to death by the heavy hooves of a massive, black horse—would take me. I fell to the ground in a heap of terror, and the second that my body hit the dirt, the ground erupted into a series of shakes. I kept my eyes closed, holding onto the blades of grass for stability and hoping that the earthquake would somehow prevent the horses from reaching me. The rumbling subsided, but the neighs and cries persisted, though they didn't appear to be getting any closer. I reluctantly opened one eye, and found that the ground had broken apart and the horses had fallen into it. I clambered to my feet, leaning over the edge to inspect further. The thought of stumbling into the surrounding pit frightened me still. How had that happened? One minute they were tearing toward me, and the next minute the horses were swallowed up by a bottomless pit. Had their stampede caused the earthquake? I could be certain it wasn't Riley's doing. He would've been more than happy to watch me die by my biggest fear.

"Luke?" I cried into the distance, holding onto a glimmer of hope that this was his doing. But when no answer came, I resolved to the notion that I was still alone.

Suddenly, an ear-piercing scream split the air. I knew that scream. I had heard it just today . . . in the classroom. It was Maddy! Her screams wafted through the air until they penetrated my eardrums, sending deep chills down my spine. Was this part of Riley's production? Or was Maddy really there?

"Maddy!" I hollered.

"SARAH?!" her faint cry carried back to me. "SA-RAH, HELP ME!"

I detoured around the pit and pushed my way through the trees. Maddy's screams seemed to awaken the forest, and soon a melody of howls, grunts and growls surrounded me. If I could only find Maddy first, then maybe I could help wake her, or at the very least, enlist her to help me fight whatever came next.

The deeper I travelled into the woods, the darker and colder it became. Soon, the forest was so dim that there was barely enough light to see the circles my breath made when I exhaled. My body trembled, but was it from the cold or from fear? Something was following me—I could hear the broken sticks underneath its steps. Something else was lurking in the woods to my right—its eyes glowed a pale green. I found a tree and hid behind it, pressing my back into its stiff, unforgiving bark.

The rustling of earth from the thing that was following me was getting closer until it was right next to me. I held my breath. *Please don't kill me.* Then it let out a deafening roar, akin to the sound a black bear would make. I fell over and scrambled from the creature, catching a glimpse of it for the first time. I was right—it was a bear. But not just any bear—this one stood twice as tall and wide as any bear I had ever seen. It stood on its hind legs with its paws reaching out toward me. Its claws were longer than my hands and its teeth were sharper than knives. . . . My knife! I thrust my knife toward the bear, but he wasn't intimidated by the blade. He pushed me further into the woods as he closed in on me. Suddenly the creature that was lurking in the forest appeared next to the bear. It was a wolf almost the size of the bear. Its grey-black fur stood on end as it held its head low and circled me. *Oh, God, now would be a good time to save me.*

The ground began to shake as another roar covered the air. I closed my eyes tight. *Not another creature!* Was I going to die by bear today? Or wolf? Or whatever else was about to join the feast?

Heavy footfalls pounded the ground, louder and louder. In the distance, trees began to crack and fall. The giant roared and I had to cover my ears from the cruel sound. The only good thing was that the bear and wolf seemed unnerved by it, too. They still circled me, but their attention was swaying to the giant storming toward us.

With a stroke of luck, the giant tripped and fell heavily on the ground, his head only feet from me. The performance catapulted me into the air and I landed, indecently, about thirty feet away. The wolf was now gone, having been mercilessly crushed by the weight of the huge giant, but the bear was still in play, and the interruption seemed to aggravate him further. I clambered to my feet and he raced toward me, the same time I ran as hard and fast as I could toward the giant. It appeared as though we were running toward each other, but I knew I would veer off at the last second and dive into the giant's collar. Whether that would be a mistake or not, I wouldn't know until it was too late.

My plan worked, but barely. I could still smell the bear's breath from when its teeth grazed only inches from my face. I buried myself into the shirt of the giant, hoping to lose my scent in the stench of the giant. It may have worked initially, but my leg was bleeding quite severely and I could hear the bear fervently sniffing the air.

Without warning, the bear's paw came crashing down on me, ripping away at the giant's shirt. I cried out in pain and slid further down the giant's back as he started to move. The giant roared and thrashed around — was he angry that his dinner was inside his shirt bleeding all over him? Or angry with the bear for attacking him, too? Regardless, I had little choice but to crawl my way through his shirt until I found the rim of his pants. I held on tightly as the giant wrestled with the bear. It was too far of a drop to just let go. I would never make that fall without breaking bones, but maybe I could climb down. I took my dagger and used it as a hook as I rappelled down the giant's pant leg. His irregular movements made it more than a difficult task, but soon I was close enough to the ground to let myself fall. As I hit the ground, my arm twisted behind me at an awkward angle and I stifled a cry as I heard a snap. The bear, who had been lucky to have avoided the giant's grasp, caught my scent, let out a roar and abandoned his fight with the giant to finish me off. Just as he was closing in on me, the giant's foot came down on him and the symphony of cracks and snaps made me vomit. I fell behind a tree to catch my breath.

What had just happened? I avoided death by horses, a wolf and a bear, and was now lying bleeding and broken while a giant searched for me to claim as his prize.

The edges of my vision were darkening, and the centres fading in and out. I closed them for a minute, feeling the comfort of just letting myself go, when I was startled by Maddy's scream. This time it was much closer. *Maddy!* I thought, desperately. *I have to help Maddy.*

I listened for the giant, but I didn't couldn't hear his deep breathing or heavy steps. Had he left? I peeked around the tree and confirmed that I was really alone. Had I fallen asleep? Passed out? Maybe I had, and he couldn't find me. Whatever the reason, I was happy to be alive. I forced myself to my feet and headed, once again, in the direction of Maddy's screams.

CHAPTER 27

The Vault

~ DREW ~

IT PROBABLY ONLY took twenty minutes to get there on dragonback, but it felt like hours.

"We're almost there," Luke shouted over his shoulder as we glided above a thick forest. Devon was on a smaller dragon behind us, and I was thankful that Luke still had enough authority here to summon us the transportation.

"Thanks for this," I said.

He didn't answer, and I knew he felt like he didn't deserve any thanks.

"It's not all your fault, you know," I told him.

The dragons started their descent over the stone wall and into the field.

"I screwed up," Luke said, his admission surprising

me. "She would've been better off with you."

I wasn't about to deny it. She was definitely better off with me. I not only loved her, but I knew how to keep her hidden and safe. I knew how to protect her. In the five years I had known her, she never once had an accident. Then he came into her life, and three weeks later we were here. Doing this. My body tensed. I would never let her out of my sight again.

The dragons landed in a field just inside the thick, concrete wall that surrounded the vault. I slid off the back of the larger dragon while Luke climbed down the side.

"So here's the plan," Luke began. "The vault will have at least two dragons at the entrance, and once we make it past them, there will be six guards just inside at the interior. The beast will be in the arena, which is straight ahead down a long, but wide, corridor and through two large metal doors. There are two guards stationed at every twenty feet down this corridor, which means there'll be at least twenty more guards that we'll need to take out before we reach the arena. The beast is tethered in the middle of the arena. Hopefully the protections around him will be strong enough to bide us enough time to add more."

I was calculating and planning as he spoke. Two dragons, twenty-six guards, then the beast. Riley would show up at some point, too, and if he had even half the power he had when he was on Earth, we'd need to reserve some strength for him.

"Seems like an awful lot of trouble for a girl," Devon grunted.

"She's not just a girl," Luke said firmly.

"I get it. She's *special*. But Luke, man, come on. I'd be the first one to tell you Riley's an idiot, but he's also your family. He's just looking out for Etak, which is what you should be doing. Not chasing after some girl like a love-sick fool."

"You don't understand, Devon," Luke growled.

"Then help me understand, Luke. Why are you willing to risk *everything* for this girl? You've had girls before and you'll have girls again. This is just another notch on your belt and it's time you realized that."

Luke had Devon by the throat. "Devon," he hissed, "shut the fuck up."

"What the hell's gotten into you?"

Luke dropped him and pushed his hands through his hair.

"We made a deal," I inserted. "Luke promised nothing would happen to Sarah in Etak. He's just trying to honour that promise."

"Okay," Devon said, "but a deal goes two ways. What does he get out of this so-called deal?"

Luke's eyes flickered to mine. I hadn't thought that far ahead. I was just trying to steer Devon away from asking more questions about Sarah, or worse, convincing

Luke that she really wasn't worth saving.

"An alliance," Luke said, finally. "Earth will back Etak in the event of a crossfire with another world."

"Great," Devon said. "So we have backup from Drew in the highly unlikely event that we'll be ambushed. And in the meantime, we may all die today to hold up *your* end of the bargain." Devon pushed ahead of Luke and took the lead. "Like I said—seems like an awful lot of trouble for a girl."

I nudged Luke's arm and when he looked at me, I mouthed, "Thanks." He nodded and kept walking. He was frustrated and angry with himself, and I could see that the more time we spent in Etak, the darker he turned.

THE VAULT WAS an impressive dome made entirely of stone and steel. A faint haze stretched over top like a blanket with sparks of lightning travelling through it every few seconds.

"Is that the field of protection?" I guessed, eyeing the irregular currents.

"It used to be much stronger," Luke answered.

"Riley spends a lot of time here," Devon said. "His plan was to release the beast the next time the girl came."

My fingers tightened around the hilt of my sword.

"For whatever reason," Devon continued, "he seems to think she's getting in the way of everything." When no one answered, he said, "I always thought he was crazy, but now I'm beginning to wonder if he was right."

"Devon," Luke warned, "I know what I'm doing."

"And I've never had trouble believing that, Luke."

"Then trust me now—help us take out the dragons and the guards."

Devon shook his head, but then pulled his bow. As he loaded an arrow, he muttered, "I hope you're right. I hope you know what you're doing."

With the three of us shooting, the two dragons fell quickly, but not before warning the guards of our arrival. We ran toward the front gates, unloading arrows whenever a new guard appeared in the entrance, and soon, with two dragons and four guards down, we were alone at the gates.

"Now what," Devon said as Luke pulled on the large metal doors, which were barred and not budging.

Luke banged his fist against the gate. "This is your keeper! Open up!"

Nothing happened. No one came.

Luke stepped back and swirled his hands together, forming a tornado. When he was satisfied with the size of it, he hurled it toward the front gates. They rattled and shook but failed to open.

Devon nodded toward me. "Got any tricks up your sleeve, keeper?"

If Luke's craft didn't work in his own world, I was sure mine wouldn't. Besides, airbending was something he could at least use to try to blow the door down, but my craft was useless here. How would bending gravity be useful in this situation? The gates were made of solid metal. It would've taken a hundred men to lift even one of them.

"How are the doors put on?" I asked, trying to think through the mechanics of our situation.

"They pivot on steel rods," Luke answered. "It took three giants to lift each one into place and slide them onto the rods."

"Okay," I said, studying the hinges, "what if I flipped the doors' gravity? They would slide up. There's nothing stopping them from coming off their hinges."

Luke considered this while Devon studied the hinges, too.

"He's right," Devon said. "They'd come right off. Drew, I don't know how strong you are, but if you can do that, you're freaking superman."

"I was thinking that once I get them off the ground a little, Luke, you could bend the air to give them the lift they need."

Luke rubbed his hands together. "Worth a try."

"You're going to want to save some energy for when we get in there," Devon reminded us.

Reversing the weight of the doors was more of a challenge than it sounded. They were a lot heavier than I imagined and even with zero gravity, the hinges were old and rusted into place. Slowly they moved, inch by inch, and when there was enough space between them and the ground, Luke let out a grunt and pushed his hands toward the doors and then up. The doors moved up several feet, but got stuck on the next hinges.

"Again!" Devon shouted. Luke took in a deep breath and again shoved his hands in an upward motion. His arms were shaking like mine and I wondered if my face was as red as his. The doors slid up another couple of feet, enough for Devon to take up a sniper position, picking off the guards that showed their faces in the opening.

After another minute, the doors slid past the last hinges. I let go of my hold on them and collapsed as the doors slammed into the ground and toppled over, revealing two dozen surprised guards.

"No time to rest, superman," Devon said, pulling me to my feet. I shook the exhaustion from my arms and grabbed my sword, which now felt as though it weighed an extra hundred pounds. Luke was moving slower too, and I wondered if exerting all our energy on removing the doors was our smartest move. It wasn't as if the doors were going to be any match for the beast, anyway. The only thing holding that beast back was the field of protection, which was looking more pathetic by the minute. If that beast got out, there would be no survivors.

When Luke took the lead in the entrance, the guards

hesitated, retreating slightly. "Stand down," Luke ordered.

One stepped forward. "I'm sorry, My Lord, but we serve your brother now. He wears the key and if we disobey his orders, then he'll—"

"He'll kill you," Luke finished for him. Then he took his sword, and in one swift movement, beheaded the foolish guard. "So you can either risk my brother's wrath later, or die by me right now. It's your choice."

The guard's head rolled around on the floor as his body crumpled in a heap next to it. My eyes widened to Luke's. "Was that really necessary?"

About half of the guards dropped their weapons and raised their hands. Luke stepped aside and let them escape through the entrance. Then he said quietly, "If I hadn't done that, we wouldn't have been able to beat them. There were too many."

The remaining guards held their swords high and roared, "For Etak!" Then they charged us. Devon and Luke didn't seem to have any trouble killing the guards, and I wondered if I were in Luke's position, if I would have any reluctance. These were his loyal guards not long ago. I supposed he felt somewhat betrayed. My sword sliced and jabbed as we made our way through the corridor, and before long we were at the end, with only a pile of bodies in our wake.

The door to the arena was locked on our side. Devon

and Luke lifted the heavy metal bar and slid it out of the way.

Luke backed up and traded his sword for his bow. "Get ready, Drew," he said. "Put on as much protection as you can." They pulled open the doors. "Riley will be here soon, and then—"

"Already here!" Riley's voice sang out from inside the arena as a blast of wind hit us in the face. He pulled us in with his strength and the doors slammed closed behind us. I tried to reach my sword but the wind was now a vortex around us and we were caught in the eye of the storm.

"Drew, get out of here," Luke gasped as the wind reached for our breath and whipped at our faces.

"I'm not leaving without Sarah!"

"He's persistent, I'll give him that," Devon inserted.

Riley circled us, enjoying the fact that we were on our knees and unable to move. "I'm not gonna lie," he began, "the power from this key is pretty intense. I can't understand why you ever gave this up, brother. I mean, there's no way in hell I'm ever giving this back to you now."

Luke fought hard against the invisible hold around his throat. "You don't have to give it back, Riley. I'm taking it."

"Luke, I don't want to have to hurt you, but I will." He pressed the tip of his sword under Luke's chin. "You know, there was a time when I had myself convinced that maybe, just maybe, you were the right man for this job. But now that I know how much power is inside this key, and you never let it out. . . . You're not worthy of the title."

"Anyone can wield power from a key, Riley. But it takes a real keeper to know when to use it and when to *keep* it under control."

"I think you're just scared of what it'll turn you into. It's okay, little brother, with your strength and my courage, we could make a damn good team. I'm proposing I let you live, and in exchange, you and I rule Etak together."

"What?"

"Think about it, Luke. Think of what we could accomplish together."

Luke shook his head. "You think I could trust you after this?"

Devon grabbed Luke's arm. "Hear him out, Luke."

Luke considered Devon for a moment, then turned his attention back to Riley. "So then what? What happens after I agree to your terms?"

Riley smiled and the hold on our throats weakened. I grabbed my sword and with a loud roar, ran toward Riley, but when I hit the tornado wall, I flew back into the circle with Devon and Luke.

"He's strong," Devon noted. "Don't waste your energy."

"Well, we get rid of the girl first, of course," Riley answered, ignoring my attempt at his life. "She's just in the way, Luke, and you know that. Besides, she knows too much now."

Luke struggled with something inside, and his eyes just stayed glued to Riley's as he dealt with this internal conflict.

"Come on, Luke," Devon urged. "Take the deal."

"Luke, don't do this," I said. His silence was unsettling, and although I believed that he loved Sarah, I was starting to worry he would choose the dark side.

"He doesn't have a choice, Drew," Devon hissed. "Riley's won. That key is far too powerful for any of us. We're not walking out of here alive."

I hated that he had the key. I tried not to blame Luke for this, but it was clearly his fault. In the wrong hands, a world's key could unlock a deep darkness that was impossible to control. I looked down at my key. But in the right hands, it wasn't quite strong enough. At least not in Etak. . . . But what if *my* key was in the wrong hands, but for the right reason? What would happen if I gave Luke my key—just so he could fight Riley? Would it unlock something in him that would make him strong enough to overtake his brother? Or would he turn on me? Earth would be his. He and Riley would destroy it. None of that seemed to matter as much as Sarah, though. If Riley won, Sarah was dead. If I trusted Luke with my key and he turned on me, Sarah may still survive. My best chance for saving Sarah was to trust Luke with Earth's key.

"I have an idea," I muttered, hesitantly, noticing the darkness in Luke's eyes that wasn't there a minute ago.

Devon sniggered. "If you have any tricks up your sleeve, by all means—now would be a good time to honour your end of your so-called alliance."

"What is it?" Luke said.

"If you wore my key—would it give you enough power to challenge Riley properly?"

"Your key," he repeated, disbelievingly. "That's insane, Drew."

"Take it," Devon said, his eyes glowing with greed. I knew what was driving his thoughts—control and power—but I ignored him and focused on Luke.

"Just whatever happens, make sure you save Sarah."

"Sarah's my priority, Drew."

At that, I slipped my necklace off over my head and handed it to him. The second his fingers closed around it, his eyes turned to black coal and he grinned with a darkness that made me regret my decision almost immediately.

Luke unsheathed his sword and held it against my neck. Then he turned to his brother, a wicked grin on his face. "Imagine what we could do with Earth's key."

Before I could object, the hilt of his sword came at my face and everything went black.

CHAPTER 28

The Fiery Pit

~ SARAH ~

MADDY WAS JUST up ahead through the trees. She was perched on a boulder, a gigantic spider taunting her with its hasty movements as she screamed desperately for help.

"Don't be afraid, Maddy," I coached. "It's just a dream."

Maddy shook her head incessantly. "It's not a dream, Sarah. My dreams are real now. They're so real."

"I know they *feel* real, Maddy, but you have to believe me—you are still in control of this. You can wake up from this."

"Then *you* wake up!" Maddy jumped back in an effort to avoid the spider's pincer coming at her.

I picked up a stone and threw it at the spider, trying to keep the fear from reaching my face as it snapped its head of eyes in my direction.

"Look out, Sarah!" Maddy cried.

The spider took chase after me, and I ran into the jungle, searching for something I could use to fend off the creature. A stick? A rock? . . . A vine hanging from a tree blew slightly in the distance, catching my eye. I raced to the vine, grabbed onto it, swung into a tree so that I could kick myself off, back toward the spider. When I was close, I sliced the vine free and landed on top of the spider. I wrapped the vine around the creature's neck and then drove my knife into its head. It wavered, but did not fall, so I slid off the spider's back and wrapped the vine around all eight of its legs, then pulled tight, ensuring a snug fit as the creature finally fell.

Maddy slid down from the boulder and ran to my side. She held onto me, weeping into my torn and dirty shirt. I ignored the pain covering my whole body. I didn't even know where my injuries were anymore.

"It's okay," I told her. "It was just a dream and you're okay."

"Why does it feel so real?" she sobbed.

"Because it's a nightmare." I looked around at the gloomy forest. "Nightmares are dark. They're vivid. They're meant to stay with you even after you wake."

"Sarah, if this is a dream, why can't I wake up?" she

cried.

"I don't know," I admitted. It had something to do with Riley, but how could I tell her that Luke's brother was a psychopath? That trusting Luke may have been a mistake? That being my best friend may cost her her life?

"Sarah," Maddy gasped. I followed her eyes to my hands and saw, for a split second, a flicker of light in the palm of my hand. It licked up my fingers like a flame, and then extinguished at my hesitation.

"That's right!" I exclaimed, an idea stirring inside. "You're dreaming, Maddy."

"You said that already."

"But as a dreamer, you have powers." I searched my memory for the mini lesson Luke had given me about how to protect myself in the dream worlds. "Luke said dreamers can alter the ground, air, water and fire." I rubbed my hands together, still feeling the warmth from the light. "You just need to believe in yourself."

A faint snipping noise came from behind Maddy and as I hesitantly peered around her, I found the mutant spider biting its way through the vines.

"Maddy," I said, "go to the top of that hill. I'll try to keep the spider down here. Drew will find us. He will. I promise!"

Maddy hurried up the hill and crouched next to a rock. "Will you be okay?" she called down to me as I prepared myself for the fury of the spider.

I nodded, but kept my eyes on the creature. "Maddy, just have faith that you can do this. You are in control of your dream." Yes, Riley was making it extremely difficult to escape the dream, but she had to still be in control of it, didn't she?

The spider lunged at me and I dropped to the ground, dodging its pincer. It came at me again, and I dived away, narrowly missing its sharp teeth, although I could still taste its stagnant breath. I hurried to my feet and scrambled underneath its body, making a futile attempt to recapture my knife which was still protruding from the creature's head. Infuriated, the spider came at me again, with more force. I tripped over the branch and before I could regain my footing, the spider had one of its legs pinning me to the ground. I tried to move, but it was like a sword digging into my stomach, deeper and deeper, piercing and pinning me to the ground. It hurt to breathe and it hurt even more to struggle. Its slimy mouth was getting closer and closer as it gnashed its ugly fangs. And slowly I realized that I was done. This wasn't a dream for me, and I couldn't make myself stronger. I couldn't turn myself into a slippery snake and get away. All I could do was await my untimely death.

My body began to tremble uncontrollably. Was this what death felt like? But then I loosely noticed rocks and pebbles around us were moving and bouncing in response to the vibrations. This didn't seem to faze the spider as its mouth was now agape and only inches from my face. Remnants of its last meal clung sickeningly to the back of its throat.

My eyes found Maddy who was holding tight to a tree, her eyes squeezed shut. Was she doing this? Was she causing this earthquake?

With every ferocious shake of the ground, the sharp leg dug deeper into my stomach so I could no longer breathe. I was okay with this, though. I'd rather die this way than be eaten alive.

Then as quickly as the rumbling began, it stopped with a deafening crack, and the ground opened up and pulled the creature into its fiery depths, dragging my skewered body with it. Maddy screamed one last time and as my eyes found the place where she balanced on the hill, I saw through the thick haze the silhouette of a man dressed in black, an intense dark energy surrounding him. I had only seen that ring of darkness around one person before—Riley. Had he come to witness my death? Had he come to finish off Maddy? I struggled to pull free from the spider, pushing against him and arching my back as far as I could, but to no avail. I grabbed at everything I could on the ground to keep me from falling into the fiery pit, but it was too late.

CHAPTER 29

Alliances

~ SARAH ~

THE PIT WAS deep and dark, except for the red flames that licked from its depths. We fell fast, the spider always below me by a leg's length. At least it would die first. Suddenly a branch jutted out from the wall and caught me, ripping the creature's leg from my stomach as it continued to fall, screeching and gnashing its fangs as it went. I cried out and clutched my stomach as I clung onto the branch with my free arm. The limb continued to grow, spreading its branches and creating a nest for me to rest in as I gasped for breath and focused on making the pain disappear. We reached higher and higher until I was out of the pit. The branches bent sideways, tipping me from the nest and I slid to the ground in a slump. I couldn't stand. I could hardly breathe. My whole body was on fire as my lungs searched desperately for air.

"Let me see," he said as he rolled me onto my back, and I let him because his voice was familiar. The trees around me were spinning and spiralling in and out of focus.

"Is she okay?" Maddy demanded.

"She will be." He touched my stomach now and it somehow made it easier to breathe. The warmth from his hands transferred into my body and, like a hot liquid running through my veins to each broken bone and open wound, my body slowly mended.

I gasped for air before I realized that my lungs were now working overtime. I coughed and blood sprayed from my lips. The trees were still again and their details began to emerge.

Then I saw him. My healer. Luke. He almost looked in worse shape than I felt, but he tried to smile. I reached for him and he hesitated, but then collected me into his arms and held me tight against his chest.

"How did you do that?" Maddy said. "How did you heal her?"

"I'm so glad to see you," I cried into his chest, ignoring Maddy.

"Is someone going to answer me?" Maddy shouted.

Luke raised his head and directed his response to Maddy. "You're having a bad dream, Maddy. You'll

wake now and this will be the end of your nightmares."
He waved his hand and Maddy vanished.

"Are you okay?" I asked as he stroked my hair.

"I'm fine," he answered, his breath heavy. "Are you?"
He surveyed my body, pulling me to my feet and turning
me so he could assess my injuries.

"I'm much better. What happened to you?" His face
showed signs of struggle—residual blood and faded
bruising. His jeans and shirt were both blood-stained and
torn.

"I just had a little setback." He looked away. "We
found your stalker."

"Your brother," I said, confirming that I knew.

"I'm so sorry, Sarah. I had no idea."

"Where is he now?" I asked, glancing around nerv-
ously.

"He's secured. Drew helped me."

"Drew," I gasped. "Is he okay? Where is he?"

"He's here. I told him I'd come get you and meet him
back at my place."

"He's okay?" I asked, relief washing over me.

Luke nodded. "He gave me his key so I could challenge Riley."

"He did that?"

"Yeah, I know. I was surprised, too. It unlocked a lot
of . . . strength in me." He looked down. "I may have
knocked him out."

"Wait, what?"

"I had to gain Riley's trust so he'd let his guard down long enough for me to overpower him." He shrugged. "Anyway, it worked. Drew's okay now, and I think he'll forgive me . . . once I return you to him."

"He must really trust you," I noted.

"Yeah," he said, as if this had surprised him, too.

"I'm glad you're okay," I said, noticing the closeness of his body now.

"Riley will die for what he did to you."

"No," I said. "He only acted like a dark lord would."

He looked at me, his eyebrows puckered with confusion. "How do you do that? How do you forgive so easily?"

"You can't heal hurt with hate." I smiled from the truth of it.

He grinned, regret still covering his eyes. "How are you so perfect?" Our bodies were touching and my heart hammered with a need to kiss him. But could I? Loving him nearly killed me. Being here in his world was dangerous. And it was obvious he needed to be here. He wouldn't be back to Xavier High.

Completely overwhelmed, all I wanted was for him to hold me. I fell into his arms and let myself cry while he stroked my hair.

"It's okay. You're safe now," he said, his voice calming and soothing and everything I missed. But then his brother's words returned to me. *He can never love me. Etak is a dark world. It's not made for happy endings.*

I slowly pulled from his warmth and looked into his deep, dark eyes.

"What is it?" he asked, a trace of uneasiness in his tone.

"Your brother. . . ."

Luke's jaw tensed.

"He said you never cared about me. And that you're not capable of loving anyone."

"He probably said a lot of things that weren't true."

"Maybe Drew was right about us. Maybe this . . . can't work." My voice trembled. "Maybe it would've been better if we never met."

Luke hung his head. "Sarah, I thought you were safe. I didn't know."

"Do you love me?" I hadn't meant to say it, and my face reddened immediately.

"Love," Luke said, as if tasting the word on his tongue for the first time. But he had said it before, hadn't he? At Peggy's Cove? I had overheard him and Drew both say they loved me. . . . Right? His silence made me doubt myself. Maybe he had said it to gain Drew's trust.

"You don't have to answer that," I finally said, extinguishing the agony that was enflamed by his silence.

"Drew may have been right about one thing," Luke started, slowly. "Keepers of dark worlds . . . we've never known love."

I recoiled as if he had slapped me, and my heart squeezed with a vicious intensity.

"But that doesn't mean I never loved you," he added. "I just . . . I can't be sure that's what it is. And it's not fair to tell you that I love you if what I feel for you is just an intense, unnatural attraction."

I hadn't expected him to say that he loved me, but hearing him say that he wasn't sure if he did, hurt worse than hearing nothing at all. But I understood. Maybe what I felt for him was just an intense, unnatural attraction, too. After all, how could you love someone you just met? I hardly knew anything about him—and today was true testament to that. Regardless of how either one of us felt, we couldn't be together. If anything was clear now, it was that.

Suddenly I felt a deep desire to be with Drew. To let him hold me and gloat if he needed to, but just to feel his realness. Just to know that he was still my constant.

"Can you take me to see Drew now?" I asked, fighting the lump growing in my throat.

Luke closed his eyes and slowly nodded. Then he took my hand and a minute later we were in a large room with stone walls. A massive fireplace dominated the far wall with dark leather furniture surrounding it, while an impressive four-poster bed and matching armoire stood behind us. Before I could take in more details, Drew was next to me.

"Drew," I cried, throwing myself into his arms.

He embraced me firmly for a few seconds, but then held me at arm's length. "Are you okay?" he demanded. I realized my struggles had left some obvious evidence. Apart from my torn, blood-stained shirt, my face still stung, too.

"I'm fine," I said quickly. "Are you okay?"

Drew nodded. "It's all good now. But we need to get that shadow out of you before it does any damage."

Luke laid his hand on my shoulder. "This will probably hurt but we'll be right here with you. I'm sorry we have to do this."

"You know what you're doing, right?" Drew aimed this at Luke.

"I think so," Luke said, uneasily.

"What do you mean you *think* so? If you don't do this right, she could die!"

"Would it help if I told you the shadow's gone?" I grinned.

"What do you mean?" Drew said.

"I mean that it's gone. It's dead."

"It's probably just lying low," Luke said. "It won't depart on its own until it kills you."

"Well, I'm not saying it didn't try to kill me," I said. "And it was awful. Like really awful." I remembered the darkness and despair, the cold, empty feelings, the fear, the desire to just be dead. A tear slipped down my cheek. "But I fought it, and then I got violently sick and . . . threw it up."

Both stared at me as if I had grown an extra head.

"And then it turned into a snake and I cut its head off."

They still stared, neither saying a word.

"So," I said, rocking back and forth, "that's about all there is to tell."

"You're still alive," Drew finally said.

"Yeah, well, the shadow was nothing compared to the mutant wolf, bear, spider and giant! The horses were pretty scary, too."

Drew pulled me into him and held me firm. "That won't happen again."

I marvelled in the security of his embrace for a moment longer before asking, "So now what?"

"Sarah," Luke began, "I never should have let you fall for me, and I never should have left my brother in charge. I'm really sorry . . . for everything."

I went to him, despite Drew's resistance, and took his hands in mine. Our eyes met, and the pain in his pierced my heart. "I forgive you," I said. I wanted to kiss him. To feel his warm, salty lips just one more time, but neither of us moved. Another tear slipped down my cheek and he caught it with his finger.

"You need to go with Drew now." His voice was

hoarse, full of agony. "I have to fix what Riley's done."

I felt a deep sense of responsibility for this mess. If I hadn't convinced Luke to come to Earth, maybe this wouldn't have happened. "What has Riley done?" I heard myself ask.

Luke's face hardened. "Aside from nearly killing you, he's turned some of my own people against me, and nearly unleashed a beast that would cause more damage than I know how to fix."

I swallowed. "Will he hurt you?"

"Drew and I secured him for the time being."

"Let me know if you need any more help with him," Drew said. Luke nodded his appreciation.

"So is that really the end?" I asked.

Drew stepped forward until the heat from his body warmed my back. He placed his hands on my waist. "It is."

I couldn't help but notice Luke's eyes flicker to Drew's. Was it because they both knew it was far from the end? Or was their uncomfortable exchange because Drew had his hands on me and Luke wasn't thrilled about it?

"I don't want this to be the end," I admitted, my voice soft and meant only for Luke.

"Drew can protect you better than I can." And there it was, the reason he was letting go—I was safer with Drew.

Drew took my chin and tilted my face back to his. "I'll keep you safe."

My heart mended with the comfort of knowing Drew. The assurance that, no matter what, he would always be there for me. He would never abandon me. My arms found their way around Drew. He was the security I needed. He had always been there for me and always would be. His embrace was strong and sure.

Luke cleared his throat and put some distance between us, reminding me that this wasn't easy for him. I let go of Drew and slowly approached Luke. He wasn't making eye contact.

"Luke, I—"

"It's okay. Don't say anything." His eyebrows came down in a show of discomfort.

My heart ached. I took his hand and brought it to my face. Drew turned away while I slid my arms around Luke's body, revelling in our last embrace.

"I was wrong," he said, his voice choked. "A keeper can feel pain in his own world."

I let the silence cradle that admission, giving it the time and respect it deserved. "Will you come visit me?" I asked, my eyes pinched closed, trying to capture every detail of this moment.

I pulled away at his silence. He was looking at Drew. "Probably not a good idea." He stepped away. "This is where I belong."

Drew was at my side now. He touched my elbow and said, "We should go."

"Take care of her, Drew," Luke said, and it was more of an order than a suggestion.

"Don't need to worry about that." Drew smiled down at me. "Ready?"

I nodded as he held my waist firmly and then held firm to his key. Luke took another step back and gave a salute to us, the smile on his face failing to reach his eyes.

"Take us home," Drew said.

And we were gone. Luke was gone.

CHAPTER 30

New Beginnings

~ SARAH ~

"YOU LOOK BEAUTIFUL, Maddy," I said as she finished applying a coat of lipstick and I fixed the back of her hair one more time.

We were inspecting her through my full-length mirror, admiring her gorgeous teal dress, which accented her newly tanned legs. Caleb would lose his breath when he saw her, I knew. I was happy for her. Happy that she found happiness with Caleb, and that she was going to the prom looking so gorgeous.

"Do you think Caleb will think so? Think I look beautiful, I mean?"

"If he doesn't, he's blind." I smiled and reached for my phone to take a selfie of the two of us in my mirror.

"I think I'll give him my necklace tonight," she said, and her eyes were on mine, watching for my reaction.

"I thought you might." I adjusted her necklace properly. "I think it looks better on you than it will on him, though."

She winked. "I don't think he'll wear it."

"I'm sure he won't."

I turned away from her now and found my perfume bottle on my shelf. The one I knew was her favourite.

"Here," I said as I handed the bottle to her.

Maddy took it from me, a look of pity in her eyes. "Do you miss him?" she asked, and I knew she was talking about Luke.

I sat down on my bed and petted Lucia who was lying quietly near my pillow, listening and watching. "I do," I said, and Lucia licked my hand as if she understood my pain.

"Weird that his family had to move again when they literally just got here."

"Uh-huh." *Don't make eye contact. She'll know you're lying.*

"Will you keep in touch?"

"Probably not." A tear fell from my cheek onto Lucia's fur.

"Oh, Sarah, I'm so sorry." Maddy came to the bed and sat down next to me. She put her arm around me and laid her decorated head on my shoulder.

"Don't mess up your hair," I warned. "I spent an hour on that."

Maddy lifted her head, then said, "And you did that because you're selfless. You're the bestest friend a girl could ask for and you deserve to be happier than this."

"I'm happy," I assured her. "I'm happy that you're happy, and that you're going to have an awesome time at prom tonight with Caleb."

Maddy nodded slowly. "You know, I liked Luke, I really did, but since he's been gone I haven't had any more nightmares."

My heart squeezed, knowing the real reason for this—Riley was locked away and unable to hurt us any longer. But I knew where she was going with this. "You think you were having the nightmares because you instinctively knew he wasn't good for me?"

"Maybe," she said, "although the last nightmare ended different than the rest."

"Oh?" I said, feigning only mild interest.

"You were about to be killed by this gigantic spider, but then Luke showed up and when I thought he was going to kill you, he didn't. Instead he saved your life. It was super weird, but so real."

"I guess he wasn't such a bad guy after all," I said softly.

"Drew seems to be more relaxed now that Luke is gone," she noticed. "I guess he just needed another alpha dog to come in and shake things up a bit."

"Maybe so," I laughed.

"Now we just need him to break up with that horror show."

I nodded. We had been back to school for three days since our near-death experience in Etak, and I had hoped that since I was no longer seeing Luke, Drew would've ended things with Holly. But she was still hanging around and worse, still wearing his ring.

"You still like Drew, right?" Maddy pressed.

"Do we need to talk about this right now?"

"Just answer me."

"Of course I still love Drew."

"I said like, but love will do."

"What?" I shook my head, trying not to get too frustrated with her on her big night.

Her cell phone beeped and she looked at it quickly. With a smile, she said, "I have a surprise for you."

I curled up on the bed next to Lucia and pulled her into me. "What is it?" I was expecting another revelation about her love life and I wasn't overly eager to hear it.

"No, get up." Maddy pulled me off the bed and dragged me to my bedroom window. "Look down there."

Once my eyes adjusted to dimness of the outdoors, I found Drew standing on the sidewalk, bathing in the glow of the sunset. Seeing him standing there, looking up at me, made my breath hitch in my throat. I didn't expect to see him on prom night at all. I figured he and Holly would've gone out for dinner beforehand and I would hear all of the nauseating details from her tomorrow. So what was he doing there? His bright green eyes held my gaze, and we were connecting. Once again connected.

I smiled and he immediately matched it with his own beautiful smile. Then he raised his arm and I saw the bouquet of a dozen roses he was holding. And not just any roses—a dozen of every colour of the rainbow. They were stunning.

I unlocked the window and slid it up out of the way. "What are you doing?" I laughed.

He was dressed in a handsome black tux with a smart yellow bowtie. His hair was perfectly messy, but I knew he had enough product in there to make it stay that way all night, which was his intention.

"Sarah Marley, will you go to prom with me?" he said, his words floating on the thick late-May air.

I held my breath as if unable to breathe, then slowly turned to Maddy. "Did you know about this?"

She was giggling like mad and hardly controlling her excitement. "Yes!"

"Why didn't you tell me? I could've been getting ready all this time!" I was in my pajamas, sporting a messy, ready-for-movie-and-popcorn ponytail.

"You still have time," she said. "And I'll be helping

you, too." She propelled herself at me and we embraced.

"Thank you," I said through watered eyes. Of course I still felt a deep sense of loss over Luke, but there was nothing I could do about that. We weren't meant to be together. And in the end, this was what I had always wanted. Drew. Drew to love me. To notice me. To take me to prom.

When I went back to the window, he was gone.

"Drew?" I called outside as I searched the sidewalk, my driveway, and leaned out my window to get a view of the front walkway. No Drew. Crestfallen, I wondered for a moment if I had fallen asleep when I curled up on my bed with Lucia. Maybe it had been a dream. But no, I was still wearing Luke's school ring, so dreaming wasn't possible.

I pulled my head back in the window, turned around and nearly bumped into Drew.

"Here," he said, handing me the colourful roses. "The yellow one in the middle is from my father."

I touched the yellow petals as a pang of guilt washed over me. If it hadn't been for my insistence to go to the portal that night, Mr. Spencer wouldn't have almost died. Although Mr. Spencer would argue that if we hadn't gone, Riley and his men likely would've killed Drew, then anyone else who got in their way before finding me. I pushed the thought from my mind and tried not to think about what could've been.

"He's doing much better," Drew assured me. "He'll be out of the hospital in no time." He leaned in closer and whispered, his breath tickling my ear, "He'd be home by now if he'd just let me heal him myself."

I smiled, trying to focus on his words and not the way his breath on my ear made me shiver.

"So? Will you?" His eyes were alight with wonder and his lip was curled in an irresistible way.

"Will I what?"

"Will you go to prom with me?"

"What about Holly?" How could I pretend that he hadn't already committed to going to prom with my nemesis?

Drew opened his hand and displayed his school ring. "She wasn't my type." He smiled crookedly. "I like stubborn girls who attract danger."

I blushed and touched his ring, then looked down at Luke's ring still on my hand.

"It's up to you," Drew said. "I won't ask you to wear mine instead of Luke's, but it's yours if you want it. And not just so I can protect you. I want you to be mine, and I want to be yours. I still can't promise I can give you everything you deserve, but I will promise never to hurt you or abandon you. I love you, Sarah."

I took the ring from his open palm and set it on my bedside table. I wasn't ready to take Luke's off. I wasn't ready to finish letting him go. "I love you, too," I said, softly. "But you've always known that."

He took my hand and brought it to his lips. Kissing it softly, he whispered, "You're leaving me hanging. Will you go to prom with me tonight, or did I waste a lot of money on a tux that I can't return until tomorrow?"

"I don't have a dress," I reminded him.

Drew jerked his head to the side and Maddy hurried out of the room, returning a few seconds later with a white garment bag. She handed it to Drew and then left the room again.

"What is this?" I slowly unzipped the garment bag. Drew's smile was wide and playful, excited and impish.

I gasped when I saw the vintage yellow fabric, the intricate detail, the lace-trimmed hem, the delicate sweetheart neckline. This was the dress I had fallen in love with when shopping with Maddy . . . and Holly.

"How did you know?"

"I know everything about you, Sarah," he said, and it was as if he meant it. As if it were his job to know everything about me.

"I love it."

"I know," he said, again with an assurance that was comforting and unnerving at the same time. "So no more excuses. Will you go to prom with me?" He took my hands in his and turned me to face him.

"Yes, I will, but you need to get out so I can get ready," I laughed.

Maddy came back into the room. "Yes, yes, now get out. We have a lot of work to do in a short amount of time." She ushered Drew out of the room. "Go pick up Caleb and meet us back here in an hour."

Drew stopped at the doorway. "I just need to say one more thing."

"What?" I asked, smirking at his persistence. "You need to go—"

And before I could say another word, Drew took my face in his hands and laid his lips on mine. They were soft and warm and . . . perfect. I kissed back because it seemed right and I didn't want it to end.

Maddy cleared her throat. "Forty-five minutes now," she whispered spitefully.

Drew stepped back, leaving my lips throbbing and wanting more. "I'll see you in forty-five," he said as he walked backwards toward the door.

"Thirty," I added quickly. "I can be ready in thirty."

He smiled devilishly and then disappeared.

"Thirty minutes?!" Maddy bellowed. "Are you kidding me? We won't even have your make-up done in thirty minutes."

"She doesn't need make-up!" Drew hollered back up the stairs. "She's perfect the way she is."

Maddy rolled her eyes and then whispered, "Don't listen to him. You need make-up."

I settled into the computer chair, swirling around in

circles as Maddy plugged in the curling iron and set up the make-up on my desk. Butterflies were swarming in my belly as I thought of Drew's lips on mine, his warm touch, his soft stare. I gently touched my lips and imagined his were still there.

Without the thought process that would typically preface, I realized that I was sliding Luke's ring from my finger. I carefully set the ring down on my bedside table, letting my fingers linger on it for a moment longer than needed, then I slid Drew's ring back on in its place.

Drew was mine again. I was his. We would be happy and safe together. Here on Earth.

Dear Reader,

Thank you for reading *The Dream Keeper*. I really hope you enjoyed reading it as much as I enjoyed writing it. There are more books in this series, and I hope you continue on this adventure with Sarah, Drew, Luke and Maddy!

Please consider leaving a review for *The Dream Keeper* on Amazon and Goodreads. Reviews help other readers decide if a book is worth their investment in time, which, in turn, helps the author. So, in advance, thank you. If you would like to share your review with me, please send me a message with a link to your review(s). Thank you.

And finally, if you would like to be notified of upcoming book releases, please sign up for my newsletter on my website at **www.klhawker.com**.

Thank you so much!

Kimberley

K.L. Hawker
www.KLHawker.com

P.S. Turn the page for a sneak peek at the next book in this series, *The Buried Throne*.

THREE MONTHS AFTER the abrupt end to her relationship with Luke, Sarah struggles with her normal existence on Earth as Drew's girlfriend. When Maddy tells Sarah about her dream wherein Yelram's king is being kept prisoner in a dark world and needs their help, Sarah jumps at the chance to prove her worth. After Sarah announces her intention to become a Dream Warrior, Drew calls Luke for assistance. Realizing that she won't back down, Drew and Luke agree to train Sarah and Maddy and prepare them for a recovery mission that will push boundaries, test loyalties, break alliances, and change all of their lives forever.

The Buried Throne promises to plunge readers into an adventure thick with chaos, all while discovering secrets buried deep in the darkest worlds.

PROLOGUE

Three Months Later

~ LUKE ~

5 . . . 4 . . . 3 . . . 2 . . . 1 . . . and a splash of orange light appeared across the stone wall above my fireplace, exactly where I knew it would. Sunrise was my least favourite time of day, reminding me that the world was awake now and people would be going about their business. Sarah would be awake soon, too. Drew would probably pick her up and they would spend the hot summer day together. He'd probably kiss her on the cheek as she slid into the seat next to him. He'd take her soft, delicate hand in his and she'd feel so warm and protected and—

I slammed my fist down on the table, breaking the glass in my hand and spilling the drink. I stood up as the orange light bathed more of the wall, and walked over to the counter near the door. I pulled down another glass from the shelf above and poured the rest of the whiskey into it.

After taking a large gulp, I returned to the armchair, sat down and put my feet up. If only I could sleep, then at least my mind would get a rest from the nagging thoughts of her. Had Drew taken her to prom? He hadn't wanted to go but he knew she did. Did she get her wish? I clenched my jaw, but why? Because I didn't want to think about Drew taking Sarah to the prom? Or because I'd be mad if he didn't? He had promised to take good care of her, and to me that meant giving her everything she wanted. And what did it matter now anyway? Months had passed. I had made a promise to Drew to stay away from her, and I wouldn't break that promise. Not when it was Sarah's life at stake.

The glass was empty again and before I could decide whether to start another bottle, a knock sounded on my door.

"Come in," I called, my voice echoing off the cold, lonely walls.

The door opened and closed again and heavy footsteps came across the floor. Devon. No one else would have the guts to enter my room so confidently.

"Devon," I said. "What is it?" After Devon had proved his allegiance when he helped Drew and me slay two of our dragons, a dozen of my own men, and then challenge Riley, I made him my second-in-command and put him in charge of the vault, which meant ensuring that the beast stayed inside.

"It's the beast," Devon said.

I watched him with narrowed eyes. "What about it, Devon?"

"It's getting stronger, Luke."

I set down the glass. "Then I'll put more protection around it." I crossed the room and went to the window, peering out at the vast kingdom below. "The beast isn't going anywhere."

When the door didn't open and close again, I turned to find Devon pouring himself a drink.

"Is there something else?" I asked, my stomach churning slightly with the look of uneasiness on his face.

"I think it's time we discuss the girl."

"I'm busy," I said, then returned to my chair by the fire, picked up my glass and rotated it, watching how the sun reflected off its surface.

"Luke, you've been 'busy' for the last three months." He joined me at the fire so that I could no longer ignore him.

"What do you want me to say, Devon?"

"Okay." Devon took a swig of his drink then set his glass down. "I want you to tell me why we killed our own for her. I want you to tell me why your brother's sitting in a prison cell for her. I want you to tell me why she's so damn special, and why the beast wants her so badly."

The glass that was in my hand only seconds ago shattered against the fireplace. "Damnit, Devon, there's nothing to tell!"

"I wish I could believe you."

"Do you see her here now?" I stood up and waved my hand around the room. "She hasn't been here in *months*.

And I haven't gone to her. She is gone. And she won't be coming back."

Devon nodded, choosing his next words carefully. "So is that why you've been such a dick lately?"

Don't hurt him. He's your friend. "Get the fuck out, Devon."

Devon, wisely, went to the door. It opened, but he hovered in the entrance. "Luke, you know I got your back, but this girl—whoever she is—you need to forget about her." He slid through the opening of the door before it slammed behind him. The blast of wind I sent at him shook the armoire and blew pictures off the wall.

I let my head fall back and stared at the ceiling. Was I losing my mind? Why couldn't I stop thinking about Sarah every minute of every day? She wouldn't be back. Drew wouldn't have it, and after her near-death experience on her last visit and her speedy departure with Drew, I knew she wouldn't dare come on her own accord. We were done. She was safe now. Safe in the arms of Drew, but safe. And happy. Although it still haunted me to think that Riley wasn't working alone. Sure, he was in prison now and no longer a threat to Sarah, but was there someone on the outside ready to do his bidding for him? Maybe Riley would be ready to talk now that he had had some time to think.

THE PASSAGEWAYS TO the windowless cells were dank and cold, leaving nothing to be desired of the peace and quiet that kept its residents. My footsteps echoed with every step down the sloping stone stairwell to another corridor, this one darker and colder than the last. Finally, a light up ahead indicated I was near. I cleared my throat and heard the guards shuffle to their post so that when I arrived, they were standing with their backs against the wall facing Riley's cell.

"At ease," I said with a nod, and they both nodded back. "Are you ready to talk to me yet?" I called into his cell as I pressed my forearms against the bars above my head.

"I'm always ready to talk to you, brother." His voice was low, tired, and I could tell it came from the cot in the back left corner of his cell.

"You know what I mean. Are you ready to tell me who you were working for? Why you did this to Sarah and what your game plan was?"

"I didn't have a plan."

"Who had the plan then? Who put you up to this?"

I heard him grunt as he sat up and his feet shuffled on the floor. "I work for no one."

"Fuck, Riley, who else was involved?" I slammed my fist into the bars.

"You think keeping me in solitary confinement for months on end and depriving me of basic necessities will make me pour out my heart to you, Luke? You think I'm that weak?"

"Unlock this," I growled to the guards, and they hurried to oblige. I pulled the heavy metal door open, my rage a bubbling volcano, my sense of power euphoric.

"Wow," Riley said, standing up from his cot. "What's this? That door hasn't been opened in months."

"I want answers," I said, stabbing my finger into his

chest. He stumbled back a step but his adrenalin allowed him to recover quickly.

"Are you going to let me out of here?"

"You know I can't do that, Riley."

"Luke, come on, man, this is ridiculous. We're brothers."

"You tried to kill my girlfriend."

"Are you kidding me? You can't possibly still be mad about that."

"Still? That's not something people tend to forget."

"No, but I thought you'd wake up and see that it was kind of stupid for you to fall for her in the first place. I mean, seriously, Luke, she is not *your* type."

I clenched my jaw and narrowed my gaze. This excited him, I could see it in his eyes. "You know nothing."

He sniggered. "I know that you can't be with her. And you know it, too."

"Shut-up!" I roared.

Riley smiled and stepped forward. "I was beginning to worry you had no anger left in you. I was afraid Sarah made you too soft. Afraid you had no vengeance left—"

My hand was on his throat now, constricting his airways so he couldn't breathe another syllable. "I said shut-UP!" My voice was a low growl and although his face was a deep red, almost purple, and his eyes were bulging, I could see the excitement in them. He wanted me to snap. He wanted me to hate him. To be angry. To be . . . the dark prince.

"I am not who you think I should be." I let him fall to the floor and he struggled for breath.

"You," he said between gasps, "have a duty to this world."

I ignored him and paced the lantern-lit room.

"You were chosen, Luke." He slowly stood, but wisely kept his distance. "Chosen to be prince of a dark world. Not another world. *This* world, Luke. Etak." He took a step forward. "And if you don't want to accept that responsibility, then you have to—"

"What?" I shouted. "Hand Etak over to you? To someone whose sole purpose is to destroy the other worlds?"

"Yes!" Riley shouted, matching my temper. "Because that's what we do! That's why we were born. That is our purpose!"

"To hell with our purpose, Riley! Is that really what you want? Is that really what'll make you happy?"

"Ha!" Riley laughed, sardonically. "Happiness is not in our vocabulary. Damnit, Luke, it's not a *choice*. It's who you were born to be."

"You always have a choice."

Riley shook his head incessantly. "I have no idea how *you* got chosen."

"Maybe there was a greater purpose than just destroying everything in our paths." I pulled on the metal bars and the door slid open.

"You're not like her, Luke!" Riley called after me.

I slammed the door closed and nodded to the guards to lock it.

"It would've never worked between you two. She's too good for you, and you know it." He came to the bars.

"What would people think, Luke? What would they think if they found out you and Sarah were together? . . . And what would sweet little Sarah think when she found out that Etak was responsible for everything gone wrong in her world?"

"Shut-up!" I shouted as I turned around and grabbed him through the bars.

"You can't change who you are," he coughed.

I growled and threw him from my grasp, then turned to the guards who were pretending not to be listening to the exchange. A memory of Sarah flooded my brain. The last time I saw her she told me she forgave my brother for trying to kill her, and she hoped that one day I would, too. I punched the wall, cracking my knuckles and splitting a stone. "Make sure he gets plenty of food and water," I growled.

"My Lord?"

"You can't heal hurt with hate," I muttered, and I could hear her voice in my head as I said it.

I led myself through the stagnant hallways of the dungeon while Riley yelled after me, "You *are* the dark prince, Luke! And one day you'll see it! One day it will overpower you!"

ABOUT THE DAISIES

SEVENTEEN-YEAR-OLD Alexis Fletcher is the artist and creator of this beautiful trio of daisies that you will find at every chapter heading in this book series. In December 2015, after an unforgiving struggle with mental illness, Alexis ended her life. A close friend of my son's, Alexis was a beautiful, caring, outgoing, funny, smart and very talented girl. She is loved by all who knew her. As light and delicate as a daisy, Alexis's spirit now blooms freely and without suffering.

MY HOPE IS that you will consider educating yourself on mental illness and suicide prevention. If not for yourself, then for someone you care about, because we all struggle at one point or another. Alexis's family started a non-profit foundation in Alexis's memory wherein they help to provide much-needed support for other young people like Alexis. You can find out more about this foundation by following the link below. You can also purchase a piece of jewellery for just $20CDN and wear this trio of daisies proudly in support of mental health. All proceeds will go to the foundation to ensure youth get the help they need.

www.BelieveInHopeForAlexis.com

ABOUT THE AUTHOR

K.L. HAWKER grew up in Nova Scotia, Canada, where she spent her childhood writing stores that took her imagination all over the world. All grown up, Hawker is still an avid daydreamer and writer, and enjoys travelling the globe with her family, visiting all the places she once only dreamed about.

Follow along on Facebook:

www.facebook.com/KLHawker

For more information, please visit:

www.KLHawker.com

ACKNOWLEDGMENTS

I am always quick to thank the Creator first for any and all creativity that lives inside of me. The time, the energy, the ideas—they are all blessings from above, and I don't take any of them for granted. I may have some shortcomings, but I am thankful for my love of writing.

Next, I owe a big thanks to my husband and three amazing kids. They are the greatest supporters as I hide away for hours to create characters that require my undivided attention. They listen as I run ideas by them, and they give feedback on each chapter. They love my stories as much as I do, and their enthusiasm is what keeps me going some days.

Thank you to my beta readers and editors—Janet, Annette and Melanie. Every bit of time, advice and feedback you give means so much to me.

And a humungous thanks to you for reading this novel. I hope you enjoyed reading it at least half as much as I enjoyed writing it.

Made in the USA
San Bernardino, CA
06 July 2020

74850909R00263